ALICE in CONDOLAND

Liz Bieler

3 SWALLYS PRESS

BOSTON

Dedicated to Morris A. Bieler, my father

CONTENTS

Acknowledgments

I would like to thank my writers' group: Marcy McNally, Sue Sussman, and Peter White for their suggestions and support. Our weekly meetings kept me on track and made writing fun.

I am grateful to my beta readers for their patience and honest feedback. It takes a special kind of friend to listen as you did. Your encouragement motivated me.

I'd also like to thank Nivi Nagiel, my editor, for her big picture thinking and attention to detail. Thanks also to 3 Swallys Press for making this book possible.

Lastly, I wish to recognize my mother for instilling in me a love of words and language. Looking back, I see the two dollars she paid per memorized Shakespearean sonnet were a wise investment.

Condoland's Cast of Characters

Aflac — An opinionated neighbor

Alice — The narrator who moves to Condoland from New York City

Bad Firm — Association's law firm

The Barbies — Bleached blond women of a certain age, dressed in denial of gravity and decorum

Bookkeeper — Condoland's bookkeeper

Bulldog — Secretary, Board of Drektors

Ceevil Engineer — Architectural Committee Chair, husband of the Connector, member of the Resistance

Champion — Commercial real estate lawyer in the inner circle of the Resistance

Circle of Trust — Alice's inner circle: Champion, Connector, Ceevil Engineer, Florence Nightingale, Harvard, Joanna Rivers, Panamanian Prince, Paul Revere, and Sherlock Holmez

Connector — The wife of the Ceevil Engineer and member of the Resistance

Cookie — The Champion's dog

Corpse — Appointed to Board of Drektors after the Mobster dies

Daredevil — Cute guy in the gym

Drekorator — Mobster's friend decorating common areas

Drektors — Board members with questionable ethics

Fab Five — Resistance candidates running against the Drektors: Champion, Florence Nightingale, Harvard, Paul Revere, and Panamanian Prince

Florence Nightingale — Alice's friend, board candidate, and Resistance member

Gassy — A member of the Finance Committee

Gladys Kravitz — Alice's nosy neighbor

Good Firm — Law firm advising the Resistance

Her Highness — President, Board of Drektors

Humpty Dumpty — Board member who becomes treasurer

Innombrable — Alice's ex

Joanna Rivers — In the inner circle of the Resistance and married to Edgar, a former board president

Long Island Lothario — Vice president, Board of Drektors

Manager — Building manager

Mobster — First board treasurer

Oracle — Gym employee with mysterious powers.

Panamanian Prince — Board candidate and member of the Resistance

Panamanian Princess — Married to Panamanian Prince and chair of Decorating Committee

Paul Revere — Aka "King of the Jews," board candidate and member of the Resistance

Peter Pan — Musician and friend of Alice

Rage Man — Resistance supporter

Red Hats — Men at the Condoland pools rating women on a scale of one to ten

Sherlock Holmez — In the inner circle of the Resistance

Tokyo Rosenberg — Double agent

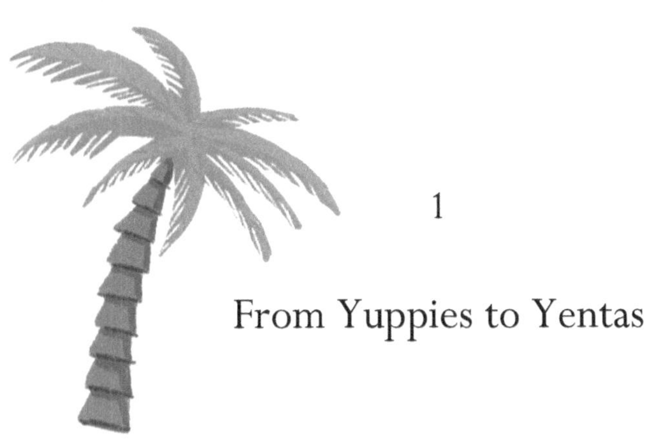

1

From Yuppies to Yentas

I never planned to live in Florida. I first visited Boca Raton on a business trip. My employer, Big Fucking Card (BFC), had a call center there. It was a warm, sunny escape from winter in Manhattan, and SPF 70 was a small price to pay for three days in paradise.

My cousin fixed me up with a charming Cuban in Miami Beach. Forewarned of his womanizing, I expected nothing more than a good-looking tour guide. He must have charmed the front desk clerk, because he knocked on my hotel room door unannounced.

"Just a minute." I ran to the bathroom, sprayed my honey-colored bob against the humidity and put on mauve lipstick. My favorite little black dress hugged my trim figure. Whatever curves I had were on display. I opened the door.

"Where's the funeral?" he asked. *Not the reaction I envisioned.*

"What do you mean?" I looked down at my dress. He put his finger under my chin and lifted my face. He was six feet tall. Even with my three-inch heels, he had six inches on me.

"Why's a beautiful girl like you wearing black?"

"I'm from New York!"

He flashed a dimpled smile. "I'm teasing you, *flaca*. You look stunning!" *This is some tour guide!*

We dined and danced at a famous Cuban restaurant on Lincoln Road in Miami Beach. Palm trees grew between the tables with skylights overhead. I'd never seen anything like it—or him. He lived in the moment, and in that moment, so did I.

I returned to Florida a few weeks later for a wedding in Key Biscayne. An Argentinian friend from business school was marrying his childhood sweetheart, and I invited the Cuban as my date. The ceremony started at 7 p.m. My date picked me up at 7:15. Seven fifteen!

"*Flaca*, you're wearing color!" I'd bought a red dress for the occasion. *Does he own a watch?*

"I start the ceremony singing 'Ave Maria,'" I said. "We're late! I've ruined my friend's wedding!"

"Relax, *flaca*. It's an Argentine wedding, right?" I nodded. "They're on Latin time." *Time is time, and the ceremony started 15 minutes ago!* I took deep breaths; they didn't help. "We'll be early. Don't worry."

I couldn't look at him, I was so angry. We arrived at 7:30. I ran to the hotel door while he sauntered past the palm trees, hands in the pockets of his beige linen suit, admiring the birds of paradise and the bougainvillea spilling onto either side of the sidewalk.

Panting, I opened the door and ran inside to apologize. The equipment room was empty. Guests started arriving an hour later, and I began singing at 9 p.m.

Back in New York, exhaust fumes greeted me at the pickup area outside LaGuardia. In the taxi to my apartment, I stared out the window. The weather, the buildings, everything was dull and gray. I hadn't noticed before.

But I love New York! I had a coveted marketing job at BFC. Great friends. Still, I worked long hours. And my yearly raise barely covered the increase for my one-bedroom, rent-stabilized apartment on the Upper West Side. I couldn't imagine ever being able to afford something bigger. I'd just turned 28 and wasn't meeting anyone. I was in a rut.

The next morning on my way to work, I hit gridlock in Midtown. I jumped out of the cab at Times Square and ran toward Sixth Avenue just as a drizzle turned into a downpour. Weaving through the crowded sidewalk, I dodged an umbrella aimed straight at my head. I was cold, wet, and miserable when it dawned on me; I needed a change. Color and warmth. Sunshine. I saw myself dancing in the Cuban restaurant, singing at the wedding, wearing a red dress. I was ready to live in the moment . . . *Florida! But I can't just up and move . . . can I? I'm not seeing anyone . . . my landlord would love to end my lease and jack up the rent. But I'd need a job . . .*

I was 29 when my transfer finally came through. I moved to South Florida as one of BFC's directors covering Latin America. At first, I rented an apartment on the beach. I bought my first car—a hardtop convertible. No more subway for me!

When black mold seeped out of the walls of my apartment, I complained to management, who sent a maintenance guy to inspect.

"Mold? I don't think that's mold. Have you tried cleaning it?" A lady down the hall was in the hospital with a lung problem. When her dog got sick, I knew I had to get out of there. There was no point arguing with the building. Two months before my 30th birthday, I paid off the remainder of my lease and bought my first home—a condominium.

My one-bedroom, rent-stabilized apartment on the Upper West Side cost more than my South Florida condo mortgage *and* monthly maintenance combined. I bought a two-bedroom apartment with a balcony overlooking the Intracoastal Waterway in a place called Condoland. It had FOUR closets, an in-unit washer and dryer, floor-to-ceiling views, and a garbage disposal! *UNBELIEVABLE!*

I moved on a Friday. My parents flew down from Newton, Massachusetts, to help.

"I still don't understand why you want to live here," said my mom. "This is where *alta kahkers*[1] go to die."

"No, it's not," I said. "It's changed. It's full of young people!"

She got to what was really bothering her. "You're so far from us!" Her face grew somber. "What if we have an emergency?"

Being an only child was a blessing and a curse: I had my parents' undivided attention. My mom was 65, and my dad was 72. He'd had bypass surgery, but they were both still strong and independent.

My dad turned to her. "Look, it's a four-hour drive from Newton to New York and a three-hour flight to South Florida. She'll actually be *closah!*" My mom pursed her lips. My dad grabbed my hands. "The most important thing to me—to us—is yah happiness, Alice. Don't worry!" I managed a smile, wiping my eyes, the same hazel green as his. He pulled some tissues from his shirt pocket and mumbled about allergies. "Yah mothah and I will be just fine." His voice softened. "Yar only young once, *bubbaleh*.[2] This is an adventchah. I'm excited for you!"

By Saturday night, we'd unpacked all the big boxes and were

---

[1] Alta kahkers — Literally, it's Yiddish for old defecators. Figuratively, it means old people.

[2] Bubbaleh — Yiddish term of endearment meaning sweetie, darling

ready to celebrate. As an owner in good standing, I had access to Condoland's Club House, replete with a movie theater, gym, spa, game room, swimming pool, basketball and tennis courts. Its crown jewel was a residents-only restaurant. As we entered, the Restaurant Manager greeted me by name (word of the new "young girl" had traveled fast). I was home.

Saturday nights in the Restaurant were festive. A wooden dance floor in the center of the room filled with diners moving to the sounds of a one-man band. Couples were swinging. When the "band" played "*Hava Nagilah*," dancers joined hands, weaving sideways in the traditional circle.

That Saturday was Lobster Night. Seated in a cream leather booth in the upper section—perfect to see everyone and everything below—a group of widows attacked heaping plates of lobster. Their sequins and diamonds caught the light. One wore a white fur cape (this was June). Another wore four-inch Jimmy Choo shoes, her feet dangling above the floor. Thick makeup covered their Botoxed, Restylaned faces.

My dad observed them attack their shellfish.

"The ladies who lunch," he said with an amused smirk.

"They look like clowns!" said my mom.

"They don't have your skin, Diane," said my dad.

Below this kosher crime-in-progress and two tables over, Sol Rabinowicz was celebrating his 90th birthday. His wedding picture sat on an easel beside him, surrounded by balloons. Several of his shellfish-eating guests wore yarmulkes. When it came time to toast, they wished him to live "*biz a hindut und tzfuntzik*."[3] My dad beamed; I was happy he approved of my new environs. *Did I just move to the*

---

[3] "Biz a hindut und tzfuntzik" is a Yiddish toast wishing the person to live for 120 years.

Florida Catskills?

The next morning, we ate breakfast on my balcony watching boats and yachts go by on the Intracoastal. In the afternoon, we explored the property. Manicured walking paths with exotic flowers and palm trees encircled each of Condoland's three residential towers. There were water fountains everywhere.

My favorite path ran alongside the Intracoastal where unit owners moored their boats. It was so beautiful, I pinched myself to be sure I wasn't dreaming. The water, clear as glass, broke into waves, crashing against the seawall as a yacht the size of a cruise ship passed. My mom cringed as smaller boats followed, filled with teenagers blasting Latin pop music.

"How inconsiderate!" she said. *Maybe, but it beats honking horns and garbage trucks.*

My dad hooked her arm, leading us toward the Club House overlooking the Intracoastal. "Let's see the gym," he said.

The gym was on the lower floor of the Club House. The lobby's floor-to-ceiling windows maximized spectacular views. The floors were marble. Our footsteps echoed as we walked toward the elevator. My mom frowned at the dated décor. I wasn't complaining. It was a HUGE step up from my pre-war New York building where double locks and a basement laundry room were the only amenities. We walked past the Restaurant to the movie theater. My mom ran, childlike, to the upper section, sinking into a plush chair.

"I could get used to this!" she said.

We took the elevator down to the gym. There was a room for fitness classes with mirrored walls, and an equipment room with outdated but functional machines and free weights. Use of the Club House facilities was included in my monthly maintenance.

Outside, we passed people dining al fresco under large umbrellas. There was a lap pool, around which deeply tanned, leather-skinned unit owners sunned in chaises. *They look like raisins!*

An attendant went from raisin to raisin offering pitchers of water and lemonade. Another brought fresh towels.

"Better they should offer sunblock," said my mom.

"You can do laps here," said my dad.

We followed a rock-lined path to the tennis courts behind the Club House. Even with sunglasses, the glare was blinding. *How can anyone play in this heat?*

Returning to Condoland I, we explored the public rooms in the lobby: a party room, game room, conference room, and a card room filled with ladies sitting four to a table. My mom wandered into the wood-paneled library. Searching shelves of donated books, she pulled out poetry by Emily Dickinson.

"Mommy, take it with you."

"Really?"

"We're on the honor system. Just bring it back when you finish."

"I can't get over it!" she gushed. "My daughter has her own library!"

"Come on, honey," said my dad. "Let's help Alice finish unpacking."

He checked my mailbox while I took my mom to the ladies' room. We joined him in the mailroom just in time; the widows from last night were encircling. He was the perfect trifecta: breathing, ambulatory, and alone. He seemed oblivious, and I pulled him out of there before my mom noticed. One widow turned to another and whispered loudly, "Oy, he's married." I glared at her. She glared back, defiant.

The night before their flight home, I served drinks on the balcony. As the sun set, the ocean changed colors—green near the shore, to aqua to sapphire to navy near the horizon. The sky flared bright orange as the sun set, filled with white cotton balls. My dad said he wanted to reach up and touch them. I'm still tempted.

2

Adjusting

M y mom was right about one thing; Condoland was full of *alta kahkers*, but I got a kick out of them. I was traveling to Latin America twice a month, so when I was home, I wanted to relax. The neighbors were welcoming, but nosy. I was the youngest person living in Condoland, and they wanted to know how I got here.

"Are you visiting your parents?" a woman asked as I entered the elevator.

"No." *Was that rude?* "They live in Massachusetts."

"Oh. So, your grandparents live here?" *She's not stopping.*

"No." *Can't a working woman own her own home?* My brevity killed her, but she caught me off guard. In New York, people minded their own business. To put her out of her misery, I offered, "*I* live here."

"Ahh. So, is this your parents' apartment?"

"No, it's mine."

"Reeeally?" I smiled yes. She shuffled closer. "Whadda you do?"

"I work at BFC."

"Oooh," she said. "Are you single?"

9

"Yes." *Hate that question.*

"Maybe I'll introduce you to my grandson. He's coming during the holidays."

This scene repeated itself until word reached critical mass and I had the prospect of many blind dates, the results of which would surely be grist for the Condoland rumor mill if I accepted them. Within days, I was known as the single young girl from New York who worked at BFC.

Speaking of BFC, I soon realized my new region operated more loosely than our New York headquarters. For example, an executive invited employees over for a barbecue so he could submit the cost of his new landscaping to be reimbursed by the company. Another slept with his employee's wife. The employee said nothing; he had mouths to feed. I was stunned by these and other flagrant violations of our company's code of conduct. One day, I confided to a Canadian coworker about the transgressions I observed.

"That's nothing," he told me. "The last regional head was a cocaine addict."

"You're kidding, right?" I asked.

"'Fraid not."

"What happened to him?"

"He crashed his corporate car under the influence. KILLED someone."

"No!"

"Yes! He 'retired' after that."

The double-dealing was inescapable. When I reached my limit, I decided to act. As a cultural outsider, I had to be careful. If I confronted a "superior" directly, I might get canned. Instead, I slipped through a labyrinth of doors during lunchtime to the hidden Office of the Ombudsperson, where I reported myriad violations.

"Thank you, Alice," said the soft-spoken ombudsperson. "You were right to come to me." She took off her glasses and looked up from her notes. "I won't be able to share the outcomes with you, but I assure you that each potential infraction of our code of conduct will be investigated by our compliance officers, and your name will never be used."

I made it back to my office unnoticed and ate at my desk before the others returned from their two-hour lunches. Whether or not my complaints made a difference, I took comfort in taking this small stand against pervasive corruption.

During a business trip to Mexico, a colleague saw I was struggling. Over lunch, he explained the ethical differences between the U.S. and Latin America.

"If someone at a party in New York said his accountant helped him cheat on his taxes, most people would walk away. They wouldn't want to be seen talking to him."

"Sounds right," I said.

He smiled. "Alice, in Latin America, that guest would be the toast of the party! Everyone would ask for the accountant's phone number." He put his hand on my shoulder. "You're used to doing things by the book, and that's not the way it works here."

"But you're not like that."

He smiled again and shook his head. "No, I'm not. And no— you can't fix this!" *So much for a poker face.* "Things won't go well for you in this region if you try. Focus on what you *can* control, and never let colleagues or superiors think that you—a *gringa*—are judging them." I hated but appreciated his advice. It was key to my survival in this region.

It's clear now that my work experiences were warnings of everything to come in Condoland. But back then, I was too busy adjusting to see the bigger Florida picture.

I was also adapting at home. In New York, we looked straight ahead in the elevator, avoiding eye contact. Impatient fingers rubbed most "close door" buttons bare. In Condoland, people greeted each other as they entered the elevator. Many neighbors were friends who socialized.

One morning, a redheaded woman in her late 60s with an unmistakable New York accent turned to me in the elevator and asked, "Yaw the girl who works at BFC, right?" This time, it didn't feel intrusive. She wanted to place me.

"Yes, I'm Alice."

She held out her hand. "Nice to meet you, Alice. I'm Joanna. Joanna Rivers."

"Nice to meet *you*, Joanna," I said, shaking it.

"Aw you going to the bawd meeting tonight?"

"What time?" I'd never been to a condo board meeting.

"Seven o'clock in the Pawty Room. The bawd will answuh questions about the assessment. You should go." I'd heard the assessment would mean a big up-front payment.

She's right. I should go. "If I can get home in time, I will. Thanks!"

I left work early to tend to my new investment. Just before 7 p.m., I joined the crowd slowly making its way through the lobby. The Party Room was in the basement, with a basement entrance accessible by elevator for the handicapped. The more agile, upright owners entered from the lobby, descending the wide spiral staircase to see and be seen. At its base, owners for and against the assessment pounced on new arrivals to make their case.

A woman grabbed my arm before anyone else could speak to me. "You're not going to vote for this assessment, are you?" Barely five feet tall, she had a short, butch haircut, pitch black hair, and a voice like the Aflac Duck if he chain-smoked. She squeezed my arm so hard it hurt.

"I don't know," I said. "I'm here to learn about it." I tried to pull away, but she was stronger than she looked.

"You don't want new railings! They're wasting your money— and changing the design of the building. It's too modern!" She spat as she spoke, then started coughing, maintaining her grip, when Joanna Rivers came to my rescue.

"Let go of huh awm!" said Joanna. My assailant dismissed her. Joanna turned to me. "Alice, I'm glad you made it. Ignaw huh. Listen to the bawd and the engineer and decide fuh yourself. Awl the buildings in aw neighborhood have glass railings. If we wait, it'll cost a lot maw latuh." She spoke so Aflac could hear. "Pay no attention to that woman. She pinches a nickel so tight, the Indian rides the buffalo!"

Aflac wasn't having it. "I'm not giving you \$12,000!" she yelled. "There's nothin' wrong with my balcony! You and your fancy husband can't tell me how to spend my money!"

Joanna grabbed Aflac's wrist, freeing me. "Go fuck yourself!" *That's one way to end a conversation.* "Ignore huh," said Joanna. I rubbed my arm as we walked to the seating area.

Folding chairs were arranged in rows, separated by two supporting columns running from the basement up to the ceiling. I sat with Joanna and her friends on the left side of the room. Aflac sat on the right. In front of us, two men sat across from each other, yelling between the columns. Their wives' heads swiveled, hoping no one was watching.

"I should care about property value?" yelled Mr. Hatfeld. "I'll be dead before they finish!"

"Buildings don't maintain themselves." Mr. Macoyle's face was coronary red. "You always were a selfish prick! If you want to neglect your property, go buy a house." *Does anyone here have a filter?*

"Back on Lawng Island," said Joanna, "they were best friends—pawtners for 30 years in an appliance store chain. Two yeuhs ago, they went to the two-for-one happy hour with their wives. Aftuh, they went skinny-dipping in the pool. It was dawk, and Hatfeld can't see without his glasses. He slapped Macoyle's wife in the *tuchus*.[4] He said it was a mistake, but Macoyle didn't think so—especially since his wife wasn't complaining. They've been feuding ever since."

The room was rife with cliques, quarrels, and conspiracy theories punctuated with Yiddish curse words. Thanks to my grandmother, I understood most of them. Board meetings were better than a Broadway show. If they'd asked, I would have paid for admission. After 15 minutes of *kibitzing*[5] and *kvetching*,[6] a man holding a gavel at the dais in front of the room called the meeting to order.

"That's my husband Edguh," said Joanna. Her brown eyes filled with pride. As the room quieted, she whispered, "He's the bawd president!" In Manhattan, Edgar had been a high-powered attorney. He argued cases before the U.S. Supreme Court. He came to Florida for a case and never left. He bought a house, and his wife and children joined him. A few years later, he was elected to a Florida District Court of Appeals. When their kids grew up and left home, he and Joanna were among the first buyers at Condoland.

I wondered why they left New York so suddenly, and why someone so nice had such a tough exterior. I sensed sadness, but I

----

[4] Tuchus — Yiddish for gluteus maximus
[5] Kibitzing — Yiddish for informal chatting
[6] Kvetching — Yiddish for complaining

wasn't one to pry. She'd share what she wanted me to know when she was ready.

Edgar was matter-of-fact, suffering neither fools nor foolish questions. Listening to him, I was convinced the glass railings were a necessary investment. Three weeks later, the unit owner vote was close, but the cheapskates won. It would be years until we replaced the railings, and by then, the cost—and weather damage—would be much greater, just as Judge Edgar had predicted. Condominium living was political, and I found the board meetings hugely entertaining—at first.

The board asked for volunteers to serve on committees. I signed up for the Sports Committee. It was tasked with recommending new equipment for the gym and tennis courts in the Club House. Everyone else on the Committee was retired and preferred morning meetings. I explained that I couldn't make it before 6 p.m., and they grudgingly agreed. They elected *me* the Committee's chairperson, and just like that, I became an insider.

3

Hellos and Good-Bye

Gradually, I made friends at work, both in South Florida and in the countries I visited. I made friends in Condoland, too—older and wiser friends who would become members of the Resistance.

The Champion: Condoland sat along a picturesque walking path shaded by trees yearning for each other. I walked it whenever I came home before dark. One evening, I met an adorable Westie named Cookie on the path, and that's how I met the Champion. After petting her dog, I noticed Cookie's mother walking up the driveway toward my building. I ran after her.

"Cookie's mother! Cookie's mother!" She turned. "Do you live in Condoland?"

"Yes. Do you?"

"I just moved here," I said, catching my breath. "If you ever need a sitter, I'd love to do it. I dog sat for my neighbors' Westie in New York."

The Champion was a lawyer specializing in commercial real estate. In her early 50s, she was strikingly pretty. Tall with shoulder-

16

length blond hair, she looked like a Jewish Candice Bergen, but she was unconcerned with her appearance, which I respected. Tough, smart, and direct—very direct—she was a Condoland board member.

A half hour after my walk, Cookie's mother called to conduct a security check.

"How long have you lived here?"

"Three months." *I already told you this.*

"Do you own or rent?"

"I own." *What is this,* Law & Order?

"My husband says I'd be crazy to give a key to a stranger." *Am I a suspect?*

"You know, dog sitting should be fun, so if you're not comfortable, let's not do it."

She paused. "You're absolutely right." She sounded embarrassed. "My husband worries about me. He travels a lot, and I'm alone. But I got carried away. You live here. Where are you going to go?"

"Are you sure? If you'd like, you can speak to my New York neighbor and ask for a reference. I'll give you—"

"No. No, no. It's not necessary. Cookie and I would love for you to dog sit."

The first time Cookie stayed with me, the Champion gave me the key to their apartment. I eventually gave her the key to my apartment, and we've been good friends ever since.

Florence Nightingale: When I wasn't traveling, I either walked outside or went to the Condoland gym. Florence and I both exercised after work. In her early 60s, Mrs. Nightingale had a high, squeaky voice that matched her petite frame (she was no more than four foot eleven). She spent much of her workout apologizing. If she used a machine, she apologized to everyone who might have wanted it. If she watched one of the shared TVs, she apologized in case anyone preferred to watch something else. She was as nice as she was sorry, and I found it hard to take her seriously.

Florence was a therapist with an Ivy League education, married to a forensic pathologist and Rhodes Scholar. Her demeaner and vocation were products of an emotionally abusive childhood. She had learned that a soft voice *did* turn away wrath. Determined to be nothing like the mother who raised her, a determination I understood, Florence's excessive kindness was sincere. She devoted her life to helping others in emotional pain.

There would come a time in Condoland when knowing how to deal with the psychologically challenged would prove essential. That's when the limelight Florence Nightingale avoided for most of her life would shine upon her.

Sherlock Holmez: Sr. Holmez came to Condoland from Colombia. A retired rancher and businessman, he exercised in the gym each afternoon while his wife Shilah napped. She was the American daughter of a famous Italian-born painter. In Colombia, she hosted large parties to support her husband's business interests.

They made a stunning couple. He was about five foot eleven, with curious brown eyes, a full head of salt-and-pepper hair and a closely trimmed, gray beard. She was five foot six, with chin-length blond hair and green eyes.

As conditions in Colombia deteriorated, Sr. Holmez worried his *gringa* wife would be kidnapped and held for ransom. His concern proved well-founded the day drug lords threatened him at gunpoint on his ranch and stole his new Jeep. Relieved not to be abducted, he wasn't hurt. As he walked toward his ranch, the drug lords taunted him, asking if his wife needed a ride. Soon after, when the same gang made a surprisingly generous offer to buy the ranch, the couple didn't hesitate. They moved full-time to their vacation property in Condoland. Since moving back to the U.S., Mrs. Holmez seldom left the safety of her apartment, leaving Sr. Holmez with a lot of time on his hands.

He noticed everything and everyone, but only engaged with people he found interesting. In the gym, he chatted with and teased the Oracle, a college girl working at the gym. She was smart and hungry to learn, and they made each other laugh.

"You eat all that?" he asked, pointing to her ramen noodles.

"Why not?" she answered. "I'm not the one with a pot belly!" The Oracle smiled.

"You hear how she talks me?" Sr. Holmez said in his imperfect English, bringing me into the conversation. "She call me fat!"

"Eh . . ." I muttered. "Maybe she's just saying *she* doesn't have a pot belly!" He noticed I said "eh" like a Spanish speaker and reverted to his native tongue. He didn't subscribe to the *yenta*[7] interrogation protocol. Sr. Holmez explained the architect's vision for our property, describing subsequent changes that had violated its artistic integrity.

Wearing his cowboy hat, Sr. Holmez strolled the perimeter of the Condoland property each morning as he had on his ranch. He dressed meticulously in slacks and a guayabera. He had a facile, respectful way with Spanish-speaking employees and vendors. They gave him behind-the-scenes information which neither the board nor building management would share. He substantiated or dis-

---

[7] Yenta — Yiddish, meaning a woman who is a gossip or busybody

missed each tidbit after extensive online investigation. Sr. Holmez worked the internet like a private eye. If anyone at Condoland was up to something, Sherlock Holmez knew about it first.

Many of my neighbors thought Sr. Holmez was eccentric; I found him fascinating. He helped me with my Spanish, and he made me laugh. He was in his early 60s and had lived in the U.S. for five years. While he understood more English than he let on, he liked to be in control, which is why Sherlock preferred to speak in his native tongue. Due to the language barrier, he and his wife Shilah didn't socialize with Condoland's gringos. Having faced down Colombian guerillas, he wasn't afraid of confrontation. He rubbed a lot of people the wrong way, which was fine by him.

The Oracle: A pretty 20-year-old with dreads down her back, the Oracle assisted owners and their guests in the exercise rooms and spa. She encouraged unit owners to stick with their exercise regimens and set goals, which they met in large part because she checked on their progress. Each day, she greeted these souls with a big smile, listened to their stories, and left them feeling hopeful and valued.

Even the most entitled unit owners liked the Oracle. One of Condoland's Barbies (women with frozen faces who refused to act or dress their age) gave her a grocery bag full of worn designer shoes as a holiday gift. It's bad juju for a Jamaican to wear another person's shoes, but she thanked the Barbie for her generosity and waited for the end of her shift to toss the "gift" in the trash.

The Oracle was putting herself through college. She was a voracious reader, and we found common ground in literature.

I discovered she had special abilities. First, I noticed her total recall. If I lost track of my machine repetitions, she knew how many

I'd completed, even if she was helping someone else across the room. She could remember who said what when, going back months or years.

One day, as she helped me adjust the chair on the biceps/triceps machine, the Oracle revealed a more intriguing talent. "Has something changed in your life?"

"Why?" *Nothing good begins with that question.*

"Your aura has changed."

"You see auras?" I'd heard of people who do this, but I'd never met one.

"Yes." She waited for my answer.

"Well, I met someone." I felt myself blush. "Are you intuitive?"

She smiled. "It depends on what you mean by intuitive—"

"Are you psychic?" I loved stuff like this!

"Let's just say I see things. I usually get messages in dreams about what is going to happen. And—"

"I met a guy at work, and I really like him."

"I know you do." She wasn't smiling anymore. "Be careful."

Soon after moving to Condoland, I began dating a Cuban guy (half Jewish—the wrong half) from work. People say love is blind for a reason. He was going through a divorce and didn't want to be alone. Before long, we were in what I thought was a committed relationship. I fell hard. We spent most of our time together, and I lost interest in the goings on in my building.

One night at the Restaurant, a bent old man with a kind smile and a halo of white hair walked across the dance floor directly to our table. My new boyfriend had just left for the restroom.

"Hello," I said, wondering if the man mistook me for someone else.

He skipped formalities. With one hand on the back of my chair and the other leaning on the table, he whispered in my ear, "If that man loves you, if he truly loves you, he'll never leave you. Remember, when it's right, it's easy."

I nodded. I don't know why, but I didn't ask questions. "Thank you," I said, but he had already turned and was walking back to his table just as my boyfriend came back to ours.

"Who was that man?" he asked.

"I don't know."

"He has such a light." Like the Oracle, my boyfriend had a highly developed sixth sense. "What did he say to you?"

Call it women's intuition, but I kept the message to myself. "He came by to say hello," I said. "Maybe he mistook me for someone else."

When we first met, my soon-to-be boyfriend told me to "assume positive intent" if ever his actions made me question his commitment to our relationship. I did, unaware I was nothing more than a post-divorce rebound. Right after we got engaged, he pulled away.

Around that time, *El Innombrable*, Spanish for "He Who Shall Not Be Named," ran out of career options at BFC. A sketchy friend looking for someone like-minded threw my fiancé's name into the hat for a job at a shady bank in a shady country in Eastern Slavia. They threw crazy amounts of money at him, and that was all it took. He moved halfway around the world, away from his family, his friends, and me. I was devastated. The words of that old man were painful, but they helped. El Innombrable didn't love me; I had to let go.

On the third anniversary of our first date, El Innombrable broke up with me IN A TEXT MESSAGE. I remembered the Oracle's advice. Two people had tried to warn me, but it was too late.

4

Pursuing Happiness

I hid in an emotional cave after the breakup, avoiding friends and postponing travel. Condoland's gym was my sanctuary. I went there for the endorphin rush. Getting toned was building my self-esteem. I was 34 but looked 24 and was, by decades, the youngest person in my building. The friends I made there gave me perspective my contemporaries could not. My biological clock was ticking, but my new friends assured me there was always time to meet the right man.

"What do you want?" asked the Champion one evening as we walked the path. "I'm not just talking about a relationship; what makes you feel happy? Accomplished? Don't answer me. Think about it and put your energy there. If I spend eight weeks a year with my warband"—that's what the Champion called her war correspondent husband—"it's a lot. When the kids left home, I thought about divorcing him. A therapist gave me the advice I'm giving you. It saved my marriage, because it taught me to take responsibility for my own happiness and fulfillment."

I took the advice to heart and focused on work. I had an idea for a new service. For a modest fee per day, travelers could have a doctor visit their hotel room if needed. In the land of Montezuma's revenge,

23

it would sell like hotcakes. I secured the network of doctors and discussed the idea with my boss in New York.

"I could have used your service when I crossed Montezuma!" she said. "You have my blessing. In fact, I'm going to put you in charge of this *globally*." It was a home run! Well, almost.

After my American boss approved the project, a vice president from one of the countries in my region arranged to meet with me.

"I hear you're working on a new kind of travel insurance," he began, his black eyes cold above a disingenuous smile. *Uh-oh. How could he have a problem with this?*

"Yes." I smiled. "It'll make millions for BFC, *and* travelers will love it! So will the hotels." How could he object?

"Maybe it is a good idea," he conceded, "but that's not the point. Those profits won't accrue to me locally." *Has he no shame?* "Listen to me, and make sure you understand what I'm saying to you." He was scary serious. *Is he threatening me?* "You work for THIS region!" His hand banged the table. "I don't care how much it makes for BFC if it doesn't help ME." He pointed a finger at my face. "If there's one nickel you can contribute to my bonus, that's where you focus. *¿Entiendes?*"

"Yes, you've made yourself clear." I ran to the bathroom and threw up. There was no way around him. He was married to my regional boss's daughter. This guy was bulletproof. It was only a matter of time before I was hauled into his father-in-law's office to make sure I'd gotten the message.

I'd overlooked a lot of unethical behavior since coming to South Florida, but now it was stopping me from doing my job. I thought of E. E. Cummings. *"There is some shit I will not eat."*

Two days later, the regional president—my local boss—summoned me to his office. I was calm; he was ready for an argument. Having built up a head of steam, he released it as soon as I sat down.

He and his son-in-law were in full agreement.

"Are you going to stop wasting time on this project of yours?" I nodded. He looked puzzled. He changed his demeanor, smiling sheepishly. *He's wondering what I'll tell headquarters.*

"Yes, I am." I smiled, too. I'd had two days to think about it, and I no longer cared. He relaxed into his chair, reaching for a cigar in the humidor on his desk. "I've prepared a letter of resignation," I said, placing it on his empty desk. "It gives you four weeks' notice——" He slammed the humidor shut.

"Nobody wants you to leave!" He hadn't seen this coming. *New York will get an earful, all right.*

"Four weeks will give me time to prepare my team," I continued calmly. "It's their chance to shine." He was stunned as I kissed him on the cheek. "Thanks for everything, Mr. President. I've always been proud to work at BFC. I'd like to think I've made a difference here, but it's time for me to go."

The day I left was a blur. I remember a cake. Phone calls and goodbyes. Why was I leaving? Where was I going? My coworkers wondered if they should leave, too.

My hands shook as I loaded two boxes and seven years into my car and drove home to Condoland. BFC was my identity. I made great friends there, but the breakup with El Innombrable left me intolerant of people I couldn't trust. I was raw, and I needed to heal.

On the drive home, my phone rang. "Did you quit?" It was a Florida friend from BFC.

"I did!"

"I heard a rumor, but I never know what to believe around here. Good for you, sister! If *I* had fuck-you money, I woulda quit a year ago."

"I don't have fuck-you money." *Gulp.*

"What're you gonna do?"

"I'll consult. I lined up three clients . . . And I'm going to do voice work."

"Nice. Hey, we should celebrate! You free tonight?"

I just quit my job. I have no boyfriend, so yah. "Free as a bird."

"Great. I'll see who can make it and text you the details."

We met in Ft. Lauderdale at a low-key Irish pub with a big mahogany bar and cheap drinks—perfect for my mood. I didn't have second thoughts, but I was starting to realize the enormity of my decision.

A commercial on the TV over the bar got my attention. One of those law firms with the 24/7 hotlines asked Floridians to call if they'd been victims of condo fraud. "Is condo association fraud endangering your building? Millions of dollars are stolen each year! If *your* association is stealing your hard-earned money, we can help. Call NOW at 1-800-GET-EVEN!" I laughed out loud.

"What's funny?" asked a friend.

"Nothing—just a crazy ad about condo associations stealing from people."

"I don't get it."

"I live in a condo. That stuff can't happen. There are laws and rules to protect us. I dunno. I guess it was the way they exaggerated."

"Glad I live in a house," she said.

Our drinks arrived. "Let's make a toast!" said another friend. "Here's to Alice Miller Independence Day!" The five of us toasted with the house white.

"Thanks, guys. You're the best!"

They said they envied my decision. We laughed and gossiped and went around the table asking what each person would do if she weren't afraid. I *was* afraid, but at least I didn't need to say "woulda" or "coulda." *Hopefully, there'll be no "shoulda."*

"Alice, tell us about this voice work. What do you want to do?"

My turn. "You know the voices you hear but don't see in comercials? Those are voiceovers. I want to do that, and now I'll be able to audition during the day. Also, I want to sing jazz—professionally."

"Wow! Where'd this come from?"

"I didn't know you sing!"

"I grew up listening to my grandparents' records, and I fell in love with musicals and jazz standards. I sang in school—took lessons, too. I stopped when I started working," I said, "but now I'll have time."

"That's so cool."

"You've got guts, Alice!" *I do?* I just wanted to be happy.

"Let us know when you have a gig. We'll be cheering in the front row!"

Since I was technically unemployed, they insisted on paying. "Here's to Alice! And courage!"

There was no turning back.

Six months later, when Bigger Fucking Card—a key competitor in the region—advertised its launch of *my* idea, I knew leaving BFC was the right decision.

5

The Board of Drektors[8]

Two weeks after my emancipation, Joanna Rivers stepped onto the treadmill next to me.

"Hi, honey. What's doin' with the Sports Committee?"

"The board met with the other buildings and approved our wish list for gym equipment. Actually, they want to renovate the whole Club House!"

"The Club House? Aw you kidding?" she said in her Bronx accent. "Idiots! While they're futzing around here, aw building is on life support!" Joanna panted as she increased her pace. "Do you understand the structural problems we have and what it'll cost to fix 'em?"

"What problems?"

"The air conditioning pipes aw corroded. The A/C could conk out any day—in this heat! We need new coppuh pipes, and that's not cheap. And the watuh pipes—have you noticed the leaks? We're spending a fortune in cleanup, and that's not in the budget."
I had no idea.

"When Edguh was on the bawd, he tried to replace the balcony

---

⁸ Drek — Yiddish for fecal matter

28

railings, remembuh?" I nodded. "Now, they're not up to code. And the rebar that holds up the balconies is rusting—that's a safety hazard, and expensive to fix. Meanwhile, this *farkakteh*[9] board wants to renovate the Club House? What the fuck is wrong with them!"

If these problems were so serious and urgent, wouldn't the board have mentioned them? *Maybe she's exaggerating.* "Can we remodel the Club House now and do the other projects later?" Joanna hit the stop button on her treadmill and marched to the cooler. *Did I say something wrong?* I followed her, hoping she'd answer my question.

She crushed her cup and dropped it in the wastebasket. "You tell me," she said, hands on hips. "You want A/C? Watuh? Balconies that don't collapse? Aw would you prefer a new treadmill?" She stomped off. *Oy! But how could the board ignore our safety?* It didn't make sense.

The board turned over when I started dating El Innombrable. Back then, I was oblivious. Now I had time to observe, and the new members didn't compare, either in credentials or professionalism. On the other hand, they hadn't raised our monthly maintenance payments, and they hadn't imposed special assessments. I figured they were spending our money prudently, which is why I voted to re-elect them.

The Board of *Drektors*, as Joanna called them, announced a January meeting soon after their fourth election victory in December. They would present the Club House renovation project. Immediately— and with no other information—unit owners began to argue the pros and cons.

---

[9] Farkakteh — Yiddish for crappy, becrapped

The night of the meeting, I arrived at the Party Room early to get a good seat. Sr. Holmez was wearing his cowboy hat—part of his Condoland *shtick*.[10] The gringo board dismissed him as an eccentric foreigner, giving him free reign to discover and document what he wished. He waved me over, and I sat next to him. The Champion joined me a few minutes later and I introduced her to Sr. Holmez.

Any time a special assessment was on the board agenda, unit owners showed up to hear what it would cost them. This meeting was no exception. There were more people than seats, so the board waited to start while the staff set up more folding chairs.

We strained to hear each other over a dull roar from the *fressers*[11] surrounding the refreshment table. Older unit owners filled plastic baggies with cookies "for later." The last people in line reached the table to find the cookies were gone. Macoyle called Hatfeld a "*chaza*."[12] Seeing tensions rise, the Manager dashed to the house phone, raising his voice over the noise.

"Gimme the chef . . . I told you! That's right. We're out of cookies . . . a big tray . . . bigger . . . maybe two . . . any dessert . . . I understand, but we have a situation here . . . Eighty-six 'em from tonight's menu . . . trust me . . . *fast* . . . remember Valentine's Day? Hurry!"

"What do you guys think of this board?" I asked my friends in Spanish and English. Sr. Holmez and the Champion gave me an earful on what can only be described as a cast of characters. When they finished, that law firm commercial seeking condo fraud litigants didn't seem so ridiculous. *Should I have written down the number?*

Here's what I learned:

---

[10] Shtick — Yiddish for gimmick
[11] Fressers — Yiddish for gluttons
[12] Chaza — Yiddish for pig

Her Highness: The board president was a *farbissina*,[13] a 70-something Chicago transplant who shed her Heartland values long ago. The lone WASP in a hive of East Coast and Latin American Jews and Catholics, she formed alliances, not friendships. Notoriously short-tempered, she kept a fierce hold on both her power and the meeting gavel, which she pounded whenever someone asked a question she didn't want to answer. She covered her thinning hair with a rotation of White Sox baseball caps, a perpetual annoyance to the building's Red Sox and Yankees fans.

Childless, she'd recently put her husband in a nursing home, creating a drain on her wallet. My friends suspected her role on the board helped fill the gap. Her sour face and nasty demeanor made it hard to feel sorry for her.

Her Highness held illegal board meetings on Saturday nights at her corner table in the Restaurant. According to Florida's Sunshine Law, gatherings of a majority of board members must be announced 48 hours in advance and be open to all unit owners. She routinely defied this law by dining with the other board members, who were "just neighbors eating dinner."

The Restaurant Manager knew where his bread was buttered. The Champion observed him placing unopened wine bottles in Her Highness's oversized bag. Condoland's unit owners paid for that wine! Sr. Holmez and the Champion's assessments fell into "trust" or "don't trust" columns. Her Highness was the first in the latter column, but she wouldn't be alone for long.

The Long Island Lothario: The board's vice president was a big

---

[13] Farbissina — Angry, bitter woman

and tall man with a booming voice. He sucked oxygen from any room he entered. He wore his hair slicked back and his polyester shirts tight; the top buttons open to display chest hairs and the gold chains adorning them. The shirts weren't tight when he bought them, but now they struggled to contain his basketball of a belly. He had the cheeks of a trumpet player. His face was usually flushed and his gray eyes bloodshot. He was Willy Loman, Long Island style.

In the months before board elections, Lothario went on a charm offensive. He sat for hours watching tennis matches, even offering himself as a doubles partner. He complimented the ladies while his wife, the head Barbie, worked the interior of the Club House. She befriended women in her exercise classes, bragging about her Prince Charming while soliciting votes. Glad-handers, the Lotharios agreed with everyone's ideas for the building, which may explain how Mr. Lothario got re-elected four years in a row to a volunteer job no one in their right mind would want.

He had no visible source of income, and his wife was a public school teacher. The couple *outrageously* name— and brand-dropped. On the surface, they seemed like over-the-top yet nice-enough people, but the fact that all three of their daughters lived in the Pacific Northwest, as far from their parents as possible, made us think there was more to this story. For Sr. Holmez, the Champion, and me, the verdict on the Lotharios was still out. Our greatest concern was Mr. Lothario's relationship with the Mobster.

The Mobster: The board treasurer, he moved to South Florida from New Jersey decades ago upon release from prison for grand theft auto. Sr. Holmez had it on good authority that the Mobster's employers made him a nonnegotiable relocation offer. In South Florida, they believed he was less likely to draw scrutiny from law enforcement.

The Mobster flaunted his connections to organized crime. Rumor had it that his business partner was a captain in one of New York's crime families—the one that rhymes with crazy. To repeat, he was the board TREASURER.

A jewelry consortium near Condoland was the perfect cash-friendly spot for his lending business. He recruited the Long Island Lothario as an apprentice and errand boy, schooling him in the underworld arts. Soon, his pupil was seen driving a Lincoln Navigator, followed by a black Cadillac, followed by an Audi, a BMW, and a Hummer. The Mobster was the father Lothario never had.

Now in his late 80s, the Mobster was feared by Condoland residents and management alike, and for good reason. When challenged, he brandished his connections like a weapon, but he didn't rely on threats alone. On a day that shall live in infamy, a unit owner asked the "wrong" question. Our treasurer got up from the dais and punched the man in the face—in front of 100 witnesses. No charges were filed, and the injured man was never again seen at a board meeting. Of all the Drektors, I would come to fear the Mobster the most.

Humpty Dumpty: The board secretary was as short and round as her name suggests. She accentuated her sun-damaged cleavage with plunging necklines on her wardrobe of brightly colored muumuus. As a young girl, she helped her father keep two sets of books for his New York garment business. There was nothing Mrs. Dumpty's father wouldn't do for his little girl. He was serving as Condoland's treasurer in the building's early days when an amount equal to four years of his only grandson's college tuition went missing, along with our general ledger. Condoland's recordkeeping was manual.

Without that ledger, there was no way to prove the money missing. The unit owners were assessed to cover what became known as the Tuition Heist.

Humpty Dumpty inherited her parents' condo. She was in over her head on the board, and she knew it. She lacked the mental wherewithal to mastermind fraud, but she also lacked the moral fiber to stand up to it. After all, she'd grown up with it. If it was good enough for her father, it was good enough for her.

I was surprised to learn the Dumptys socialized with Joanna and Edgar Rivers. From what I could see, they had nothing in common. Despite that friendship, the Champion, Sherlock, and I put Mrs. Dumpty in the "don't trust" column.

The Bulldog: This member-at-large hailed from Philadelphia. A boxer in his youth, he was squat with a disproportionately heavy torso and no neck. He dressed to convey respectability, but Brooks Brothers slacks and button-down shirts could not disguise his quick temper and street-fighting instincts. A consummate bully, he revealed his true nature in the company of anyone with less power or influence. He shouted when challenged, even in polite company. It was his tell.

To cut costs in the Club House, the Bulldog tried to discredit its staff members to get them fired. He left lights on and water running, only to accuse the employees of negligence. He'd raise the volume on the hanging TVs in the equipment room and make noise complaints to the Club House manager.

The worst was when he went after the Oracle, the spa's hardest working and most beloved employee. Fortunately, she was onto him. She kept a checklist of what she inspected when, which she reconciled with the Bulldog's visits to each area. When things went awry during her shift, her detail proved a successful defense.

The Bulldog was an attorney. He knew right from wrong and tried to cover his tracks. We put him in the "don't trust" column.

Just before the meeting began, I asked, "Sr. Holmez, have you heard about problems with our pipes and balconies?"

"Yes," he said in Spanish. "The previous head of maintenance told me we're living on borrowed time."

This is scary! "Then why's the board pushing the Club House renovation? Will they fix the structural issues in our building concurrently? How much will it all cost?"

"Those are my questions, too, Alice," he said. "Would you do me a favor? My English is no good. The people no understand me." He was proud, but practical. "Would you translate for me?"

"Of course." I was flattered to be asked.

"Order! Order! Order!" Her Highness banged her gavel, and the meeting began. Last month's minutes were approved, and each committee head gave a report. The next item on the agenda was the proposed Club House renovation. It was protocol for board members to talk amongst themselves when considering an initiative, but it was obvious they'd met in secret and reached a consensus. Most of my neighbors were retired and living on a fixed income. The board expected pushback, particularly from people who never used the gym or spa.

The Long Island Lothario pulled his pants up over his girth, walked in front of the dais and forced a big smile. His gold tooth caught the light. "When our property was built, it offered unparalleled luxury living." *Unparalleled luxury? I'm thrilled to have a garbage disposal!* "We were the envy of the neighborhood. Outsiders used to beg to eat in our restaurant or buy passes to our spa." Unit owners turned each other, eyes rolling. Our presenter was loving the spotlight, oblivious to his audience. As the Yiddish expression goes, you could spit on him, and he would think it was raining.

"Our Club House needs to be updated," he continued. "Take the gym. The equipment is ooold. Treadmills are out of service. You complain when you wait for machines, complain the room is crowded. I agree! We need new equipment. A bigger, better space! And the tennis courts—who wants to fry like an egg in this sun? What's your health worth to you? Covering the courts will protect you from skin cancer—and wrinkles!" He winked.

The vice president paced, yelling. "We need to renovate the spa, because it's . . ."—he stopped for dramatic effect, bending then straightening his arms—"DISGUSTING! Why should you need flip flops to take a shower? Why's the mani/pedi station next to the toilets?" He grinned. "You deserve a state-of-the-art salon! A place you can be proud to take your friends!"

He scanned the room to see if anyone bought what he was selling. The younger residents—in their 50s and 60s—were listening. Some looked interested. A tennis player touched a bandage on her leg. *Basal cell?*

The walker and cane contingency, however, was distressed. They complained loudly to each other. Lothario was losing them. He looked over to his wife. She gestured to him using her left hand as a plate and her right hand as a utensil, scooping up imaginary food and pretending to chew it. He took the hint and changed topics.

Leaving his mic on the dais, he strolled down the center aisle, where the older unit owners sat (it gave them easier access to the bathrooms). "The Restaurant needs an update. The chairs are stained. The stuffing is falling out of them! Our chef says our kitchen isn't up to code. Our stove isn't reliable." Our "chef" was a cook. I called him Death by Garlic.

The Champion whispered to me, "The city inspector just cited the kitchen as a fire hazard and gave us a warning."

Lothario made eye contact with the elder unit owners, particularly the women. They stopped whispering to listen. The Restaurant was their stomping ground. Though they complained about *everything,* they liked going there. Seeing his opportunity, he continued with renewed confidence.

"I've seen you beautiful people kick it up on the dance floor. Have you noticed that floor is chipped?" Lothario walked to a group of women and stood close. "One of you lovely ladies could catch your heel and fall. You could break a hip!" They nodded. It was working. I heard Music Man's "Ya Got Trouble" in my head.

"And what about your children and grandchildren? What do they think of our *farkakteh* Club House? Or that smell from the bathrooms!" The bathrooms got me. There was something wrong with the Club House plumbing.

"What's this gonna cost?" yelled a snowbird. The money question opened a floodgate. I tried not to laugh as people shouted over each other.

"Why should I pay for you to exercise?"

"Speak into the microphone. We can't hear you!"

"Why so fancy?"

"Anybody speak eh-Spanish? *¡No entiendo!*"

"I'm on a fixed income!"

"The Restaurant looks fine. Just change the chairs!"

Before Lothario could respond, an unmistakable Bronx accent broke through.

"Yes, aw equipment is old. And sure, it'd be nice to update the Club House." Joanna stood, and all eyes turned to her. "But befaw you spend money on the nice-to-haves, fix the necessities! I'm tawking about the air conditioning and watuh pipes in *this* building. They're on life suppawt. Why haven't you mentioned them?" The audience gasped with alarm. Questions raced through the Party Room in English and Spanish.

"Pipes? What's she talkin' about? Is that true?"

"I'm on oxygen!"

"*Por favor*, in eh-Spanish, please!"

"What's all THAT gonna cost?"

"What did she say?"

"Speak into the microphone!"

I watched the Drektors seated at the dais. They shuffled papers, darting knowing glances at each other. *They're hiding something!* The meeting was getting out of hand.

Her Highness grabbed the gavel. "Quiet! Quiet! Our vice president is presenting this important project to you as a courtesy. If you keep interrupting, I'll adjourn the meeting!"

The Champion whispered to me again. "It's no courtesy. The renovation he's describing includes structural changes—they need two-thirds of the unit owners to approve it."

The Long Island Lothario looked at Her Highness, unsure of himself. She nodded, and he continued, making light. "Don't worry," he said, flapping his hand. "That's just routine pipe maintenance. Our 40-year inspection is eight years away. We have plenty of time to take care of it. Same with the balconies. There's no rush!" *Nobody mentioned the balconies.* Sweat stains grew under his armpits. *He's lying.* "Right, Manager?" If our building manager had an independent thought, he never expressed it. The board could fire him at will, and he knew it. With a forced smile under lifeless brown eyes, he stood.

"Yes, that's correct, sir. The A/C and water pipes are low priority." Her Highness nodded at him, and he sat down, eyes toward the floor.

Satisfied with the Manager's opinion, the unit owners settled— until someone repeated the paramount question: "What's this gonna cost!" We waited. Lothario stood tall, shoulders back, his buttons at war with his shirt.

"Four million dollars—remember, we only pay a third of that. Condolands II and III each pay a third." Condoland II and Condoland III were smaller, newer buildings on the property. Their units were larger and fewer. They were expensive, but poorly built. The developper went bankrupt during their construction and cut corners. As part of the settlement, he'd left $2.7 million in escrow for upgrades to the Club House. *Amazing how those numbers align.* The money was burning a hole in their board members' pockets.

"That's not bad considering the upgrades," I whispered to the Champion. I wanted us to have it all.

The Champion shook her head. She stood, her voice firm. "Your budget's unrealistic. How did you get to that number?"

"We have estimates for everything we're gonna do," said the Long Island Lothario. "That's the number. It's $1.3 million for our building."

There were 400 condominiums in Condoland; that would cost each owner an average of $3,250. I'd pay less, since mine was one of the smaller units. *Not peanuts, but manageable.*

The Champion sat down. "He's out of his mind if he thinks he can get that done for $4 million." I translated for Sr. Holmez. He nodded in agreement. *But Lothario has signed estimates! We need new gym equipment. The Restaurant sounds nice, too. Why's everyone so pessimistic?* After three years on the Sports Committee, I wanted something to show for it.

A bald man in his 70s with a lyrical Argentinian accent stood and introduced himself. He spoke slowly and deliberately.

"I am a ceevil [civil] engineer. As many of you know, I am the head of the Architectural Committee, and I agree with thees lady." He pointed to the Champion. "The project jew [you] describe should cost more than $4 million. I would like to review the es-teemates—"

"I guarantee it won't be more than $4 million!" said Lothario as if his life depended on it. "I *personally* guarantee it! That's how sure I am. Ladies and gentlemen, we must protect our investment! We can't leave our Club House in disrepair! We can't be embarrassed to invite guests there!" He wasn't wrong. Softening, he switched from stick to carrot. "This project will raise our property values! Vote yes for the renovation, and I promise you, it'll pay for itself." With that, the Long Island Lothario exited central stage, chin up, and returned to his chair behind the dais.

"The meeting is adjourned," said Her Highness, giving her gavel one last bang.

We stayed in our seats as the crowd dispersed. "If he has esti-mates and guarantees the cost," I asked, "wouldn't it be nice to fix our Club House?"

"Sure, it would," said the Champion, "but he's dreaming if he thinks it'll be $4 million. Why would he guarantee that number?" I made a disappointed face. "I'd love the refresh, too, Alice—espe-cially a roof over the tennis courts." She'd had several bouts with skin cancer. It was a fact of life down here. "But they can't pull the numbers out of thin air. I see it all the time at work. South Florida contractors give 'made to order' estimates to get the job."

"What do you think?" I asked Sr. Holmez.

"I here 32 years," he said. "Condoland design by excellent architect, but property no take care of herself. I agree with Champion. Price no realistic. I watch this board tonight, and I watch the Manager. Something is no right."

"Why didn't you say something?" I asked. "I would have translated."

"Thank you, Alicia. Today, is best to listen. When is time to ask questions, I hire you." He tipped his hat, and I smiled. Sherlock could be serious and funny at the same time. He had lifetimes of wisdom and experience at the ready for those who took the time to know him.

Joanna Rivers passed us on her way to the staircase, and I waved her over. The Champion and Joanna knew each other from the previous board. I introduced her to Sr. Holmez.

"Nice to meet you." She shook his hand. *Why don't the English and Spanish speakers know each other?*

"What you think of thees meeting?" asked Sr. Holmez.

"They're full of shit!" said Joanna. "Those pipes can burst any time. When my husband was on the bawd, he had the head engineer evaluate the building, and that was the conclusion faw years ago! Of caws, *this* board foyud [fired] the engineer and replaced him with a yes man. And the Managuh," she flapped her hand. "Fuhgeddaboudit. He's a puppet."

Sr. Holmez looked surprised. He was unaccustomed to women cursing. "I agree," he said after a moment, smiling.

"So, what do we do?" I asked. *I quit my job, and now the building falls apart?* "How do we know what to believe?"

"I'll tawk to Edguh," said Joanna. "Maybe he has the report from the previous engineer."

"I talk to people, too," said Sr. Holmez. He knew every employee and vendor in the building. If the board was up to something, the workers would tell him.

"Alice," said the Champion. "The board chooses new committee members this month. You've done your job for the Sports Committee. Why don't you volunteer for the Finance Committee instead? You have the background. If they pick you, you'll get monthly reports. You can tell us how our money's being spent."

"That's a good idea," I said.

"I'll dig into things from a legal perspective," she said. "Let's share information as we get it. We can meet in the Condoland Coffee Shop. Once a week?"

It was a plan. It was nice to be part of something. I hadn't felt this comfortable with people since I left New York.

"I heard you're working from home now," the Champion said as we walked up the stairs. "What are you doing?"

"I . . . I'm *trying* to make a living with my voice—singing and voice acting, maybe some writing." I braced for judgement. It didn't come.

"You go, girl! Have you done vocal work before?" She was genuinely interested.

"I sang in school, acted in the musicals. In New York, I read the news on the radio for the blind. Oh! And last month, I recorded three voicemail greetings!" We reached the top of the staircase and moved away from the traffic. "I dreamed of singing on Broadway, but my mom said female leads could only get cast on a couch." I dropped it and majored in economics.

"I'm proud of you."

"You are?" I asked.

"Yes! You found what makes you happy." She paused. "And for money in the meantime?" It was everyone's inevitable question.

"I cashed out my BFC stock options, and I'm consulting." She gave me a look. *I'm not unemployed. I really am consulting!* "I have three marketing clients so far—companies I know from BFC."

She beamed. "That's terrific. I admire your courage!"

"Thank you, Champion. That means a lot to me," I said. *If only my mother could be so encouraging.*

6

The Floods

The last board meeting filled me with doubt. I owned a condo over a thousand miles from home in a building that might be falling apart, with management I couldn't trust. I quit my job, and my boyfriend quit me. Most of my friends were back in the north-east. I felt . . . unmoored. I called my dad.

"Hello?" It was my mother. *Shoot.*

"Is Daddy there?"

"Is it urgent? I'm going shopping, and the boy who usually shovels is *skiing* this weekend. Your father's clearing the driveway." *I forgot; it's winter.*

My heart sank. "No . . . never mind. It can wai—"

"Hold on. I hear the door. Ben! It's Alice." She lowered her voice. "She doesn't sound too chipper." Speaking into the receiver, she said, "You're in luck. He came in for his scarf, but since it's you, he's coming right over." Back to my dad. "Take off your boots!"

"How's your 'work' going?" she asked me, her voice dripping with sarcasm.

Really? "Fine."

"Alice?"

"Hi, Daddy." Tears stuck in my throat. I couldn't help it.

"What's wrong?"

"I'm scared. I'm taking so many risks. What if I can't do it?"

He thought for a moment. "Being scared is normal," he said softly, so my mother couldn't hear. "If you weren't scared, I'd think something was wrong!" He tried to laugh, but my pain was his pain. "Listen, sweethaht, you gotta give it yah best shot. Yar a smaht girl, yar talented. I believe in you!" I smiled and wiped my eyes. "But *you* gotta believe in you. Success takes time. That's why yar consulting, right?"

"Right."

"Don't look back, and never look down. Just keep yar eye on the prize. Sometimes, you'll take one step fahwahd and two steps back, but you keep going. You understand?"

"Yes, Daddy. I do. Thank you!"

"I love you, sweethaht." I heard a door open and shut. He whispered, "You need money?"

"No. I'm OK."

"Ya sure?"

"Yes. Thank you, Daddy!"

"Remembah, you can always come home."

"I know." I grabbed a tissue.

"Wanna talk to yah muthah?"

"No, that's OK." He believed in me. Always. Without judgement. It was enough.

"See ya latuh, alligatuh!" he said.

"After a while, crocodile!" I answered. We'd recited this reptilian rhyme when he put me to bed as a child, when we ended each phone call, and whenever we said good-bye.

I brought a list of questions to my first Finance Committee meeting. This was an opportunity to understand how Condoland was spending our money. Hopefully, my friends and I were worrying about nothing.

Two board members—Humpty Dumpty and the Bulldog—walked into the meeting like they were in charge. They sat across from me at the Conference Room table.

"What are they doing here?" I asked the Committee member next to me.

"He's on the Committee," he said, pointing. "She's the board liaison."

"What's that?"

Mrs. Dumpty overheard me. She and her cleavage leaned over the table. "I'm here ta represent the bawd's views during yaw meetings and share yar idears back with the bawd," she said. "I'm a non-voting Committee membuh." She looked at the Manager to ask if she said it correctly. He nodded, and she sat back in her chair, arms folded.

The other Committee members and I looked at the Bulldog as if to ask what *he* was doing there. He looked up, startled to see us staring at him. The Manager intervened. "Mr. Bulldog is a voting member of this Committee. Board members are allowed to serve on committees as long as no more than two—that's a minority of the board—are in attendance."

"That's correct," said the Bulldog, chest out. *He's here in case Humpty Dumpty has a big fall.*

The Manager explained the Committee rules and protocols to us. Our first order of business was electing a chairperson.

"Who wants to nominate someone?" asked Humpty Dumpty.

Gassy's hand shot up first.

"I nominate Alice," she said. *Me?* Maybe that was my reward for making the rookie mistake of sitting downwind of her at the conference table. Before I could decide if I wanted the job, the other six Committee members voted unanimously, and I was elected chairperson.

I called the Champion after work to give her the news. "Is that right? Well, congratulations!"

"You don't sound surprised. Did you do something?" I asked.

"Last night, Gassy and I took the same yoga class. She made a rather large announcement during downward dog. Even *she* was embarrassed. Only for you, kiddo, I moved against traffic and lay my mat next to hers. Walking back to our building, I mentioned what a finance whiz you——"

"Seriously?"

"What do you care? As chair, you——we——have access to more information."

The Champion was right. Everyone on the Committee got monthly reporting, but as chair, I could meet with the accountants and all the department heads to question the numbers. I would make recommendations to the board. Now, we had leverage.

My relationship with the board began amicably. At 34, I was younger than most of their kids, and nobody saw me as a threat. I asked polite questions about expenses they assumed I wouldn't understand.

"What's this $450,000 in unbudgeted 'Water Restoration' on line 36?" *Is this the flooding Joanna mentioned?*

"That's what we paid to Water Pro," said the Manager. "We've had several indoor floods this year. Water Pro stations pumps to get rid of the water and prevent mold."

"Is this expense recurring?" I asked. *Two weeks ago, he told us pipes were low priority.*

"No," knee-jerked the Manager.

"Has maintenance inspected the pipes?"

"Those were one-off situations, Miss Miller. We patched those spots—"

"I see. Can we hear from the engineer?" I asked.

"The engineer reports to the Managuh," snapped Humpty Dumpty, "and he just told you the spots have been patched." *I hit a nerve.* She tried to sound good-humored, but I got the hint and pulled back.

The Conference Room had several rows of seating available for interested unit owners. Because finance meetings were usually booor-ing, only a brave few showed up. Sr. Holmez was there— he attended all Committee meetings—along with a handful of re-tired businessmen.

Unit owners watched the conversation like a tennis match, re-peating my questions when they weren't answered. Apparently, drilling down to understand specific expenses was new. The at-tendees went home and told their wives, who told their friends in the Card Room, who went to the spa still talking about this myste-rious young girl who asked tough questions.

Over the next few months, I continued querying while trying not to trigger the board. Attendance grew, as did the rows of spec-tator seats in the Conference Room. At the time, I didn't realize people were talking about me. After getting dumped by El Innom-brable, I built a wall around my heart that gossip couldn't pene-trate.

Long after it mattered, the Oracle told me that when I joined the Finance Committee, unit owners saw me talking to her in the gym and grilled her about me. She flipped back her long ponytail, speaking softly out of habit. "Alice, you were the new girl on cam-pus! You wouldn't believe the rumors about you."

"What rumors?"

"They said you had a boyfriend who doesn't live here." *He did just leave for Eastern Slavia.* "They said you worked for a Fortune 500 company." *I had.* "They asked me how old you were. I told them to ask you."

"Thanks," I said. "It's none of their business!"

"Exactly," said the Oracle.

"Is that it?"

She shook her head. "They wondered how somebody so young could head the Finance Committee. The head of the Decorating Committee figured out your gym schedule and used to stop by to 'run into' you! She wanted money for wallpaper, but you always had your headphones on."

"What is she, a lobbyist?"

The Oracle smiled. "You were an overnight celebrity. People popped their heads in the gym to see if you were there, and if you weren't, they'd leave!" *Why didn't she tell me back then?* "I know how private you are. I didn't tell you at the time because the gym was a good outlet for you. You were sad, and I wanted you to keep exer-cising." *She's right. If I knew, I would have stayed clear.*

I enjoyed more than exercise at the gym. I took a salsa class and was paired with the Daredevil, an extreme sportsman in his 30s. He was broodingly handsome, and I was human. We kept bumping into each other after that. I liked talking to him. He was five foot ten with short dark hair and dark eyes. He looked like a Latin Don Draper with a five o-clock shadow—a *Jewish*, Latin Don Draper.

One crowded evening at the gym, the Daredevil watched me

struggling to clear a path as I lunged across the room with 10-pound weights in my hands. "Try the shoulder press. It's great for leg strength. *Ven*," he said, motioning me toward him. "I'll spot you."

"OK. Be right there." I put away the weights and swiped on lip gloss from my fanny pack.

He adjusted the bar to my height and removed two heavy plates from either side. "You're in good shape!" he said, giving me the once-over. "The bar itself weighs 45 pounds. We'll build up when you're ready." He added a 10-pound plate to each side of the bar, and I placed my shoulders under it. "Bend at the knees." He put his hand on my back. "Nice and slow," he said, as I lifted. "That was easy right?" I nodded. "Wanna go higher?"

Yes! "I'll try." I blushed, feeling the heat where his hand had been.

"Did you put on lipstick for me?"

"It's ChapStick," I said. He smiled. *Busted!*

He added 15 pounds on each side. "How does it feel?" He leaned over my shoulder.

You mean your breath on my face? "Good," I smiled. His hand slid lower down my back, sending sparks up and down my spine.

"You wanna try more? Or should we save it for next time?"

Next time? "Let's try it," I said. *How hard can it be?* He added a 20-pound plate on either side of the bar.

The Oracle passed by. "Alice, you need anything?" She sounded bothered.

"No, I'm all set . . . Thanks!" *Why is she interrupting?* I gave her a look.

"You're welcome." She took the hint and left the equipment room. I inhaled and pushed up. It was too heavy. As my knees buckled, the Daredevil grabbed the bar and set it in its groove. He put his hands around my waist, pulling me up to sit on the bench. *Is that musk?*

"That was 135 pounds." *That's more than I weigh!* "Too much, too fast. I'm sorry. You'll build up to that. You all right?"

"Yep," I nodded. "Building up sounds good."

He never overtly hit on me. We met at the gym and talked. Music, movies, history, even politics. I got hooked on those conversations. He compared the U.S. to growing up in Uruguay. We talked about his passion for skydiving and mine for singing.

He didn't pry, and he never asked superficial questions. He spent hours with me at the gym but didn't ask me out. I was confused. I wasn't ready for a relationship, but a friendly dinner and a movie would be nice.

"We close in five minutes, guys," the Oracle told us one Sunday afternoon. I'd lost track of time. The Daredevil and I had been talking for hours, alone in the gym. I went into the locker room to get my things, and the Oracle followed me. "He's not capable of a relationship, Alice. He's trouble." *Relationship? She sees the attraction. I'm not imagining it.*

"We're just friends," I told her, embarrassed. *We are just friends!*

"Best keep it that way." She sounded serious. I didn't listen when she warned me about El Innombrable. This time, her advice gave me pause. The Daredevil bragged about women, and that was a red flag. Since his wife's death six years earlier, he buried his grief in a string of flings and short-term girlfriends.

At first, the references to women past, present, and future didn't bother me. I felt safe, and I empathized with his heartbreak. *There's nothing here, Alice. He enjoys our conversations, and that's all you need right now. He's not into you.* But the closer we got, the more those references irked me.

In March, I traveled to Lima, Peru, on business with a client who was also a friend. She made an appointment with an astrologer and asked if I wanted to join her. Always open to that sort of thing, I said yes.

The astrologer's home was in an upscale neighborhood with armed guards at every street corner. *Yikes!* Thanks to those guards, we could walk safely from our hotel to the astrologer. Her home was cheerful, with lots of brightly colored cushions. In her backyard, exotic butterflies flew from flower to flower.

"It's a butterfly garden," she explained. "Come, let's sit on the patio." I followed her outside. As I sat down, an electric blue butterfly sat on the back of my hand. "Don't move!" I stayed still for 15 minutes before it flew away.

"Do they normally do that?" I asked.

"Once in a blue moon," she said. "It's a sign."

"What kind of sign?"

"I can't say for sure. When you see that color again, you'll know." *One hundred dollars to tell me I'll see the color blue?* Before the reading, I sent the astrologer the date, exact time, and location of my birth. She opened a folder with charts and told me what the stars told her.

"Have you lost weight recently?" *It's the exercising. Lucky guess?*

"About five pounds."

"You're going to lose more, and you're going to fall in love." She studied my face. I tried not to react. *She sees I'm not wearing a ring. She could say this to any single woman.* "Soon, you'll be head over heels in love. In fact, you're going to feel like you're flying. Yes, you're going to be flying!"

I thought about the astrologer's predictions on the flight home.

The Daredevil jumps out of planes. She couldn't know that . . . Is he the one? Does flying mean skydiving? Am I ready to fall in love again?

Whether it was infatuation or true romance, over the next few weeks, I spent more and more time at the gym. The Daredevil and I both worked out in the evening on weekdays, but on weekends, it was hit-or-miss. Seeing him became an obsession. I spent hours at the gym on Saturdays and Sundays hoping to "bump into" him. According to the Oracle, the Daredevil did the same. Despite my doubts, I wanted the astrologer to be right.

Condoland's indoor flooding continued. I was home during the day now and heard noisy fans—the kind that Water Pro used—on several floors as I rode the elevator. *How much are they costing us? Why not fix the pipes?*

I brought up the floods the next time my friends and I met in the Condoland Coffee Shop. "Last year, we spent $450,000 on water restoration. At the rate we're going, it'll be more this year. Does anyone know what's causing them?"

"I spoke to my friend in maintenance," said Sr. Holmez. He spoke in Spanish, and I translated. "Half of the floods are occurring on two floors. Know who lives on those floors?" He sipped his espresso, eyes dancing, waiting for us to guess.

I played along. "Who?"

"The Mobster and the Long Island Lothario." Sr. Holmez sat back, smiling, as I translated for the Champion and Joanna.

"What about the other half?" I asked.

His cheeks gave way to a full grin. "Know who lives on *those* floors?"

"No! Who?"

"Two *other* board members: Her Highness and the Bulldog.

Also, Lothario's friend who flips apartments. What an opportunity to buy flood-damaged apartments below market, renovate, and sell at a profit!" Sr. Holmez sat back, waiting for me to translate and for everyone to digest his accusation.

"Those bastuhds!" Joanna slammed her coffee cup, which over-flowed onto our table. The Champion stacked napkins on the spill.

"I get the flipping part," I said, "but why would Drektors flood their own apartments?"

"It's fraud, Alice." The Champion dealt with insurance claims in her law practice. "Say someone wants a new floor but doesn't want to pay for it. The flood destroys the floor, and the claim check pays for a new one."

"If that's true," I asked, "why doesn't our building get a claim check for flooding in the common areas? I don't—"

"Look what I brought!" Joanna handed the Champion a copy of Condoland's flood insurance policy. "Edguh got it from the Office."

The Champion skimmed the policy. "So far, flood damage to the common areas has been less than the deductible per incident," she said. "That's why."

"*¡Que coincidencia!*" said Sr. Holmez.

"Indeed," said the Champion. "Florida insurers are squeamish. If the building submits a claim for a big flood, our premium will spike. They might even cancel our policy."

"That's not good fuh 'business'!" said Joanna. "But I think there's more to this story. What do we know about the watuh res-toration company? Aw they paying kickbacks?"

"There's no money for kickbacks," I said. "Water Pro gives us a 30 percent discount."

Joanna graduated magna cum laude from the School of Hard Knocks. She gave me a pitying look. "Thirty percent off *what*? If

Watuh Pro doubles its price and takes 30 percent off, there's plenty of money for kickbacks." I flashed back to a BFC executive's backyard business barbecue that paid for his new landscaping. *I am so naïve!*

The Champion saw me slump. "Here's what you do: Call the Bookkeeper and ask to see the other two bids for the water restoration contract. The board should get three bids for any service to compare prices and quality. Act like it's a routine question. See what she says."

I called the Bookkeeper the next day. When I asked about the bids, she asked me to hold while she checked the files—the paper files. Records *still* weren't digitized at Condoland.

"Thanks for holding," she said. "I don't see any bids for water restoration."

"What about the Water Pro contract?" I asked.

"Don't have that, either. Do you want to ask the Manager?" I thanked her, told her not to worry, and hoped she wouldn't say anything. I wasn't ready to tip my hand.

At the next Finance Committee meeting, the Manager reported $200,000 in water restoration expenses year-to-date through April. *This is moving in the wrong direction.*

"Manager, how does Water Pro's pricing compare to the other companies who bid on this contract?" My eyes were wide. I was going for innocent.

The Manager sputtered. His face went from pink to crimson. "Well, ah, what do you—"

"You get three bids before you award a contract, right?" The manager glanced at the three dozen unit owners in the audience waiting for his response. He spoke carefully.

"Usually, we do."

"Usually?"

"Well, you need to understand, Miss Miller, a flood is an emergency." *You don't say?* "We don't have time to ask for bids when our hallway is filling with water. Water Pro is extremely responsive. Last month, they came here at 3 a.m. to help us with a flood on the 10th floor." *In the middle of the night, when no one's watching.* You could hear a pin drop. Nobody even coughed, and that's saying a lot for this crowd.

"I understand the urgency," I said, "and it's great that Water Pro's responsive. But we've had floods for 16 months now, and we've spent hundreds of thousands of dollars on water restoration in that time. Why not get bids *now* so when the *next* flood comes—and hopefully it won't, since you told us there's no problem with the pipes—we'll know our money's being spent wisely?"

Clapping erupted from the observation seats. It felt great, but it made me a target. I motioned them to stop, and they did. Humpty Dumpty glared at me. There were too many witnesses for her to ignore my question.

"The Manager will look into that, Alice. Thank you," said Mrs. Dumpty. He nodded, and Sr. Holmez tipped his cowboy hat at me from the audience. *Baby steps.* We were making headway.

I found a voice teacher on the internet. I hadn't sung much since college, and I had a lot to relearn. He toured with a big band before settling down and teaching. He knew jazz as a business. He told me to make a vocal career plan and follow it. He helped me create music videos, which I posted to social media. At his suggestion, I built a website with the help of a friend from BFC. Once I had the site, the videos, the demos, and the social media pages, I was ready to get gigs.

The Oracle was my biggest cheerleader. She gave her boss the link to my website. He gave it to someone in the Condoland Management Office, who shared it with the Restaurant Manager. The Oracle gave me the update.

"He likes your voice and your music."

"Really?"

"Yeah—"

"What's wrong?"

"He said, and I quote, 'She can sing here, but she doesn't expect to be paid, does she?'"

"What! Don't they pay the one-man band?"

"That's what my boss asked. He said you're a professional. Of course, you want to be paid!" *I'm a professional? If they pay me, I guess I will be.*

The one-man band had a standing gig on Saturday nights at the Restaurant. His keyboard had levers to add bass, drum, and horn sounds to his piano playing. Linking to his laptop, he could play backing tracks when someone requested a song he didn't know. He blended like wallpaper, but he got the job done. Condoland diners danced to his music until closing at 9 p.m.

The Restaurant Manager called a few weeks after my conversation with the Oracle. "Our entertainer is going on vacation for a week. Would you like to fill in?"

I did a happy dance. "Yes! I would!" I needed enough to pay an accompanist. He agreed to my price.

"We look forward to having you at the Restaurant. You'll start at 6:30. Come by that afternoon for a sound check."

"Thank you! I sure will."

We made the evening elegant. I wore a sleeveless black gown, and my accompanist wore a dark suit. At my request, the grand piano was brought into the main dining area. I sang standards from the American Songbook, mostly in English, with a few in Spanish and Italian. "Fly Me to the Moon" and Burt Bacharach's "Close to You" were the highlights of the evening. Nobody seemed to notice how nervous I was. Even weeks later, neighbors stopped me to say they enjoyed the performance. Making people happy is the best part of singing. This gig would help me get other gigs. It was happening. I was a professional singer!

My performance did not escape the board's notice. When the Dumptys dined with Joanna and Edgard Rivers the following night, Mrs. Dumpty mentioned it to Joanna, who called me as soon as she got home.

"So, Dumpty says, 'What does she know about finance? She's just a singuh!'" Mrs. Dumpty hailed from Brooklyn. "'Just a singuh!' Alice, I gripped the table so hawd my knuckles turned white. 'Just a singuh!' You know what I told huh?"

Whatever it was, I'm glad I wasn't on the receiving end. "What?"

"I says, 'She's got maw degrees than you have hairs on yaw head!'"

"What did she say?"

"She dropped the subject, but I gotta tell ya, I'm not lettin' it go so fast." A crack had formed in their friendship.

After a vote, the Drektors and the respective boards of Condolands II and III approved a combined $4 million special assessment for the Club House renovation. The Club House closed in May when the renovation began. During construction, the Long Island Lothario snagged the still-functioning exercise equipment and had the maintenance crew move it to the Party Room in the Condoland I tower.

Passing through the lobby one evening on my way to work out, I saw four Water Pro fans running at full blast. A few people watched while maintenance men standing on 20-foot ladders installed vertical beams reaching the ceiling.

"What are they doing?" I asked a neighbor, yelling over the fans.

"Tryin' to keep the ceiling from collapsing." *Great!* I hurried to the Party Room, skirting yellow folding signs that warned, "CAUTION! Wet Floor" and "¡CUIDADO! Piso Mojado." *They really did it this time.*

In the Party Room, buckets around the floor were filling with water falling from the ceiling. *How many floors are leaking?* Only the Daredevil, the Oracle, and I were there. The carpet squished as I slushed toward the Oracle. "When did this happen?"

"Last night, around 3 a.m.," she said.

"Why's it always 3 a.m.? Why not 4 a.m.?"

"It's the perfect time," said the Daredevil, sloshing toward us. "Think about it." He moved a hair off my face, watching me like prey, oozing testosterone. *Alice, snap out of it. He does this with everyone. He can't help himself.* I looked away, watching water drop into a bucket to concentrate on his words. "The night owls are asleep by 3 a.m., and the early birds aren't up yet. It's the least likely time to get caught." I looked at him. *How does he know this?* "Remember, I grew up in Uruguay." We both smiled.

I pulled away from that animal's magnetism toward the Oracle. "Who did it?" I asked her quietly, my focus returning.

"It's who you think it is," she said. Her grandmother schooled her to give direction, not a blueprint. People with their gifts were meant to guide the seeker to her destiny without changing it. "This time, somebody made a mistake. The flood wasn't meant to be this big. Condoland will have to report it to the insurance company."

She was right. The adjuster estimated the cost of cleanup and repairs at $900,000, obligating the Manager to file a claim with our flood insurer. Given the obvious damage, the claim was approved. *This time, we know the payout, and we know what repairs we need. Finally, we can hold the board to account!*

7

Rattling the Snake

There are 613 commandments in the Old Testament. Condoland's Book of Rules and Regulations had almost as many. When Security called me on a Saturday night, I learned one of those rules the hard way.

"Alice, the unit owner below you said she hears people walking in your apartment." It was 10:09 p.m. "Noise disturbances are not allowed after 10 p.m." I had two BFC friends over for drinks.

"Walking is a noise disturbance?"

"I have to relay the complaint."

"Are you saying I'm not allowed to have company?"

"No, but would you and your guests take off your shoes?"

In a building filled with professionals and professional complainers, Condoland's largely retired population served as an informal neighborhood watch reporting rule infractions to the Management Office. They bordered on vigilantism. Arguments with offenders were frequent, but to their credit, the retirees were equal opportunity enforcers. Most residents ultimately complied, as the alternative was a $50 fine per infraction per day.

Rules were the price of living in a community. From time to

time, they were disputed and reconsidered. Change petitions were reviewed monthly by the Rules Committee. If approved, a recommendation was presented to the board for a vote.

During one of our Sunday get-togethers in the Condoland Coffee Shop, my friends and I discussed a do-as-I-say, not-as-I-do pattern among the Drektors.

"For the last 10 years," said Joanna, "I have a canasta game on Tuesdays and Thursdays. It's me, two women from the building, and one woman who lives in the next complex. Around noon, we go to the Restaurant for lunch.

"My friend from the othuh complex invested with Madoff, that son-of-a-bitch! Poo-poo-poo!" She spit on the floor. *Who's gonna clean that up?* The waitress looked askance. "Keep ya pants on," said Joanna, dropping a napkin on the floor and wiping the area with her foot. "All gone, see?" The waitress shook her head and walked quickly to the entrance to greet arriving guests. "So where was I?"

"Your friend in the next complex," I said.

"That's right," said Joanna. "She and huh husband lost eh-vree-thing." She leaned forward and whispered, her face contorted, "Their son sends them money. Can you imagine?" We shook our heads. "Last week, she asks if we can bring sandwiches to the Cawd Room so we can 'play longuh.' My heart goes out to huh, but I explained Condoland doesn't allow eating in the Cawd Room."

"What's your point?" No one ever accused the Champion of being polite.

"I'm getting there. You got a train to catch?"

"Her husband's in town," I said.

"Ohhh!" Joanna grinned knowingly. "OK. I'll make it fast. Now where was I? I know. I wanted to help my friend, so I told huh Condoland has a new rule. Only unit ownuhs can pay in the Restaurant. Remembuh that in case you see huh and she asks you——"

"And?" The Champion looked at her watch.

"And I've been treating huh. I tell huh she's doing me a favuh coming heuh, since I don't drive." *You can't walk next door?* Joanna saw we were all impatient. "Hold yaw damned horses! I'm going as fast as I can. Heuh's the point. Yesterday, we were packing up aw cawds to go to the Restaurant, when in comes two waituhs *delivering lunch*! And they didn't bring sandwiches. They had eggplant Parmesan and pasta with red sauce. Tawk about a mess!"

"Who order?" asked Sr. Holmez.

"Huh Highness! There wuh six at huh table, and they sat there eating in front of us."

"Did you say anything?" asked the Champion, taking notes.

"Whaddayou think?" said Joanna.

"You said something to her," I said, rubbing my hands together.

"You bet I did! I told huh, 'There's no eating in the Cawd Room! Yaw the board president. Don't you know yaw own rules?' And lemme tell you, the whole room was looking at huh."

"What'd she say?" I asked from the edge of my chair.

"She told me ta mind my own business. I told huh I was going to report huh to the Office. She tells me SHE's the president, and SHE makes the rules. For awl the work she and huh board do for Condoland, she says she's entitled to a few 'privileges.' Can you believe that?"

"Then what?" *This is some story.*

"I says, 'We'll see about that!' I went back into the Cawd Room after lunch to look at huh table. There were sauce stains on the chairs. I took a pikchuh. I'm gonna insist the Office sends huh the cleaning bill."

"No, no. Don't do that," said the Champion. "Write down

every detail, with the dates and times and everyone who was there. And print out that picture. This is really good work, Joanna." Joanna smiled, sitting tall in her chair.

"What do we do with the notes?" I asked. Now *I* was impatient.

The Champion hesitated. "I don't know . . . Let's see what else we find. Depending on how bad things are, we may need to see a lawyer."

"You're a lawyer," I said. *Lawyers are expensive.*

"I'm a commercial real estate lawyer. We need a condominium lawyer. Besides, I'm too close to this. We need an objective third party. But we're not there yet. Let's keep gathering information and documenting it. Agreed?" We agreed.

My parents had different reactions to my new professional pursuits. My mother's concern was palpable on the phone. "What exactly are you doing?" she asked.

"I'm consulting and becoming a singer and voice actor."

"What do I tell my friends? They ask about you. Will you be able to support yourself?"

My father wanted me to be happy. He wrote me a letter expressing his thoughts. When he was 50, he quit his job as vice president of sales at a manufacturing firm to start his own company selling robotics. For six years, he put everything into that business while my mother supported us. (I give her credit for that.) He worked 18-hour days when I was growing up, until his business took off.

He understood pursuing a dream. He had *terrible* handwriting, which made letters an ordeal for him. He only wrote when it was important, and I cried when I read it.

Dearest Alice,

I've thought a great deal about your frustrations at BFC and realize that in dealing in the Latin market, besides being a *gringa*, you're a 5'3" tall woman, and the macho men don't respect you. This is their culture. Obviously, this attitude made it very difficult for you to do what you knew was necessary to grow your business. Until these men learned to respect and listen to your ideas, you would always have had a difficult time with them. This also goes for the Florida people.

Your idea of forming your own company is a good start for your independence and self-respect. Now, you can control your destiny, and your hard work can pay off.

Being without a paycheck is not only devastating, it's demoralizing. I'm glad you are making this change with money in the bank.

You are a beautiful girl with a beautiful, unique voice. I can see you voicing commercials for airlines, autos, department stores, cosmetic companies, etc.

People need a lift. When you sing, your sense of humor and your personality give you appeal. You can make your audience feel good. They will remember you and want to hear you again.

I wish you the very best, sweetheart. If you would like to discuss this matter, we could do it by phone or when you come home.

I send you all my love,
Daddy

P.S. I hope my writing was not too difficult to decipher.

My dad's faith in me helped me keep going. Once I had a little voice acting experience, I submitted my demo and résumé to a website that only accepted "professionals." I was approved! Advertising agencies and casting directors went to that site to cast local talent.

A few weeks later, I received an email from an advertising agency in Fort Lauderdale. The casting director heard my demo on that website and liked my voice!

His agency was producing a series of orange juice commercials and he wanted me to audition. The email included a script for me to record. Auditions were due by 5 p.m. the day my computer was being repaired at the Apple Store. *I can't lose this chance! Maybe they'll give me more time.* I called the agency.

"Hi, this is Alice Miller. You sent me an email about the orange juice audition. I'd LOVE to submit a read, but my computer's being fixed. I can't send you a compressed file today."

"I see . . . You know what, that's OK. Our client really likes your voice. Do you have an iPhone?" Apple equipment was generally used for recording.

"Yes." I closed my eyes, hoping.

"Great. Record the audition on your phone. We'll make that work." *Thank you!*

Thirty-one takes later, I had a read of the script that was as good as I was going to get. I hit "send" at 4:50 p.m. *Throw it out to the Universe, like the Oracle says.*

The Universe responded the next morning, and the next few days were a blur. I got the gig! I rehearsed and rehearsed and rehearsed. The morning of my recording session, a friend called. I explained that I couldn't talk because I had to "get to the studio." *Did I just say that?* It was true!

The client was patched in during the session, listening to every utterance I made. I stood in a stuffy, soundproof recording booth, and the agency and studio people sat outside with air conditioning. The studio engineer synched my audio to the visuals of each of four commercials. He spoke into my headphone to say, "That's a wrap," and we were done.

The agency people were gossiping as I gathered my things.

"Can you imagine how long we'd have been here if they'd picked Famous Actress?" *The client wanted Famous Actress and ended up with me?*

"'Til midnight—at least."

"And her husband would insist on approving every word of every spot. Nightmare!" *They prefer to work with me?*

A month later, I turned on the Sunday morning news and heard a familiar voice. I stared at the screen. *Who is that?* It was my commercial! I was on TV! I called my parents.

"What channel is it on?" asked my mother.

"It's on NBC, but I think only in Florida."

"Oh. So, we can't see it?" she asked.

"I'll put it on my website, and you can watch it there."

"Sounds complicated."

"Alice will show us, honey," said my dad. "Alice, I knew you could do it. I'm so proud of you!" I felt like crying. My father had that effect on me. He always understood.

The four commercials—two 30-second spots and two 15-second spots—were on frequent rotation across 15 channels. I heard them on the evening news, and my neighbors heard them during the day in the gym. The Oracle told everyone who would listen that I was the voice of the campaign. I think my neighbors were as impressed as I was—most of them, that is.

Over the course of my 34th year, my fellow detectives and I documented numerous examples of the board breaking its own rules. But we knew we'd just scratched the surface, because our building was run in secrecy.

The Manager kept his office door shut. I went to see him to discuss the costs of the Club House renovation. Sitting down in front of his desk, I noticed Her Highness hiding in the far corner to my right, behind a bookcase. Our board president was visible only if someone walked into the Manager's office and sat in the chair I was occupying, far enough to the left to see past the bookcase. *What is she doing there?* "I'm sorry to disturb you," I told the Manager. "I didn't realize you were in a meeting."

"Not at all," he said. "Mrs. Highness won't mind listening to our conversation."

"I'd like to hear it," she said. *I bet you would.*

"No, thanks," I answered, surprising myself. "I'll make an appointment when we can meet privately."

The valets told Sr. Holmez they washed the Drektors' cars free of charge. He shared his recording of their conversation with us at one of our Sunday meetings.

"Does the board know you're doing this while you're on the clock?" Sr. Holmez asked the valets, in Spanish.

"Sí, Sr. Holmez. They tell us to wash their cars every week. They don't pay us because we do it during our shifts. But we lose tips."

"Why do you do it?" He knew the answer but wanted to hear them say it.

"We need our jobs, Sr. Holmez. If we don't help them, the board can fire us." The answer made my skin crawl. Not only were the Drektors stealing from these poor valets; they were stealing from each unit owner—*we* paid for the valets' time!

While the Club House was closed for renovation, Sr. Holmez snuck in often, right before lunchtime. One day, I accompanied him, pretending to measure things across the room while he spoke to the tradesmen. I wore my only Lilly Pulitzer dress—pink and green. It screamed English speaker, assuring potential witnesses that whatever they told Sr. Holmez would fly over my head. I wore earbuds with the sound off as I noted imaginary numbers. He gave the men *arepas*—corn pancakes fresh from the oven, filled with ground beef, avocado, and cheese. As they ate, he took pictures and asked questions.

"How's the work going?"

"There is a lot to do, Sr. Holmez."

"Anything you didn't expect?"

"Well . . ."

"I promise you, I will never use your name. What's troubling you?"

"We find mold, and the man from the board said to leave it. He said fix it later. He said not to tell anyone, or he'll fire us. Also, we found termites. We leave them, too."

"Which man from the board?"

"The big one, with the gold chains." *The Long Island Lothario!*

"Thank you. What else?" The men looked at the floor.

"*Parceros*, I am here to help. Your secret stays with me. *La unión hace la fuerza.* [Union makes strength.]"

"*Dale*," said one of the tradesmen, nodding to another, a carpenter. The carpenter surveyed the others, who nodded their approval.

At first, the carpenter stared at the floor, wringing his hands as he spoke. "We call the man Mr. 20 Percent, señor."

Sr. Holmez' eyes widened, and he chortled. "And why is that? Please, tell me. If I don't know, I can't help."

The man looked Sherlock in the eye. "Because he asked each of us—the carpenter, painter, the mason, etc.—to add 20 percent to our invoices."

"Did he pay you the extra money?"

The carpenter shook his head. "The treasurer pays us, then we pay *them* the 20 percent—in cash."

"So that I understand, who is 'them'?"

"The treasurer and Señor 20 Percent." *The Mobster and his pro-tégé.*

"*Gracias, mi amigo.* Please, enjoy your lunch."

Sr. Holmez, the Champion, Joanna, and I continued to document and share infractions at our Sunday get-togethers. For example, the board had gym staff reserve specific machines for the Drektors' use. They had first dibs on the tennis courts. According to Sherlock's friend in the Restaurant's kitchen, Her Highness was getting food delivered without paying for it.

I told the group what the carpenter said about Lothario. "If they steal 20 percent from $4 million, how do we finish the Club House on budget?" Everyone gave me a look. *Naïve again?*

"Alice, it was NEVER getting done for $4 million," said the Champion.

"And? Do we let them get away with it?"

"I didn't say that, but it's hard to prove. Before we accuse anyone, we need witnesses—workers—willing to testify. Confiding in Sr. Holmez—in Spanish—is very different from taking the stand in court." *She's right.* "We also need documentary evidence. And we'd have to pay our own legal fees. The Drektors have Condoland's law firm to defend them. You know who pays *their* legal fees? We do. All the unit owners would pay. How many owners you think want to chip in to pay our lawyers?"

"But—" I said.

"I don't like it any more than you do," said the Champion, "but let's not get ahead of ourselves. For now, we document. Anyone else?"

"*Sí.*" We turned to Sr. Holmez. "Alicia, you translate?"

"Of course." He explained what he found, and I relayed it. "He saw the head maintenance guy loading wood and carpeting into one of the storage rooms marked 'Association Use Only.' When Sr. Holmez asked what the materials were for, the guy didn't answer. Eventually, he said he was converting the Lotharios' second bedroom into a . . . cat jungle gym?" Sr. Holmez nodded, confirming my translation. "That's it. A cat jungle gym."

"Who is she, Catwoman?" asked Joanna.

"You know what that's about, right?" asked the Champion.

"What?" I asked.

"They're estranged from their daughters. I don't know what caused the rift, but I do know she named her cats after them." *Ew.* "So much for the one-pet rule." The Champion wrote a note to herself.

"How do you know this?" I asked.

"I ran into her once when I was walking Cookie, and she bragged about her 'girls'—the four-legged ones. I feel sorry for her."

"Let's get back to the maintenance guy," I said. "Are the Lotharios paying him?"

"No. He do thees to keep hees job," explained Sr. Holmez.

My father might be right about Florida people. "And we just sit here and take it?" I asked.

"Write it down. That's all we can do now," said the Champion. I implored her with wide eyes. "I feel the same way, Alice, but think about it. Can you imagine that maintenance worker testifying against the Drektors? They'd fire him just for talking to us." I shook my head. "That's the problem. Don't give up. *I'm* not giving up. But know it's an uphill battle."

"I'm not goin' anywhere," said Joanna. "Sooner o'latuh, these *gonifs*[14] are gonna pay."

As we left the Coffee Shop, Sherlock pulled me aside. With my parents in Massachusetts, he'd become a surrogate father. His wife, Shilah, told me he felt the same way.

"*Artista*," he said. I earned that nickname after he heard me sing in the Restaurant. "Yesterday, the Mobster came up to my parking spot in the garage. I was unloading groceries, and Shilah was still in the car on the phone with her door shut."

Uh-oh. "Did you speak to him?"

"He spoke first. That's important."

"What did he say?"

"He told me we had much in common. We should be friends."

"And?"

"I said we have nothing in common, and I don't need new friends! I told him I don't accept corruption, and I hope he dies!" *OMG.* Sr. Holmez was macho. He didn't see just how dangerous the Mobster was. I slapped my forehead. *Sherlock thinks he's Tony Montana.*

"What did he do?"

"He asked if I know who he is, who his friends are. He told me to be careful. He said in Hialeah, there are people who kill for $500." I covered my mouth. Sherlock poked his chest with his finger as he spoke. "I told him he doesn't know who *I* am. He doesn't know who *my* friends are, and HE better be careful!"

---

[14] Gonif — Yiddish for thief, dishonest person, or scoundrel

"Do you understand who his friends are?" I was frightened. Not only for him, but for all of us.

"I don't care who his friends are! In Colombia, I stood up to the drug lords. Nothing happened to me."

"Then why," I asked, "are you living in Florida?" Sherlock was quiet. I had a point. "This man is an associate in a New York crime family! These are not drug lords. They're organized! Bigger than— never mind. The point is, none of us should mess with him!"

He saw the look on my face. "Don't worry, Alicia. I'll be careful. But understand something." He narrowed his eyes. "All we've done is ask questions, and those questions have rattled the snake. Now, the snake is rattling back."

Sr. Holmez was right. There was a lot more going on at Condoland than met the eye, and the Drektors knew we were onto them. We'd have to be very careful.

8

Do You See What We See?

Our Sunday afternoon meetings in the Coffee Shop continued. We sat in a corner on leather couches, thinking we
were discreet. But this was Condoland. Everyone saw everything.
It took little for people to talk, especially as we approached the
board elections in December.

In mid-November, Gladys Kravitz, a neighbor on my floor,
quizzed me while we waited for the elevator. "I've noticed you in
the Coffee Shop with the Champion, Joanna, and that Mexican
guy—the one with the cowboy hat."

"He's Colombian, Mrs. Kravitz."

"OK, Colombian. How do you know him?"

"He's my neighbor, like you."

"Mm-hmm. What do you guys talk about?"

"We visit. We're neighbors."

"Uh-huh." She lowered her nasal voice. "What do you think of
this board?"

Careful, Alice. "I have some concerns, like the floods, that I don't
see being addressed."

"Hmm . . . I have some concerns, too." She pursed her lips and

74

crossed her arms. "Maybe I can join you and your friends for coffee sometime—you know, as neighbors?" *Touché, Gladys.*

"That'd be nice," I lied. The elevator arrived with enough passengers to end our conversation.

Gladys wasn't the only neighbor expressing concern. "My friends ask me about this board," said Sherlock the following Sunday during our afternoon meeting. I knew he meant his Wednesday lunch group friends—Spanish-speakers from the building. The Ceevil Engineer, head of the Architecture Committee, was one of them. Mrs. Holmez called it Sherlock's kosher lunch because everyone but her husband was Jewish. More importantly, they were all Latin, and they were emigrants. They understood each other. For one hour a week, they remembered how it felt to belong.

"What did they want to know?" I asked. A woman walked into the Coffee Shop. He waited until she was out of ear shot before answering.

"They ask if I trust this board. I say 'no.' Two friends have mold in they apartments because the flooding. They are angry. They ask what I think of you, Alice." *Me? Why are they talking about me?* "Don' worry." Sherlock smiled. "I tell them you are a smart and honest young lady. They go to the Finance Committee meetings; they like your questions." *That's a relief!* "They trust me," he leaned forward, "and now they trust you."

Like it or not, I was attracting attention. These were successful businessmen. They'd had enough experience with real estate to know when something wasn't right. I mentioned my encounter with Gladys Kravitz.

"People have approached me, too," said the Champion. "One of my neighbors is a banker. He lends money all the time to condos that delayed maintenance. The longer they put off the work, the more urgent—and expensive—the repairs become." The waiter brought our biscotti. He lingered to listen, so we sipped and chewed until he left. The Champion spoke softly. "He worries we may need a loan."

"He has a point," I said. "I've asked about the pipes several times at Finance meetings, and the Drektors think the repairs can wait. All they care about is the Club House."

"Anyone know what the Drektuhs aw doing with the insurance money?" Joanna asked. "I heard they hired a Drekoratuh. She wants to build a *farkakteh* wall sculptchuh in the lobby. What does that have to do with flood damage?"

The Drekorator had already replaced leather chairs in the lobby with pleather, and a Moroccan rug with a nylon imitation, neither of which could hold up to commercial use. *How is this rational?*

"I asked Humpty Dumpty about it at our last meeting," I said. "She says they're using what's 'left over' from the payout to 'enhance' the building. How can money be 'left over' when they haven't fixed the flood damage? I don't get it. I pressed Humpty for an answer, but I'm hitting a wall."

"Don't take this the wrong way," said Joanna, "but you look 12 yeuhs old. You ask a lot of questions—in public—and you embarrass the board. Of course, you're hitting a wall!" *Ouch. But she's right.* "No one's gonna go on record. Lemme help you. How 'bout you and I go to the office and ask to see the receipts for the restuhration work?"

"Before you two do that," said the Champion, "you have to submit a written request that spells out exactly what records you want to see. Otherwise, they won't show them to you. The Florida Sunshine Law requires Management to provide requested information to unit owners, but they can take up to two weeks if they want to."

"Sounds like legal mumbo jumbo to me!" said Joanna. I shrugged my shoulders.

"I'll write it for you," said the Champion.

Joanna called me a week later, upset. "Edguh and I had dinnuh with the Dumptys last night. What a disastuh!"

"What happened?"

"Humpty asks me, 'What aw you doin' with that singuh and the lawyuh and that Spanish guy?'"

"She asked you that?"

"She sure did. I told huh, 'I like them.' Then she asks me, 'Whaddayou have in common?'"

"What did you say?"

"I asked huh, 'What's it to *you?*' It's none of huh fuckin' business! She tells me she's 'just curious.' She thinks yaw a trouble-makuh, and she tells me nobody liked the Champion when she was on the bawd. Besides my husband, the Champion was the smartest person there. I told Humpty don't tell me who my friends aw be-cawz I know them much bettuh than she does." *She really is fearless.* "You know what she says ta me?"

"What?"

"She says, 'yaw FRIENDS?' Real sarcastic. 'YEAH, my friends!' I told huh. Then she says, 'What about that Spanish guy?'"

"What did you say?"

"I said, 'First of awl, he's not Spanish. He's Colombian. And what aboudim?'" Joanna was shouting. I held the phone from my ear.

"What were your husbands doing?"

"Abso-fuckin-lutely nothing. They both sat there staring at

their menus."

"Sorry, I interrupted you. What did Humpty say about Sherlock?"

"She says he's sneakin' into the Club House, and the general contractuh saw him taking pikchahs. I asked huh, 'What the fuck do you care? He's an ownuh. Why shouldn't he take pikchahs! You gawt somethin' to hide?'"

"You said that?" *That's chutzpah.*[15]

"You bet I did! And get this: She tells me, 'Be careful, Joanna. I wouldn't want to see you get involved with troublemakuhs.' Can you believe huh? She's THREATENING me!"

"I'm so sorry." I paced in my living room, thinking about what the Mobster told Sherlock. *"In Hialeah, there are people who kill for $500."* But I didn't mention it. I didn't want to scare her.

"I told huh we bettuh change the subject. Edguh and I didn't say a word on the drive home. When we pulled into the garage, I said, 'Edguh—' and he said, 'I know.' I said, 'Good!'"

"What does that mean?"

"It means that's it. A 20-yeuh friendship . . . and it's ovuh."

Two weeks to the day after Joanna and I submitted the Champion's information request to the Management Office, we were given an appointment with the Manager. We arrived at 11 a.m. sharp. The Bookkeeper greeted us.

"We have an appointment with the Manager," I said.

"He's in a meeting. Can I help you?" Joanna and I looked at each other. Something was up. "What can I do for you?" asked the Bookkeeper, motioning us into her office. Due to Joanna's propen-

---

[15] Chutzpah — Yiddish for intestinal fortitude, guts

sity toward profanity, we agreed I'd do the business talking. When we reached the editorial portion of our program, she could let it rip.

"We sent an information request two weeks ago," I said, "and we're here for that information." She looked at us blankly. "We asked to see how the insurance payout for the Great Flood is being spent, especially what's been spent to fix the water damage."

"Sure," said the Bookkeeper, walking to her file cabinets in the next room. Ten minutes later, she plopped a manila folder in front of us on her desk. "Here's what I have. These are the Drekorator's invoices." Joanna inhaled to speak. I gave her a look. Too soon.

"Thank you." I scanned each invoice and added the amounts on my phone. "It looks like you've spent $325,000 on . . . furniture and artwork. Is that correct?"

"If that's what it says, then yes."

"You're not sure?" Joanna did another big inhale. I bumped the side of her foot with mine, and she exhaled quietly.

"Well, that's what I have. The work's ongoing, you know. We'll get more."

"I understand. I have a few more questions." I handed her a copy of our information request. "Would you like to take a—"

"No, I have it," the Bookkeeper said. I smiled politely, sneaking a glance at Joanna. *The Bookkeeper's in on it!*

"Great," I said. "What's been spent on flood restoration? The stains on the Party Room ceiling are still there. The rugs in the Card Room are stained, and the marble floor in the lobby is cracked and uneven." Joanna nodded adamantly. "We need the claims money to fix the damage. Why would we redecorate before completing the repairs?"

"Alice, we negotiated a great deal with Water Pro," said the

Bookkeeper. "They're giving us a 30 percent discount. And some of the work we can do ourselves, so there're more than enough. No need to worry."

"I see." There was no point fighting with her; this was a reconnaissance job. "Thank you. There's one more thing we requested; we'd like to see the receipts to date."

"Receipts?" I gave Joanna a prophylactic kick.

"Yes, the receipts for the items purchased," I explained.

"I . . . I don't have receipts." *Huh?*

Joanna couldn't take it anymore. "Whaddaya mean you don't have receipts?" I jabbed her with my elbow.

"How do you know what you've spent without receipts?" I asked.

"The Drekorator lists what she bought and how much she paid for it on her invoices. They're in that folder."

"And you take her word for it?" I asked. *We're in the Twilight Zone.*

"Yes. Of course." Before Condoland, the Bookkeeper worked for a residential management company. She wasn't a CPA, but she knew better.

"Does this mean any vendor can submit an invoice for any amount, and we cut a check?" I wanted her to acknowledge how crazy it sounded.

"Well, no. We trust the Drekorator." The Bookkeeper leaned forward, elbows on her desk. "She comes highly recommended by the treasurer, so we know she's reliable." *Our MOBSTER treasurer? Hello?*

"Tell me you realize that's not an acceptable business practice." She stared blankly again, as if reason had left her body. I had to get through to her. "What happens if the new furniture is defective?

80

Which store do we call? Where's our proof of purchase?"

She leaned back into her chair and crossed her arms. "Ladies, I've given you what I have. If you'd like, you can make an appointment with the Manager to discuss the matter further." *Earth to Bookkeeper!* Having drunk the Kool-Aid, she wasn't budging, and I was out of ideas.

It was Joanna's turn. "We *made* an appointment!" she said. "The Managuh doesn't have the bawls to see us, so he sent you to do his dirty work."

"That's not fair!" said the Bookkeeper. "He—"

"I see you gawt a holiday card from the Lotharios," said Joanna in what the Bookkeeper mistook for a friendly tone. The card was taped to the wall behind her desk. It was a photo of Mrs. Lothario with three cats wearing tiaras sitting in her lap. Mr. Lothario loomed overhead. The perfect family, blatantly violating Condoland's one-pet rule.

"Oh, yes," answered the Bookkeeper. "They're such nice people!"

"Ya think so?" asked Joanna. I smiled. *Friends close, enemies closer.*

The Bookkeeper grew somber. She leaned forward, her hands on her desk. "Are you going to visit the Mobster at the hospital?" she asked, her eyes welling.

"What happened to him?" I asked.

"He had a stroke."

"Oh, wow. That's too bad," I said. "We aren't acquainted, so I won't visit."

"Me, neithuh!" said Joanna.

The Bookkeeper reached for a tissue, and I noticed her Rolex watch. "He's a wonderful man." *They're all working together.*

"Oh, yeah?" said Joanna. "He beats his wife! You think that's wonduhful?" On that note, our meeting adjourned. We trudged toward the elevator.

There has to be a bright side . . . "So, the books are a disaster," I said, "but that meeting confirmed the power of prayer."

"Whaddayou talkin' about?"

"I prayed the Mobster would die," I smirked. "I'll keep praying."

A few days later, I was watching TV when the doorbell rang. I figured it was a valet on the wrong floor. I looked through my peephole. It was the Daredevil. *I'm in my pajamas!* I spoke through the closed door, buying time.

"Who is it?"

"It's me."

"Hi! Can you give me a minute?" I ran to my closet. Clothes flew until I found my fitted jeans and an olive-green shirt that accentuated my eyes. "Coming . . . one sec." Mascara. Lip gloss. And earrings!

"Hi," I said, opening the door. "What's up?"

He looked me up, down, and up again. "Hi there. You on your way out?"

"No. Watching TV."

"Can I borrow a DVD disk?" *He knocks on my door at 10 p.m. for a DVD disk? What happened to dinner and a movie?*

"Sure. Come on in. I'll see what I have." I stood on a stool and looked in the cabinets above my office desk. "I don't see them—" As I stepped down from the stool, he grabbed my waist. I turned to face him, inhaling his aftershave.

"That's OK—" He was about to kiss me. I was tempted, but the voice in my head stopped me.

No, no. This doesn't feel right. Be the prize, Alice. Be the prize. "Wait. I haven't given up yet." I pulled away. Let me look in a few more places." I went through some drawers. "I have some old CD disks. Would that work?" *I hate to think what he wants to record.*

"Nope. It has to be DVD. I'm making a video of my best sky-diving trips, and I need a hard copy." *Hard all right.*

"I can't find one."

"That's OK. Sorry to bother you." He stood in my living room, waiting. *What does he think? He shows up and I sleep with him? Nah. I was never that girl, and I'm not starting now.*

"No bother. Sorry I couldn't help." Another long silence. "So, I'll see you at the gym?"

"Yeah . . . I'll see you at the gym," he repeated. *That's your cue, buddy! Bah-bye!* "I'd better get going."

"OK, good night."

"Good night, Alice." I felt my heart pound as I closed the door. He wanted me the easy way. I'd just turned 35. Having learned about relationships the hard way, I wasn't going to settle for less than I was worth.

9

Forecast Hurricane

That December was a busy month at Condoland. With the snowbirds—Northerners—down for the winter, the Club House held a grand reopening a week before the annual board election. Unit owners were invited to happy hour at the bar overlooking the Intracoastal. The view was magnificent; I couldn't help but be impressed.

I went with the Champion. An overpowering scent of lavender hit me when I entered the lobby. Later, I learned they lit candles to mask the eau de toilette wafting from the Club House plumbing. Although budgeted, it hadn't been fixed.

When we got there, the Long Island Lothario was prancing euphorically from owner to owner seeking praise. His eyes bulged, and sweat glistened on his forehead as he passed us, laughing to himself. *What is he on?*

"See this floor?" asked Joanna, walking over to me. "It's papuh thin. I give it six months, tops, until it cracks."

"It's residential instead of commercial grade," said the Champion. *Marble has grades?*

"Well, it looks nice," I said.

Sr. Holmez marched up the outdoor staircase connecting the first and second floors and came over to us, scowling.

"*¿Que tal, Sr. Holmez?*" I asked. "Why so serious?"

"*Artista,* have you been downstairs?"

"Not yet. What's wrong?"

"They change rooms. Ees no right. We no vote to change rooms."

"They need two-thirds of the unit owners to approve a change in use of a public area," said the Champion, visibly annoyed. "That wasn't included in the renovation ballot."

"I want see the vote," said Sherlock. Forced by corruption to emigrate from his country, transparency—particularly in elections—was paramount for him.

"Let's go downstairs," I suggested. Sherlock, the Champion, Joanna, and I assessed the changes. The roof over the tennis courts was gorgeous. "Guys, you have to admit, they did a great job here."

"*¿Si?*" asked Sherlock. He touched one of the new walls encircling the courts and wiped his wet hand in his cocktail napkin.

Joanna used hers to wipe her forehead. "Why's it so humid?" she asked.

"Ees no ventilation," said Sherlock. "No air conditioning. Een weenter, when outside air more cool than inside air, ees bad for court surface." *What doesn't he know?* I bent down to touch the surface. He was right. Already, it was starting to marble. With trepidation, we walked to the new gym area.

The equipment was state-of-the-art but cramped in what used to be the Reception Room. Half the size of the old equipment room, it was designed for small gatherings. It offered a spectacular view of the Intracoastal, but no more than 15 people could exercise without bumping into each other. *Lothario promised more space, not less!*

The old equipment room was empty. "We'll use it for exercise classes," the gym manager told us.

"How many classes do you have a week?" I asked.

"Three." His eyes implored me to stop. *What can't he tell us?*

"So, this space will be empty the rest of the time?" Joanna asked.

"Yes, Mrs. Rivers."

"Something's not right," I whispered to my friends. "I'll ask the Oracle tomorrow."

"Good," said Sherlock. While he wouldn't admit to a sixth sense, he wouldn't discount it, either.

"What's that smell?" With no candles to mask the scent on this floor, I got a whiff of sewage.

"That's coming from the pipes," said the gym manager. He looked like a home invasion victim answering the front door with a gun at his back. I felt sorry for him.

"Yuck!" I said.

"Leave him alone. Maybe the Oracle can tell you more," the Champion whispered. "Sr. Holmez, I'll draft an information request for you to submit to the Office about the votes."

"Gracias, Champion," said Sherlock, tipping his cowboy hat.

The next day, I went to the gym. "What's that stink in the spa?" I asked the Oracle.

"They never fixed the pipes."

"But they specifically said they'd fix the plumbing!"

"They say a lot of things. My boss is scared stiff. We're all scared. If we tell anyone what's going on here, the board will fire us."

Fortunately for her, the Oracle was leaving Condoland as soon as she graduated from law school. Other employees didn't have her options.

"Why'd they move the machines to the Reception Room?"

"The Barbies like the view."

"I don't think we voted for that change. Did the other buildings overrule us?"

"No." She whispered. "Condolands II and III didn't care one way or the other. The Drektors changed the project scope after the vote."

"What!" *That's fraud!*

Reading my mind, she nodded. "They do what they want and think no one will notice. Chef told me the city inspector almost didn't renew the Restaurant permit. He found cockroaches. The exhaust fan over the oven isn't working right—it's a fire hazard. He gave us 30 days to fix everything."

"Did somebody pay off the inspector?" The Oracle nodded. *I'm catching on.*

"After he left," she said, "they had a grease fire." *This is a nightmare.* She stiffened. Ventriloquist-style, she said, "People are watching." I looked in the mirror and saw Barbies surveilling behind us. I smiled at them, and they turned away.

"Wasn't that a great movie?" I asked, raising my voice.

"I loved it! I haven't laughed that hard in a long time!" said the Oracle. "I'm going to check on the towels. Have a good workout, Alice."

"Thanks for your help!" I finished my squats and got out of there.

The grand reopening of the Club House had done its trick. Impressed with the renovations, unit owners re-elected the entire board. Two days later, the Mobster died. The Drektors chose a man we nicknamed the Corpse as the fifth board member. He was appointed vice president—in name only—in place of Lothario, who became a little ole member-at-large. If anyone were to question his spending decisions, Lothario would direct unit owners to the man whose only proof of life was the rise and fall of his chest.

"He's the ultimate scapegoat," the Champion told me. "He's too far gone to know what they're doing, let alone object to it. He'll sign anything—"

"And take the fall?" I asked.

"If they get caught." *We'll catch 'em!*

The Bulldog replaced Humpty Dumpty as the board secretary. Dumpty, whose father was notorious for his Tuition Heist, became board treasurer. This legacy appointment was a mistake. She had no idea how to be an honest treasurer, let alone a dishonest one.

The last Finance Committee meeting of the year was held on December 30th. I was surprised to see Lothario in the audience; something was up. I was about to complain about having three Drektors present when I noticed we were $1 million over budget through November.

"October's numbers were on target," I said to the Manager. "What happened in November?" *How could we spend money we don't have? Why didn't you tell us?* By law, Condoland couldn't spend money now and print it later. We had to assess the unit owners first, and we'd need a damned good reason to do so.

"There were unforeseen issues in the Club House, Miss Miller. There was no time—"

"You had *signed estimates* for the Club House renovation. What unforeseen issues cost a million dollars? And why didn't you request an emergency assessment?" I asked.

The Manager got a nod from Lothario before answering. "We found mold. Everywhere. And there were termites." *So that's why the "big one, with the gold chains" told the tradesmen to keep the problems a secret. The Champion was right. Going over $4 million was a foregone conclusion!*

"Are you saying nobody noticed mold or termites *before* the renovation?" I asked.

"No, I'm afraid not." The Manager looked me straight in the eye. Didn't flinch. "Also, we had to air condition the tennis courts. *You don't say?* The total's approximately $1.3 million. Some of the bills came in this month."

I didn't know what to do. Obviously, he was lying, but if I told him what I knew, what would come of it? We didn't have proof, and our witnesses were terrified to come forward. *Discretion is the better part of valor . . . Zip it, Alice.* I took notes.

"You mean the $1.3 million that was our guaranteed total cost?" asked a Committee member.

"No, this is additional," said the Manager.

"You mean it's DOUBLE?" shouted a less patient member. With a loud but deadly emanation, Gassy punctuated the shock. Members' heads shook around the table.

"Is that $1.3 million for Condoland, or $1.3 million for all three buildings?" asked a third member. It was a lot to take in.

The Manager stared at the age spots on his hands. "One point three million for Condoland," he mumbled. "Condoland II and Condoland III owe the rest. The total is $4 million."

I leaned toward him. "Can you understand why we're upset?"

"Yes, I can, Miss Miller. We're going to do our best to keep the total cost to . . ." He looked at Lothario, who held up eight fingers. ". . . Eight million across the three Condoland buildings." His face inflamed.

"Oy vey!" I said it involuntarily. People laughed.

"Oy vey is right!" came a voice from the audience.

"Only the Committee and the Managuh should be talking," said Humpty Dumpty. "If yaw not on the Finance Committee, don't interrupt!" *Why is she setting rules? It's my meeting!*

The Manager continued, "It costs money to maintain an older building." *Has he always been lying?* "Please look at the list of additional maintenance projects in your packets. The Committee needs to prioritize them and recommend financing options to the board."

"All year long, you said repairs could wait." I felt a rush of adrenaline. *Let everyone understand what we're up against.* "But please, go ahead." I raised my hand to the audience, motioning them to stay quiet.

"We'll increase next year's operating budget by 10 percent, but that won't be enough," said the Manager.

"Are you suggesting *another* assessment?" I asked. A Committee member's head hit the table.

Someone in the audience started hacking. "I'm OK," he managed. "Coffee went down the wrong pipe. This spending . . . I almost choked!"

The Manager was unmoved. "Unfortunately, yes," he said. "We have to pay for several urgent and nonrecurring projects, and that's usually done by assessment." His secretary put additional copies of the list on the conference table.

"Can WE get a copy?" said a unit owner in the audience.

"I want one, too!"

"Quiet, please! You'll get a copy at the bawd meeting," said Humpty Dumpty. "If you interrupt again, I'm gonna ask you to leave."

"The building needs to be painted and waterproofed," said the Manager. "It's two years past due. The bottom of the pool is cracked, and we need to resurface it. We also have to patch the water pipes where we can. Some are beyond repair, and those we must replace."

"This has to be done when?" asked a Committee member.

"Let's go through the list first," said the Manager. *There's more?* He looked at Lothario, who nodded ever so slightly. "Then we can discuss. Please turn the page." *Holy mother of pearl!* "We need to fortify the columns and some ceiling areas in the garage. They're crumbling. It's the salt air, and leaks during rainy season have already damaged several cars. These repairs can't wait." Like many South Florida condominiums, our garage supported the residential floors above it. *Is it safe to live here?* "Also, the town inspector cited 10 balconies for code violations." He saw the looks on our faces and braced the table with both hands. "There's no need to worry. Our engineer assures us our building is structurally sound. We just need to keep it that way."

"How much?" asked a Committee member.

"Hold on, I'm not done. There are—"

"Shoot me now!" It was Joanna. The audience laughed nervously.

"Be QUIET!" said Humpty Dumpty, glaring at her former friend.

"There are overages in the Club House which we've already discussed. That's the list." He pushed away from the table.

"How much?" the Committee member asked again.

"The total is aweve miyeh," mumbled the Manager. *Cat got your tongue?*

"What?" asked a unit owner.

"We can't understand you," said a Committee member.

The Manager swallowed. He mopped his forehead with a handkerchief. "The number is $11 million." He said it quickly, like ripping off a Band-Aid. "But don't worry; we're going to get a loan to make the payments affordable."

I divided by 400 on my phone. "That's an average of $27,500 per unit on top of the $3,250 we've already paid. That's a LOT of money!" I looked at my colleagues around the table. "Guys, we can't fix everything at once. Let's prioritize."

It was like choosing between food and shelter. *It can't be this bad.* I stared at the list and turned to the Manager. "Can you help us understand the $4 million for 'contingency'?"

"We have to plan for surprises. We don't want to ask for more money later."

"I think we've had enough surprises," I said. The audience erupted in applause.

Humpty stood up, her "waist" against the conference table. "Quiet! If you can't be quiet, I'll ask you all to leave! This is yaw last warning!" I looked at the unit owners in the audience. They were angry.

"Alice," said Humpty Dumpty, "if you wanna know the details of what things cost and why, go to the Architectchuh meeting. There's nothing to prioritize heuh. The Managuh just explained that everything on this list is urgent. We don't have a crystal bawl, so expect surprises! That's why we need a contingency fund." She looked around the room. "You people wanted maintenance, and you're getting it. Whadja think—it was cheap?"

"We'll go into more detail at the board meeting, when we vote on next year's budget," said the Bulldog.

"That's right!" said Humpty.

"Let me make sure I understand." I turned to the Manager. "The plan is to assess us $11 million for repairs you said—all year—could wait—"

"Well, when I said wait—" said the Manager.

"I'm not finished," I said. I glanced at Lothario. "The cost of the Club House is now DOUBLE what the former vice president *personally* guaranteed, and you want another $4 million just in case you think of something else?"

"You make it sound—"

"Please, let me finish." I attempted a smile. "How can we believe you? Will you get three bids for each project? Will you share the estimates with the unit owners?"

"They don't need detail." *Again, with the Bulldog?* "It'll just confuse them, Alice. Trust me."

"Ha!" Again, it came out involuntarily. There was nervous laughter around the table. Eleven million dollars was a LOT of money.

"Trust is earned," said a retired lawyer on the Committee.

"That's right," said another member.

Humpty wasn't having it. "Alice, when you get elected to the board, you can tell us how to do aw jobs." *Fine. Learn the hard way. You'll be crucified at the board meeting.*

"Understood," I said. I spoke to the Committee members. "Normally, we would submit a recommendation to the board for project financing. I move to leave that choice in the capable hands of the board's new treasurer." Humpty sat forward in her chair and stuck out her chin as her muumuu caught on a nail under the table. Her head disappeared as she tried to free herself. "Is there a second?" I asked.

"Second," said a member.

"Who votes aye?" I asked. Every hand went up, and the motion was approved. Humpty Dumpty was in charge.

"OK then," I said. "Happy New Year everybody. We're adjourned!"

People lingered in the room, commiserating. I never spoke in anger, so I stayed in my chair, avoiding people, until they left. The Bulldog waited, too. We were the last two in the Conference Room.

"Too much detail confuses people," he said sanctimoniously, sashaying over to me.

"I disagree. You're asking for a lot of money, and you guys have a bad track record. I know my neighbors. You'll need to be very specific if you want us to vote for a loan."

"I don't see it that way, but I appreciate your suggestion," he said. *He must be the good cop.* "And Alice, it's not up to the unit owners. If the board passes an assessment, you're obligated to pay, or we can force a foreclosure. We're offering the loan so people can spread their payments over time. That's the topic of next week's board meeting."

"I urge you to be transparent," I said. "Explain what you know, how you know it, and what it will cost. Also, tell them what you *don't* know. As for the loan, give us all the details—the interest rate, any additional fees, and tell us how much interest we'll pay over the life of the loan." I held his gaze in mine. "Please, don't omit anything. I'm trying to help."

"I appreciate that," said the Bulldog. *No, you don't.*

I left the Conference Room realizing the Bulldog and company wouldn't listen to anyone. Whatever happened at the board meeting would be their problem. I tried.

I told the Oracle about the disastrous Finance Committee meeting.

"What's going on with your singing?" she asked, changing the subject.

"Working on it," I said. "I'm taking lessons, and I'm practicing. I'm learning new songs."

"That's good. What about gigs?" By now, I knew when the Oracle was persistent, there was a reason.

"I haven't had time lately. Between consulting and what's going on at Condoland, I've been preoccupied."

"We need you to pursue your passion," she said.

"We?" She didn't answer. "Who's we?" I asked again. "Do you mean spirit guides?" She smiled. I'd read about spirit guides. "Are they your guides or mine?"

"Yours," she said. "It's important for you to keep singing. Remember, you don't sing for yourself. Your voice has the power to heal." *It does?*

"Thank you, Oracle. I'll find places with live jazz and contact them." She studied me to make sure I was serious. "I promise!"

"Good. That makes us happy, Alice."

10

Breakthrough and Blowup

Heeding the Oracle's advice, I called jazz-appropriate restaurant after restaurant asking to sing. DJs were killing live music in South Florida, and the conversations were largely the same.

"We have a limited budget. Do you use backing tracks?"

"No, normally a piano player, or a trio for a special occasion." I was determined not to sing karaoke.

"Hmm . . . maybe if we have a party. Where else have you played?"

"The Restaurant in Condoland."

"Check with us later in the season—when you have more experience."

"I will! Thanks very much." *I need experience to get experience?* Breaking in was hard, but I wasn't giving up.

"How's your new *career?*" my mom asked with unveiled sarcasm on our Sunday call. Her negativity was nothing new, but like Sisyphus forever pushing a boulder up the hill, I made a futile attempt to pass muster.

"It's good, Mommy. Any career takes time to build, but I'm on TV a lot now with the juice commercials, so that's something."

"Uh-huh. Do you think voice work can support you?"

"That's the plan."

"I hope you know what you're doing."

"I hope so, too. Nothing ventured, nothing gained, right?"

"We'll see. I'll let you talk to your father." *Thank you!*

"Hi, Daddy."

"Hi, sweethaht." He waited for my mom to hang up the other phone. "Don't be discouraged. It takes perseverance to start ovuh. It took six yeeahs befah my business turned a profit, but I stuck with it. Just keep plugging. I have a good feeling about it. Have you thought about hotels for singing?"

"I haven't."

"I see you perfahming in a nice hotel with an upscale clientele—one that appreciates jazz. Restaurants want turnovuh; hotels guests are welcome to lingah." *He's right.*

"That's an excellent idea, Daddy. Thank you!"

"Don't thank me, I'm yah fathah! Keep yah chin up, OK?"

"OK."

"That's what I wanna heah. See ya latah, alligatah!"

"After a while, crocodile. Love you!"

"I love you too, sweethaht."

I hung up the phone and Googled hotels with live jazz. The first one listed was The Alice in Miami Beach. *It's a sign!* I went there the next night. It was elegant. Palm trees grew in the lobby—that seems to be a decor down here. A grand piano stood in the corner, next to an old oak bar. Monday nights were quiet, so the bartender was free to talk.

"Hi. I'm Alice. I sing jazz and standards. I saw The Alice features live music, and I had to come and introduce myself."

"What a coincidence!" he said, leaning on the counter. He was a tall, bald man with a pleasant face. "Do you have any materials?" I handed him a photo and résumé in a folder—my press kit.

"Perfect. I'll share this with the manager, and let's see what happens. Give it a week. Things can get hectic around here, so if you don't hear from anyone, feel free to call."

"Thank you!"

"You're welcome, Alice." I left with the manager's name and phone number. Eight days later, The Alice hired me to sing! This was a five-star hotel. I called my parents from Cloud Nine.

"Very nice. Are they paying you?" asked my mom.

"Yes."

"How much?"

"Three hundred for me and the piano player."

"Each?"

She's like a heat-seeking missile. "No, we each get half." I descended to Cloud Five.

"You're making it happen! I'm so proud of you, sweethaht!" said my dad.

"I'm happy that you're happy," said my mom. *But you're not.*

I returned to Earth. "Thanks, guys." Unlike Sisyphus, I learned my lesson. *Next time, I'll keep it to myself.*

The Drektors announced a Special Board Meeting in early January. Like a call from your doctor, special board meetings were never good news. Unit owners attending the last Finance meeting spread the word about lavish spending and the tab the Drektors expected us to cover; we were braced for the worst.

The sign in the mailroom said, "The board will discuss a loan for improvements to be undertaken this year."

"This bettuh include the pipes," said Joanna.

"Let's all go together," I said. A show this good was best shared.

The old gym equipment was still in the Party Room, so the meeting was held in the Card Room. My friends and I arrived 30 minutes early.

"Look at the watuh stains!" Joanna pointed to areas of carpet. "It's almost a yeuh since the Great Flood. Why hasn't that Drekoratuh replaced this cawpet? I hate lookin' at it."

The Ceevil Engineer and his wife, the Connector, sat behind us.

"Ceevil," said Sherlock, "we should talk after the meeting."

"Yes, understood," said Ceevil. They seemed to want privacy.

"Order! Order!" yelled Her Highness. The crowd quieted. "The Manager has an announcement."

"We're out of cookies," he said in his high-pitched, nasal whine. "Those of you waiting in line can take a seat. From now on, there's a two-cookie limit per person." Empty-handed unit owners grabbed Styrofoam cups and switched to the coffee line. It was better than nothing.

The minutes from last month's meeting were read and approved. The board passed our annual budget with a 10 percent increase in monthly maintenance fees—$100 more per apartment per month, give or take. Bigger apartments would pay more, smaller apartments would pay less. No audience feedback was permitted for the vote. Next up was the loan.

Her Highness spoke into the microphone. "Does everyone have the project list? Raise your hand if you need a copy." She smiled. *I've never seen her smile before.* "You asked us about maintenance projects for our 40-year inspection, and that's what we're here to discuss. Our building is 33 years old. As you all know, living in an older building costs money." *Older? I'm older than the building, and I'm the youngest one here.* "Based on the estimates, we need $11 million for the projects on the list." There was an audible gasp. "I know, it's a lot of money. We're here to discuss a loan to spread out your payments."

The Champion wrote a note and handed it to me. "They need our votes to approve the loan. That's why she's nice." I nodded.

"Hold on!" said a voice from the audience. "We asked you about these projects *before* you renovated the Club House. If they weren't important last year, why are they so important now?" *I warned the Drektors about surprises!*

"Yeah! Why now?" asked another unit owner.

"Where's the backup? You want $11 million? I want details!"

A woman in her 80s got up, leaning on her walker. Her Highness called on her, and someone handed her a mic. She spoke slowly and emotionally. "My husband and I moved into this building the year it was built. This is my home. He passed five years ago, and I live on a fixed income. I don't go to the gym, and I don't play tennis, but I paid for your renovation. And now, because of your misguided priorities, I can't afford to live here! No board EVER spent money like you do. It isn't right!" The uproar resumed. She sat down, pulled a tissue out of her pocket, and blew her nose. *That poor woman!*

"You're running us out of our homes!"

"Hold on, hold on!" said Her Highness. "We're offering the loan to make your payments affordable. You won't have to pay it all up front—just a few hundred a month."

"I don't want a loan! I'm not paying interest!" said someone.

"Speaking of interest," said a unit owner, "what's the rate?" The question was directed to the treasurer.

Humpty Dumpty stared blankly, twirling the strand she was able to break loose from her helmet of bleached hair. *She only knows what her father taught her.* The board's shenanigans were normal to her. She couldn't know right from wrong because the good Lord hadn't burdened her with brains. She didn't expect unit owners to challenge the board's decisions, let alone ask about an interest rate. *She's scared.* My observations didn't excuse her behavior, but she had my sympathy.

Lothario's smile switched ON, his grin like a gold-toothed Cheshire Cat. "I'm glad you brought that up," he said, filling the silence without answering the question. "The loan is *voluntary*. You don't have to borrow money. We're just asking you to vote for the loan to help your neighbors who might need it." He sat down, and his smile switched off.

"A loan is a lien on our property," said a financial know-it-all in the audience. "No one wants to buy an apartment with a lien on it!"

"Unless you take a loan, there's no lien on *your* property," said the Condoland lawyer.

"Let's back up," said a unit owner. "You want us to trust you with $11 million? How do we know what you'll do with it? Look at this carpet. The flood happened *a year* ago, and you haven't re-placed it, but you have money to decorate the lobby? Now you want $11 million—with a $4 million contingency? Do you think we're stupid?"

"You told us this stuff could wait, so let it wait!"

"Somethin' don't smell right."

"It's the carpets!" Laughter broke the tension.

"We're just supposed to give you $11 million? I don't think so!"

"I don't trust you!"

"Why'd you wait 'til *after* the election to tell us?" Heads nodded in a wave across the room. The Drektors were silent, looking at each other. *Told ya to be transparent.* The meeting went downhill from there.

"You lied to us!"

"He's right. You lied to us!"

Angry, distorted faces. It was awful. Behind me sat an angel of a neighbor. She had a joyful dog named Rocky who covered my face in kisses every time I saw him. Twice a week, this woman took him to a children's hospital to visit sick kids. She tapped me on the shoulder, and I turned. She looked worried. "I can't afford to live here, Alice. We'll have to sell our place."

My friends and I were enjoying our investigations, but this wasn't a game. The Drektors' misdeeds had real consequences. *We must stop them!*

As the meeting spun out of control, I raised my hand. Her Highness didn't care for me and my questions, but she knew me to be polite. In that moment, I was her best option. "Alice, you have a question?" She spoke into the microphone. "Quiet! Quiet!" she said, banging her gavel. "Unlike the rest of you, Alice raised her hand. What's your question?" Someone handed me a wireless mic.

"Thank you." I addressed the room. "Clearly, we're frustrated." I turned to the Drektors. "I know you're working hard on our behalf, and I thank you for that." Hearing kind words, their cringing bodies relaxed. Humpty wiped her eyes. Getting yelled at is stressful, even when you deserve it. "Last year, you told us these projects could wait. Now you say they can't. Can you understand why we're confused?"

"Yeah!"

"We're confused all right!"

"Let huh finish!" yelled Joanna.

I continued. "For us to feel comfortable, we need you to be transparent. I asked for more information during the Finance meeting, and now I ask for it again." I looked Humpty Dumpty and the Bulldog in the eye and smiled. *Don't give me that look. You didn't listen!*

"That's right!"

"No more bullshit!"

"We want transparency!" I heard clapping.

With the unit owners behind me, Her Highness had to listen. "What's your *question*, Alice?"

"What details can you provide for these projects? We need specifics." I turned to face the room. My neighbors were nodding; I was on the right track. "What is the scope of work for each project? What are the costs? Are those costs guaranteed? If not, why not? And we need to know *exactly* how much money was spent on the Club House and why. Is there more work to be done there? If so, what *specifically*? How much will it cost? Most importantly, is it urgent, or can it wait?"

I faced the board. "And I have questions about the loan. You want to give us more time to pay, and that's great. But we need ALL the loan terms. That includes the interest rate, the total amount of interest we'll pay, any fees, penalties, etc. The more you share, the faster you'll restore our trust." I handed back the microphone and returned to my seat.

"Good job," said the Champion.

"You tell 'em, Alice!" said Joanna. Sherlock nodded. "Even if they give us everything, I still won't trust 'em," said Joanna.

"Neither will I," I said.

A snowbird spoke out of turn. "So, where's that information?"

Her Highness hiccupped.

"We're working on it," said the Long Island Lothario.

"Yaw working on it?" said Joanna, getting up. She didn't need a microphone. "You've gawt the chutzpah to ask faw an eleven million dolluh loan, and you don't have details? Aw you fucking kidding me? You sat there awl last yeuh lying to aw faces, and now you expect us to hand you that kinda money?"

Her Highness gulped down a glassful of water and returned to her body. "Order! Order!" she said, banging her gavel. "The Board has the authority—the responsibility—to pass assessments to maintain our building. You have until March 15th to approve the loan." Her tone changed, as if she were speaking to children. "We don't care one way or another. We're trying to *help* you! But if you vote against it, that's fine with us, too." While the Drektors talked among themselves, unit owners gathered in the back of the room, weighing their options.

"Be quiet!" said Her Highness after finishing her huddle. "We'll hold a public meeting in two weeks to discuss loan terms. We'll answer your questions, and you'll get your 'transparency.' Now I move to adjourn the meeting. Do I have a second?"

"I second the motion," said the Long Island Lothario.

"Who votes aye?" she asked. The Drektors all raised their hands. They were as uncomfortable as we were.

"The meeting is adjourned!" She gave her gavel its last bang of the evening. We sat for a few minutes, watching people leave.

"I no believe her," said Sherlock.

"Why?" I asked.

"Highness need money. Lothario need money. Something no right here."

"Nothing's right here," said the Champion. "How'd they pay

for the extra work at the Club House? Tradesmen don't take credit. If they dipped into Condoland's operating budget, that's illegal. I think it's why they want a loan and why their numbers are fuzzy. They need a slush fund to cover their tracks."

Another piece of the puzzle fell into place. "Champion, out of nowhere, our building was a million dollars over budget last month."

"So, I was right," she said. "They'll use cash from the loan to replace what they took before anybody notices," said the Champion. "Thanks, Alice. I'm gonna put the board on notice. If they broke the law, I want it on record."

"They stole from us!" I said.

"Be careful," she said. "No one here would disagree with you, but don't accuse them of anything you can't prove; they could sue you for libel."

"Oh, boy. Thanks for the advice, counselor."

"You're welcome. No charge—*this* time." She was smiling but serious.

Several neighbors stopped to talk to us on their way out. Sherlock's friend the Ceevil Engineer and his wife the Connector joined our conversation.

"Great meeting!" said Joanna.

"Ya think?" I asked.

"If we don't do something, they'll rob us blind!" she said.

"Be careful now. You wouldn't want to make an accusation," I said, glancing at the Champion. "They could sue you!"

"Bring it on," said Joanna.

"Where and when should we meet?" I asked. Our group had grown too large for the Coffee Shop.

The Latins and the North Americans in Condoland had never worked together before. Sr. Holmez nodded toward us, then gave the Ceevil Engineer the thumbs up. *We can be trusted!*

"This Saturday?" asked Sherlock. We all agreed.

"We are een the penthouse," said the Connector. She spoke slowly and with a slight accent, but her English was perfect. "We have plenty of room, and we can have privacy. Why don't you come to our apartment? Is 3 p.m. good?" We nodded. "We weel invite neighbors who also have concerns. Feel free to do the same."

Our next meeting set, we got up to leave. I walked to the main elevators with Joanna. There was no one in sight, but I whispered anyway. "These Drektors may be crooks," I said, "but if we keep the pressure on 'em, we can stop them!"

"Preshuh's good, but come summuh, we need to campaign. The only way to stop these assholes—othuh than jail—is to vote 'em out of office!"

"You're right," I said. "And now we have allies! Maybe we can."

"I hope so, honey," said Joanna. "I sure hope so."

11

The Pools

Winter in South Florida brings visitors from the North. A Boston cold spell in February brought my cousin Julie— my father's sister's daughter—down for a long weekend. We grew up together, and I was happy to see her.

Julie sought sun, sand, and sea. With olive skin that didn't burn, she could afford such extravagances. I, on the other hand, had just been read the riot act by my dermatologist on the dangers of UV rays. Julie and I made a compromise: sun for her and shade for me at the Club House pools on Saturday. She could take my car on Monday and go to the beach while I was working.

We got to the pools at two o'clock. The Daredevil often swam on the weekends. I told Julie about him but didn't mention he might be there. I kept that possibility to myself. I wore a black cover-up over my one-piece fuchsia swimsuit. Our grandmother always said a woman's best asset is a man's imagination, and I agreed with her. I brought extra sunblock for après swim. Julie wore some lotion that smelled like coconut oil. I was jealous, but one bout of water blisters was enough for this lifetime. I opened the gate, and we walked past a group of old men wearing red base-ball caps. One of them turned and watched me pass. *What's his problem?* They called out numbers to each other. *Game scores?* Julie and I found two empty chairs near a big umbrella and put down our things.

"Those chairs aw taken!" I squinted. It was Humpty Dumpty, baking below a sign that said, "No Reserving of Deck Chairs."

"You can't save chairs." I pointed. "See the sign?"

"I don't care what that sign says!" *Do as I say, not as I do.* "My friends and I always sit heuh! They'll be heuh any minute."

"Tough shit!" came a voice from the Bronx. Joanna walked up, pointing to me. "She's heuh NOW, and yaw friends awen't. Alice, keep yaw stuff right where it is."

Oh, boy. "Joanna, this is my cousin, Julie. Julie, this is my friend Joanna," I said, trying to ease the tension.

"Nice to meetcha, honey!" said Joanna. "Forgive aw neighbuh heuh." Joanna pointed her chin toward Humpty. "Can you believe she's on aw board? She fawgot she's s'posed to lead by example."

"Fuck you!" said Humpty. She eyed chairs becoming available on the other side of the deck and gathered her belongings.

"Yeah, no thanks!" Joanna said as her former friend waddled off in a huff. "Good riddance!"

My cousin's dark brown eyes were as big as saucers. I laughed. "It's OK, Julie. Think of South Florida as New York's sixth bor-ough."

"Got it," she smiled. "This place is a trip!" *It sure is.*

I caught the same old man at the entrance staring at me. "What's with the red baseball caps?" I asked Joanna, pointing to the men perched at the gate. "Is that political?"

"Worse. It's *sexual!*"

"Huh?"

"Oh, yeah. They cawl themselves the Red Hats. Did you hear them yell out numbuhs when you came in?" she asked.

"I did. Is there a game today?"

"Those aren't spawts scores, honey. Theyuh rating the women, one to ten."

"You're kidding!" I said. *Glad I didn't notice my rating.*

"Guys did that in college," said Julie.

"What can I tell ya?" said Joanna. "Some people nevuh grow up." She leaned forward, one hand covering the side of her mouth. "Even worse, they kiss and tell. Any woman stupid enough to go out with those assholes learns the hawd way."

A big splash of water hit the three of us. "Gawd damnit! I just did my hayuh." Joanna grabbed a towel and patted her wet head. "It's gonna dry like a chia pet. I gotta go. See you latuh." Hurrying toward the pool gate, rubbing her head with her towel, Joanna stopped and turned to us. "Nice to meet you, Julie!" she said.

"You, too!" said my cousin. "Thanks for the seats!"

"Anytime, hon-eee!"

"Is she a trip or what?" I asked.

"She's awesome! Hey, there's a cute guy looking at you at 11 o'clock. Is that the one? I think he's the splasher." *Gulp.*

I slowly turned toward the big pool, trying for casual.

"Hey, sexy!" No mistaking that accent. I pretended not to hear him. "Alice!" We made eye contact. The Daredevil leaned his forearms on the edge of the pool.

"Damn!" said my cousin softly. He wasn't her type—she was five foot eight and went for taller guys—but she wasn't blind.

"*¡Ven acá, guapa!*" he beckoned. He waved at Julie. "Hi, Alice's cousin!" I had mentioned she was visiting. For once, he didn't flirt.

Apparently, I was his target du jour. *Is there a decent bone in his body after all?*

She waved back and whispered, "Go over to him! What are you waiting for?"

"I'm going."

Still in my cover-up and flip flops, I walked apprehensively toward the Daredevil. The pool was his element, not mine. He pulled himself out of the water and stood up, droplets glistening over his eight-pack. He was a bronzed Adonis, and he knew it. Smiling lasciviously, he walked slowly around me with X-ray eyes. *At least I'm wearing a cover-up.* He stopped, facing me. My back was to the pool.

"What's under that smock?" He snapped the strap of my bathing suit. "Is that a bikini?" Taken off guard, I put my hand over his to remove it and stepped back. My face burned.

"It's a one-piece," I said.

He stepped closer. "Alice, why so shy? Come on, live a little!" *He's not wrong.*

A line of sweat trickled down my back. Adonis or not, there was no subtlety here—it was more like assault than seduction. I took another step back into another dimension. Disoriented. I lifted my arms above my head through what felt like a vat of Jell-O. *Where am I? What happened? Where'd he go?* In seconds, a body dove next to mine. Strong arms encircled me, pulling me to the surface. I gasped for air. I leaned against his chest, catching my breath. He wiped the hair from my face.

"Are you OK?" Julie studied me from the ledge, frightened but amused.

I coughed and looked around. "What happened?"

"You backed into the pool!" she said. *OMG. Did anybody see?*

I kissed the Daredevil on the cheek and pulled away, swimming to the ladder. As I climbed out, he yelled, "Look! You're still wearing your flip flops!" I looked down at my clenched toes. *Yes, I am.* I coughed up chlorine. "Are you OK?" he asked, climbing out of the pool. "Why don't you sit?"

"No, I'm all right." Water dripped from my cover-up. *How embarrassing!*

"Thank God!" He put his hand on my shoulder. No grabbing this time, just that wicked smile. "I seem to have an effect on you!" People behind him were jostling to get a look at me. I smiled back, waiting for the earth to split so I could disappear again. The Red Hat who'd been eyeing me was walking toward us. *Leave me alone, you lecherous creep!*

"Alice, I'm getting hungry," said Julie, opening an escape hatch. "Wanna eat?"

"Sure." I looked up at the Daredevil. "Well, that ends the entertainment portion of today's programming." Or so I thought.

"You're funny. I'm glad you're OK." He kissed my cheek. "Next time, you're gonna show me what's underneath that smock."

"Ciao!" I said.

"Ciao, bella." He dove into the pool and side-stroked toward the other end, watching me until two girls in bikinis jumped in.

Julie pointed to the outdoor showers. "Go rinse off. And take off that damned cover-up!" She handed me a Condoland beach towel. You can put this around you."

Dechlorinated but still humiliated, I came back a few minutes later with the towel saronged around me. Julie had stepped into a pair of Bermuda shorts and pulled a T-shirt over her bikini top. "Where do we eat?" she asked. "I'm starving!" I pointed to a shaded table against the side of the Club House. We ran to claim it.

"The restrooms are inside if you want to wash your hands," I said.

"Thanks. Let's order first," said Julie.

The daily menu was posted on a chalkboard. While we decided, we couldn't help overhearing the two women at the next table.

"Ho-zaay!" said one, her hand waving in the air to get the server's attention. "Yoo-hoo! Ho-zaaay!" The server didn't budge. "Do you see how he ignaws me?" she said to her dining companion. "I'm telling ya, ya can't get good help down heuh!"

The server stood at the wait station scanning the tables. I smiled and raised a finger. He came immediately and took our order.

"Excuuse me!" said one of the women at the next table after he left. Her hands on her hips, she stared at me and Julie. "We wuh heuh first! You girls just sat down and that good-fuh-nothin' waituh took yaw awduh. Did you *schmear*[16] him?" *You think I have to bribe the waiter to place my order?*

"No, ma'am," I said.

"We've been calling and calling him," said the other woman. "Why is he ignoring us?"

"You've been calling José. The server's name is Juan."

"What's the difference?" They said in unison just as Juan returned to our table with a basket of bread and ice water. He grinned at us and turned to them.

"Señoras, José's shift starts at 5 p.m. If you're still here, I'll ask him to take your order right away." He bowed and returned to his station. Julie and I turned away from the table so the women wouldn't see us laugh. When we turned around, they were gone. *Buh-bye!*

Two women in their 60s walked out of the Club House, passing

---

[16] Schmear — Yiddish for bribe. Can also mean to spread something, e.g., schmear cream cheese on a bagel.

us on their way to their deck chairs. "Can you believe that stink in the bathroom?" said one to the other.

"Feh!" said the other woman, squeezing her nose.

"It's like something died in there!" said the first, contorting her face. "Some renovation!" Julie and I looked at each other.

"I can wait," she said.

"Me, too."

Joanna walked out of the Club House as we were sipping our iced coffee. She'd wrapped a skirt around her one-piece bathing suit. I waved, and she joined us. "Your hair looks great!" I said.

"Thanks. I had 'em blow it out in the spaw. Edguh and I are goin' out to dinnuh tonight." The waiter brought her usual—a large glass of white wine. Her chair faced the lap pool parallel to the Intracoastal. Nobody seemed to care anymore that I fell into the pool, and my embarrassment began to dissipate. We girl-talked, mostly about boys. "Look at those paw bastuhds sittin' there with nothin' else to do but gawk at women. That just goes to show you girls: dating is hell at any age!" Joanna finished her drink, and Juan brought her another.

"Who are you talking about?" asked Julie.

"The Red Hats," said Joanna. "I'm not excusing theyuh behaviuh. It's just, I dunno, I kinda feel sorry for 'em."

"Huh?" I asked.

"Think about it," said Joanna. "Theyuh old and alone. They obsess ovuh women, and most of them fawgot how to get one." This was Joanna's softer side. *In vino veritas.* She took a big gulp and smiled impishly. "I gawt an idear." *Uh-oh.*

Julie and I looked at each other. "Finish your coffee," said my cousin. "Just in case."

"Oh, boooyz!" said Joanna, waving. "Booyzz! Ovuh heuh!" She

stood as the Red Hats looked our way. I had more than enough time to clear the table, because it took them five minutes just to stand up. "Come heuh!" Joanna said. *Don't encourage them!* By the time six Red Hats had gathered in front of us, Joanna had finished her second chardonnay.

My stalker spoke first. "Hello, young ladies." *Yuck.* "Joanna." He nodded. The others stood, wide-eyed. They were used to talking *about* women, not *to* them.

"Hello, boys," said my crazy red-headed friend. "I decided to give you a little present." She got up from her chair, empty-handed. "Aw ya ready?" They were mute. So was I, and so was Julie. "I can't heeeuuh you! Aw you ready?" Someone coughed. "It's now aw nevuh!" They looked scared.

"Ready," one of them yelped.

"We're ready," said another, his hands clasped in front of his groin.

"Drum roll, please," said Joanna. She must have been tipsy, but she was firmly in command and long past letting other people's opinions control her actions. She was a force of nature, and we played along. Banging our hands on the table, Julie and I were her rhythm section.

"OK, boyz," said Joanna, channeling Gypsy Rose Lee as she lowered the top of her swimsuit to reveal her breasts. *Thank God the Red Hats are hiding her from view.*

"You can look, but don't touch!" She started counting. "Five, faw, three—no pikchahs!" One of the Red Hats put his phone back in his swimsuit pocket. "—Two, one!" We stopped the drumroll as Joanna calmly pulled up her straps and tied them behind her neck. "I hope you boys enjoyed the show! Tell me, do you give me a 10?" They nodded.

"Yes!" one squealed.

"Good!" said Joanna. "So now that you've seen a poyfect specimen, why don't you stawt showing the rest of the women heuh some respect!" The Red Hats were immobilized. "Cat got yaw tongues? I'll ask again. Aw you gonna stop with the numbuhs?"

"Yes, Mrs. Rivers," said my stalker. He looked at the rest of his sorry bunch. "We won't be doing that anymore. Thank you!" He bowed slightly. As fast as their legs would take them—which was not very fast—they walked away. The man who'd covered his groin during the show sat down in the kiddie pool where two little boys were splashing.

"Are those his grandchildren?" Julie asked.

"He doesn't have grandchildren," said Joanna.

"What's he doing in there?" I asked. It *was* odd.

"That pool's not heated, honey," said Joanna. "Puhhaps his bottom half needs to cool off." We all howled. It was such an incongruous scene.

"Well, I gotta get goin'," said Joanna. "Edguh's waiting fuh me." She gave us both a kiss and grabbed the tab before either of us could stop her.

"Thanks, Joanna. Fun to see you as always!" I said.

"Any time you need a rhythm section, just ask!" said my cousin. As Joanna was leaving, my Red Hat stalker returned, cap in hand. He tried to make eye contact, and I looked away. *What's your problem?*

"Joanna," he said.

She turned. "Yes?"

"You taught us all a lesson. The boys agreed; no more locker talk." She smiled. "You know, you're still a handsome woman—not like these old ladies." He looked back at the pool's female patrons.

"And?" said Joanna. He wasn't telling her anything she didn't already know.

He stepped forward, lowering his voice. "Who did your chest?"

"Excuse me?" she asked.

"I met someone special. I'd like to give her a boob job for her 70th birthday. Did you get them done down here? Was it Dr. Schwartz? I hear he does great work."

"Nah," said Joanna, visibly annoyed. She started walking away.

"Joanna!" said the Red Hat. "Did I say something wrong? I just wanna know, who was your doctor?"

She turned and looked at him like a fly she wanted to swat. "My doctuh?" she yelled. "You wanna know who did my breasts!" He nodded. "Mothuh Natchuh, you mothuhfuckuh!" She turned and stormed out the gate.

"And you wanted to go to the beach!" I said to Julie.

By 5:00, the sun was about to set, and the pool was empty enough for Julie and me to swim laps. We put our stuff down next to a Venezuelan family I'd seen in my building. The Star of David hanging from the mother's neck signaled they were Jewish. She was engrossed in her smartphone. A woman I assumed was the nanny looked after her two young boys—the ones I'd seen in the kiddie pool. One, about four, had short brown hair. He sat quietly, tired from his "swim." I guessed the older boy to be six. He had blond curls down his neck and a big attitude. He was arguing with his nanny about swimming in the deep end of the grown-up pool. She asked him to wear a swim vest, and he was resisting. She took his arm to put it through the vest opening. "No!" he said, slapping her face.

"Did you see that?" I asked Julie.

"What?" She was tucking her hair into her swim cap.

"Little Lord Fauntleroy there just slapped his nanny!" The nanny absorbed the blow and the disgrace, her head bowed. By six, her charge had figured out that his lighter skin and his parents' bank account enabled him to act as he wished. *That poor woman!* If he jumped into the pool without the vest, she'd be blamed. If she *made* him wear it, he'd tell his mother he hated her, and she needed her job. Yet out of concern, she persisted. The older boy screamed in frustration. His mother looked up and put down her phone.

"*¡Basta!*" said the mother. "It's late. Let's go." The nanny carried their things, walking behind the boys vying for attention on either side of their mother. Just before they left my line of sight, I saw Lord Fauntleroy stick his tongue out at his nanny. It was sickening, but there was nothing I could do. *He's a Drektor-in-training.*

"Laps?" said Julie.

"Laps," I said. We swam until I heard a man's voice above me as I kicked off from the end of the pool.

"Are you speaking to me?" I asked.

"Yes." It was my Red Hat stalker. I looked around. It was just he, Julie, and I.

"Don't worry," I said, acting normal. "She says what she thinks, but I'm sure she's not mad at you."

"Joanna?" he asked. I nodded. "No, that's not it. Are you Alice?"

Where's Julie? She was at the other end of the pool. "I am. Why?"

"You're the chair of the Finance Committee, right?" *Oh!*

"Yes." I was relieved, then annoyed. Condoland was intruding on my time with my cousin.

"I like your questions," said the newly rehabilitated Red Hat.

"Thanks." I pushed off from the pool wall to finish my swim.

"One more thing!" *Damnit!* I swam back.

"What's that?"

His knees creaked as he squatted above me. "The Drektors are talking to X Bank about a loan, and—"

"How do you know that?" I asked. I didn't know this guy from Adam.

"My son works there," he said. "He signed a confidentiality agreement, so he can't tell me much. He just said to find out everything we can about that loan. Since you're the Committee chair, I wanted you to know." I wasn't in an investigatory mood, but I knew he was trying to help. Ever since I could remember, people came to me to do the speaking up. This time—for the first time—I had friends to share the burden.

"Thank you very much," I said. "I will definitely look into it."

He held on to the step ladder to get to his feet. "I know you will, Alice. We're counting on you!"

12

Birth of the Resistance

After Julie's visit, I had a particularly interesting conversation with the Daredevil at the gym. We started with politics. He explained populism to me as an all-too-frequent ploy in South America. He described how populist candidates made promises to the masses they would never fulfill. Once elected, those promises were forgotten. By the time the voters realized their mistake, it was too late. *Just like Condoland.* He talked; I listened. He had a privileged childhood, and skydiving was his passion. He invested in stocks using his trust fund. The intensity of the conversation felt intimate. I was giddy, and I remembered the astrologer's words, "You're going to feel like you're flying" *Is he the one? I hope she meant that figuratively, because I'm not jumping out of a plane!*

The Daredevil told me how he met his late wife. "Her last name was Hymen," he said, smiling mischievously. *So much for intimacy.*

"Hymen?"

"Yes. H-y-m-e-n. You know, like—"

"That's my grandmother's maiden name. Where was your wife from?"

119

"Massachusetts."

"I think I'm related to her!" He looked away. I did the generational math in my head. *She's my second cousin!* Crickets. He changed the subject.

Still talking, we left the gym together. Back in our building, we rode alone in the elevator. We passed his floor without stopping. *He didn't press his button.* As we reached my floor, he asked about me. When was my last relationship? I told him about El Innombrable. The door began to close, and he grabbed it, holding it open with his back until it beeped, demanding release.

"I'll walk out with you," he said.

"OK." We stood in the hallway in front of the elevators, sweaty, with no more than a foot between us. He smelled of musk. A portly Cuban neighbor passed us in her bathrobe and house slippers on her way to the garbage chute.

"¡Hola, Sra. Vargas!"

"Hola, Alicia."

"Hola, Señora," said the Daredevil.

"Mm-hmm." She gave him side-eye on the way back to her apartment.

Minutes flew by while we stood 100 feet from my front door. *I need to go to the bathroom . . . I wanna keep talking . . . I'm not inviting him in.*

"Your hair smells good."

"Thanks." I'd shampooed it *before* the gym, in case he was there.

"You dating anyone?"

"Yeah, nothing serious." I had to say something.

He arched his brows, observing me. "Oh, yeah? Who?"

"No one worth mentioning yet."

"You're just sleeping with him?" That didn't deserve a response.

"Them?" he asked. *Really?*

"No! I have to be in love to sleep with someone."

He stepped two feet back from the L word. "You're kidding!"

"No."

"Seriously?"

"Seriously." *How many STDs does he have?*

He tapped his foot and looked at his watch. "I didn't realize it was so late. I have to place a trade in Hong Kong." The Daredevil was a day trader.

"OK. Well, it was great talking to you!"

His smile curled, wistfully. "Yeah, you, too. Sweet dreams, Alice."

"Good night."

Saturday afternoon, I put on a T-shirt dress and espadrilles for the big meeting. I was apprehensive about expanding our circle of dissenters. Up 'til now, it was just Sherlock, the Champion, Joanna, and I putting our heads together. Sharing information more broadly was a necessary risk. *What if someone tells the Drektors what we we're doing? Alice, you can't win an election with four people!* We had to take the chance, and today was the day.

To facilitate introductions, I brought name tag stickers and magic markers. I took the elevator up to the 24th floor, then switched to the penthouse elevator. The Connector had given each of us her special code to allow access. This was what my grandmother used to call "high tone."

I exited the private elevator and found Joanna applying her lipstick in the hallway mirror. "Imagine having a private elevator!" I said.

"I know. Very fancy." She and her husband had a three-bedroom corner apartment, but even the Rivers' place didn't compare to the penthouse. The door was cracked open. We heard voices inside.

"Let's go in," I said.

"*¡Hola, guapas!*" said the Connector. She wore a flowered summer dress and a huge smile. Her dark brown hair was twisted in a chignon. "Welcome. What can I offer you to drink?" She had bottles of red, white, and rosé, each in their own ice buckets. There was American coffee, a cheese platter, crackers and dips, empanadas, fried plantains, and chicken liver with mini rye slices—a crowd favorite. The Connector was an experimental cook. "Please, help yourself! Thees is beet hummus, and thees is green pea hummus," she said with particular pride. "Alice, you have to try some!"

"Sure. Thanks."

She hovered. "Do you like eet?"

I swallowed. *Say something nice.* "Yes! It's . . . an unusual combination of flavors!"

"I'm so glad! You know the secret?" I shook my head. "Anchovies!" Gleefully, she clasped her hands together. "I made a lot; I weel give you some to take home."

No good deed goes unpunished. "Thank you so much!" I showed her the name tags. "What do you think?"

She shook her head. "Put them away, Alice. This meeting never happened, so we don't need names." She smiled patiently. *Duh.* I still had a lot to learn.

Her husband approached us. "Ladies, shall we get started?"

"Yes, of course," I said, moving into the living room. There were 12 chairs arranged in a circle. Sherlock and the Champion were already seated, along with four other men from Sherlock's lunch group, Florence Nightingale, and a man we called Harvard.

Harvard was in his early 90s. Long past his cerebral prime, he flaunted his academic credentials to camouflage gaps in knowledge and memory. Within 60 seconds of meeting him, he mentioned the school of all schools at least twice. This immodesty extended to his military service. As the self-anointed arbiter of valor, he hosted an annual dinner for Condoland's veterans and their wives. I sat between the Connector and Sherlock.

"Thanks to our hosts for having us and for the fabulous spread," said the Champion. "And thanks to all of you for being here. I don't want to assume. Are you all concerned by the Drektors' spending and their priorities?"

"Yes!" We spoke in emphatic unison. *So far, so good.*

"OK. Glad I asked!" The only lawyer in our expanding team, the Champion became our de facto leader. "First thing I think we should do is get a legal opinion. We need to know what recourse we have—if any—to address the board's actions."

"Attorney fees add up," said the Ceevil Engineer, furrowing his brow. My eyes wandered to the silk murals on the wall below the staircase to the second floor. Through French doors, I saw a garden on the roof deck which belonged to the penthouse. *He's worried about legal fees?* He looked at the Champion. "Aren't you an attorney?"

"I am," she said, speaking to the group. "But as I told Alice, I specialize in commercial real estate, not condominium law. Besides, I'm too close to this. We need a condominium expert— someone whose name will rattle the board."

"How much?" I asked.

"For an initial consult, I think $100 per unit would do it," she said.

Sherlock and his friends spoke rapidly in Spanish. "What did they say?" I asked.

"In Venezuela, they gave money to a candidate because they thought he could remove the dictator from office. He couldn't. They think the lawyer is a waste of money."

"They won't contribute?"

"They weell. I conveence them." He smiled.

"Thank you, Sherlock!" *He's our secret weapon.*

"I'm in," I said. The others nodded. We had $1,000.

"Good," said the Champion. "I'll contact the law firm. Its managing partner used to run a practice with Condoland's senior attorney. Apparently, the men dissolved their firm due to 'professional differences.'" She used air quotes. "That'll get the Drektors' attention!"

"You want the money now?" I asked.

"No. Not 'til we need it. One more thing," she said, leaning forward. "You can't discuss the attorney with anyone. This place is a gossip mill, and the Drektors can't get wind of our plans. Agreed?" We nodded. "Please, I need you to raise your hands to promise you'll keep these meetings confidential." She stared at each person in the circle.

"What about telling spouses?" asked Joanna. "Edguh was the board president. He can help."

"Use your best judgement for spouses, but make sure they don't tell anyone else. Is that fair?"

"Ees fair," said Sherlock. With his approval, his friends raised their hands. Our silence was unanimous.

"Thank you," said the Champion. "We can't be too careful."

"I'd like to talk about the loan meeting," I said. "It's next week."

"Please," said the Champion. "Go ahead."

"Thanks. At the last board meeting, I asked Humpty Dumpty to have the Drektors show us all the loan costs. Afterward, I emailed each of them a format to lay out the details." I handed everyone a paper. "This is a checklist for the loan. Have I missed anything?"

The Champion put on her reading glasses. "No, I think you covered everything," she said.

"Good. There's just one thing—and remember," I said, scanning the room, "you promised not to share anything we discuss."

"Alice, if we tawk, we're throwin' our own money down the drain!" said Joanna.

"OK," I continued. "A friend in the building knows someone who works at X Bank." It was the Daredevil's friend. "Evidently, someone from Condoland called the X Bank guy to ask if he wanted to bid on an $11 million loan."

"So?" asked Joanna.

"So, the caller requested a referral fee." Sherlock had a knowing look. He shook his head.

"Everything's a scam!" said Joanna.

"Who called?" asked the Champion

"An older woman," I said. "He thinks it was Her Highness."

"What about Humpty Dumpty? She's the treasurer," said the Champion. Sherlock laughed out loud. Humpty was treasurer like he was a ballerina.

"He said she sounded Midwestern," I answered. *Not Humpty Dumpty.*

"Do you trust your source?" asked the Champion.

"He has no reason to lie. He lives here, and he doesn't wanna get ripped off either." I thought of the Red Hat at the pool whose son warned him about the loan. "Besides, someone else with a contact at the bank warned me to ask questions before voting for the loan."

"Why don't you add 'referral fee' to your list," said the Champion, "and let's see how it goes next week. If we don't get the loan details, I'll send a letter of demand."

"You go, counselor!" I said. The Champion was a fierce advocate, but I'd never want her as my enemy. A lot of people at Condoland feared her.

"I'm not your counsel—"

"I know, I know," I said. "It's a figure of speech."

"As long as we're clear," she said.

"May I . . . say . . . something?" asked Harvard. His speech was slow and pretentious.

"Of course," said the Champion.

"Condoland . . . doesn't need a loan."

"It doesn't?" she asked.

"No. When I lived on *Fifth Avenue* . . . our building . . . had a $60 million assessment." He waited for a reaction. Not getting one, he repeated himself. "Sixty million dollars! What we did . . ." *Spit it out already!* "Was have . . . those . . . who could afford it . . . pay up front. We used . . . that up-front money . . . to pay the vendors doing the work . . . for the first . . . few years. Owners who needed more time . . . were able to pay . . . monthly. Nobody . . . paid interest. More importantly . . . we did not . . . have a *lien* . . . on our property. A loan . . . is a TERRIBLE idea!"

The Champion was nonplussed. "The laws vary by state," she said. "That sounds like a creative solution for you in New York, but in Florida, it's illegal. If we offer one group of people interest-free financing; we'd have to offer it to everybody."

"I think . . . you're wrong," said Harvard. *Aaaaaahh!*

"That's your privilege," said the Champion. "I encourage you to research Florida law before you share the idea with anyone else.

We can't afford to confuse people." *She's as tough as my mom.* I couldn't help but grin. "Any other suggestions? No? Then thanks again to our hosts for their hospitality."

The Connector beamed. This was her first gathering with both English and Spanish speakers—two groups united for the first time by a common cause.

"See you guys at the loan meeting!" I said. As people left, the Connector loaded me with beet and pea hummus to go. *My mazel.*[17]

Harvard pulled me aside on his way out. *Why me?* "I'm afraid . . . your friend . . . doesn't know . . .what she's talking about."

Be like the Champion. "Are you an attorney?" I asked.

"No . . . I'm sorry . . . I'm not," he replied with faux humility.

"The Champion's a real estate attorney. She's a subject matter expert." I'm not one to blindly defend my friends, but he was dead wrong. He shrugged his hunched shoulders, unconvinced. "Thanks for coming!"

Eight days later, we went to the loan meeting in the Restaurant, which was closed on Mondays.

We sat at square tables facing a long rectangular table near the entrance. Seated behind it were four Drektors and Mr. Complicit, there to represent X Bank.

The Champion and Joanna sat at my table. Sherlock was behind us with his kosher lunch friends. The Long Island Lothario sat in front of me.

"Why aren't you up front?" I asked him.

"I prefer to listen as a unit owner. It's not a board meeting." He was separating himself for a reason.

––––––––––––––––––––––––––––––

[17] Mazel — Yiddish for luck, fortune. Mazel tov means good luck.

The Champion whispered in my ear. "Plausible deniability that ain't plausible."

"Mm-hmm," I hummed.

The Bulldog started the meeting. *Why's he talking?* "Good evening, everyone. You should have a document for your reference during tonight's presentation. Mr. Complicit is here from X Bank. He'll tell you about the loan and answer your questions. Does anyone need a copy of the document? Keep your hands raised, folks, so the Manager can see you."

"Where's the cawfee?"

"What did he say? I need a little something to eat."

"Can we order from the kitchen?"

"My wife's diabetic!"

The Bulldog rolled his eyes. "No refreshments, folks. This is a business meeting."

Mr. Complicit droned on about his bank in monotone. He wore a gray suit and a gray tie and looked to be in his 50s. I wasn't listening. Around me, necks swiveled—instinctively—searching for nourishment. *Do the Drektors think we'll be more receptive on an empty stomach?*

"They wanna keep this short," said Joanna. "That's why there's no food."

"Alice, look at the handout," said the Champion. "It's a joke. It doesn't state the interest rate. There's no mention of prepayment penalties or fees, period."

I nodded. "And look at the branding," I said.

"What branding?"

"Exactly. There's no letterhead! It's a payment schedule on white copy paper. Who wrote this?" I spoke loud enough for others to hear. I wanted them to hear.

A man behind me raised his hand. He looked unthreatening in his sweater, glasses, and khaki pants. As this was Her Highness's sole criterion for allowing people to speak, she called on him. A waiter handed the man a mic.

"That's my friend the banker," whispered the Champion.

He stood, holding the handout, his reading glasses midway down his nose. "Hello, everyone," he began. "The stated loan amount is $11 million, but you said you may not need that much, correct?"

"And?" said Highness.

"And you can't spend it all right away, so why pay interest from day one?" *Good point.*

The Long Island Lothario guffawed. "We need it, friend!" he bellowed from the audience. "I understand where your goin', but we can't—"

"Hear me out," said the man. "We each pay a few hundred a month in an assessment, and you use the money as you go. I know, everything's urgent, but you can't paint the building while you fix the pipes, the Club House, the garage, etc. Not gonna happen, right?" Her Highness looked to her left to see who would answer. *Bueller? Bueller?* "One more thing. If we end up approving it, what interest will we pay over the life of the loan? I'd like to see that for, say, a $5 million loan, $6 million . . . up to $11 million, worst case scenario. Make sense?"

I whispered to him when he sat down. "Great ideas. I asked them about the interest, too. They don't listen!"

He lifted his hands, palms up. "At least we tried."

"The Bookkeeper doesn't have time for that," said Highness. *That's her answer?* "Look on the backside of your paper. It shows the monthly payments by apartment type—*if* you participate in the loan. Remember, voting for the loan helps your neighbors, even if you don't borrow yourself."

We all paid a percentage of Condoland's operating expenses, and the loan would be apportioned the same way. The bigger your apartment, the higher your loan payment.

"We assume an $11 million loan," said the Bookkeeper, "because that's the most we should have to borrow." *Should?*

"Whose paper is this?" I yelled it out. Nobody responded.

"Whaddayou mean?" Joanna whispered.

I stood up. They weren't going to pass me the microphone, so I used a singing technique to project my voice. "Who wrote this document? It doesn't have the bank's name on it." Silence. *Is the Bulldog chewing gum?* "Is it a secret?" I sat down. "Her Highness is ignoring me," I said to Joanna.

She stood. "Who's responsible for this papuh!" she spoke with a force that could wake the dead—but not the Corpse.

"It's general information," said the Bulldog. He got up and grabbed Her Highness's mic from its stand. His other hand crushed the papers he was holding as his inner demon fought for control.

The Long Island Lothario turned to me. "It's a summary, not a formal document," he said with a Cheshire cat grin.

"Would you borrow money without knowing what fees you were paying or who set the terms?" I asked him. "Come on. You know better." People around us listened, as I hoped they would.

"You're too serious, Alice," he said. He took his arm off his seatback and faced forward.

Joanna remained standing. "Whaddayou people hiding?"

"How many banks bid on this loan?" boomed a deep voice from a tanned, heavyset man in his late 50s.

Joanna sat down. "Don't get started with him. He's *meshuga*."[18]

"I spent 20 years in investment banking in Manhattan," he continued. "I retired early because I could." *Throw that man a parade!* "This meeting is a joke. Now, I'll ask again. How many banks bid on the loan?" It was a great question. *Meshuga* or not, politics make strange bedfellows. I caught his eye and nodded in appreciation.

Mr. Complicit from X Bank looked at the Drektors, who looked at each other and back at him. No answer.

"Simple question," said the deep voice. "What are you hiding?" No response. "Don't think you'll get away with this!"

Joanna called on herself again. "I'd like to heuh from the bankuh. Aw these yaw figures?" Mr. Complicit patted his forehead with his handkerchief. "This is a document with information the Condoland board wants you to have," he non-answered.

"Answer her question!" said the Champion, standing up. "Who's responsible for this term sheet?"

The Bulldog grabbed the gavel out of Her Highness's hand. "Order! Order!" he yelled, banging on the table, tipping over Highness's water glass. Water fell on the Corpse's lap, jerking him awake.

"Proof of life," I whispered to the Champion.

"You people asked for this meeting," yelled the Bulldog, "but we're not going to sit here and take abuse!" I tapped my fingers on the table. *I told Bulldog this would happen. Abuse?* Laughter escaped like gas I couldn't control. "This meeting is adjourned!"

"It keeps getting worse," I said to the Champion.

"That's OK," she said. "They're in over their heads. At least now, more of us are onto them."

---

[18] Meshuga — Yiddish for crazy

Three weeks after the X Bank meeting, the unit owners received a ballot asking us to vote for or against the loan. An enclosed letter from the Drektors pleaded with us to approve it for the sake of our neighbors, if not ourselves. No additional loan details were provided, but two more projects were added to the list.

The Drektors were asking for total control over $11 million. Yet, if we voted *against* the loan, we'd each be saddled with a $27,500 bill—give or take—due immediately. Neighbors would be forced to sell their homes. It was a no-win situation.

The Champion consulted our group's attorney. By law, the board was only required to tell us what our monthly payments would be. The more fees they divulged, the more likely we were to vote no, so they didn't.

The Champion issued her first non-lawyer lawyer letter to the Board of Drektors with a plea for transparency. She argued that we deserved to cast an informed vote and called their approach "ass backwards." Nevertheless, the Drektors had their way. They ignored her request and refused to move the voting date.

The votes were tallied, and the Office announced that two-thirds of Condoland unit owners, I among them, voted to keep a roof over our neighbors' heads. It was the Ides of March.

13

A Small Victory

Anyone who's watched a mob movie knows the number one rule of staying in "business": no large purchases after a big score. If you violate rule number one, apply rule number two: keep your mouth shut! Apparently, Mrs. Lothario never watched those movies. Soon after the loan was approved, I went to the gym, where it was impossible not to hear her brag about recent home improvements.

"Look!" she said, holding her phone out to a woman on the treadmill. "Marble countertops—imported from Italy! My kitchen floor's Jerusalem stone! Do you know how hard it is to get?"

I couldn't resist. "Sounds expensive, Mrs. Lothario!"

"It *is*! My husband went all out. I deserve the best, and he knows it!" *Who talks like this?* "And Alice," she said, coming closer. *Next victim!* "Look. At. This! I turned our second bedroom into a palace for my girls. They have their own ramps, lots of perches, and three scratching posts! Nothing's too good for my babies." I remembered Sr. Holmez telling me the maintenance man built her a jungle gym to keep his job. Workers served at the pleasure of the board. If a

Drektor asked for a favor, employees were between a rock and a hard place.

I forced a Mona Lisa smile. *My money is decorating your apartment.* "How nice for you."

"It really is," she said, her chin toward the ceiling as she curled her biceps. She paused, looking serious. "I feel like I can confide in you."

No, no, no! "Really?" I asked. "What is it?"

"My other girls—my daughters—they want nothing to do with me. They're mad at their father. I can't discuss why. *Because he worked for a man in organized crime?* And they're mad at *me* for staying with him. I can't mention their names in front of him. He says he worked his ass off to put them through school; how dare they judge him! It breaks my heart, but he's my Prince Charming! I could never leave him. They have their own lives now. It's not fair."

Wow. "That must be very difficult." I changed the subject. "What do your daughters do?" Normally, I hate that question, but I asked for a reason.

"They're attorneys. Prosecutors for the State of Washington." *Well, now. Everything to oppose their father.* "Very smart girls," she said. *Smart, indeed. They want to stay in the bar, not behind bars, and your husband is an indictment waiting to happen.* Despite myself, I felt sorry for her. She was in a terrible situation.

"I'm sure you're proud." She nodded, wiping away a tear. I now understood her superficiality. She was desperate to convince herself she made the right choice. We had a moment, then two unit owners walked into the equipment room.

"Hi! How are you?" said Mrs. Lothario, running to greet the yet-to-be-impressed. "Want to see my new kitchen? And here's our babies' jungle gym!" The neighbors looked at each other. "Take a look at——"

"Honey, can you come spot me?" called the Long Island Lothario from the other side of the room. "I need your help."

"Of course, my prince." She turned to her unwitting audience. "Will you excuse me?" she said and walked toward her husband, her pigtails flapping. The Lotharios argued in low tones—not low enough that I couldn't make out a few words.

"Stop talking . . . careful . . . don't . . . ammunition," said her prince. She stared at the floor. Apparently, Mr. Lothario knew both rules, number one and number two.

Sherlock Holmez came into the equipment room, and I brought him up to date in Spanish. I caught the Lotharios staring at us in the mirror against the back wall. Being bilingual was becoming a guilty pleasure. They knew I was talking about them, but they couldn't understand a word I was saying.

"Alice, I have discoveries regarding this project of ours," said Sherlock. *This project of ours?" That's how we talk now?* "I will need your help. Can you stop by my apartment this afternoon?"

"Sure. How's 4 p.m.?"

"*¡Perfecto!*"

"*Vale.* See you then."

"Hi, beautiful!" said Mrs. Holmez, opening the door. She was pretty, warm, and maternal. She looked as "American" as apple pie, but she was bilingual, having lived in Colombia for 35 years. She met Sherlock when he came to Santa Catalina Island to buy art from her father. Theirs was a fascinating love story.

"Would you like coffee?" she asked. "I just made it. It's strong, so if you're not used to it, add milk."

"Thank you, Mrs. Holmez!" I said.

"*Por favor,* call me Shilah."

"OK, Shilah."

Sherlock came into the room. He noticed me viewing the paintings covering every wall. "Alice, you like art?"

"I do."

"Come, I'll give you the tour—then we'll talk."

Compared to their properties in Colombia, their Condoland apartment was tiny. Furnishings were easy to leave, but not the art. They kept their favorite canvases, dividing the rest between their children and the Museo Nacional de Colombia. Art filled every wall in the apartment, even the bathrooms.

"This is Diego Rivera," Sherlock said.

"A print?" I asked.

"No." He brushed off the suggestion. "Everything is original. Here's a Frida Kahlo . . . this one is Velázquez . . . this caricature is José Clemente Orozco—"

"That's a Botero!" I said, pointing above their bed. Even I knew the artist's inflated female figures. They made this girl feel slim.

"*Sí, Alambrito.*" It means "little wire hanger" in Spanish. Sherlock believed in meat on the bone. "And these are paintings by Shilah's father." We were now in the living room. "And here," Sherlock lifted a thick art book, "this is an encyclopedia of her father's art. It documents each piece." We stopped in front of a still life. "See this one? Page 173." He stepped to a Madonna and child to the left. "This one? Page 225. Look in the book." I did, and there they were. *Their home is a museum!*

"Is that Salvador Dalí?" I asked, darting to a small painting in the kitchen.

"*Sí.* You know his work?"

"I saw an exhibit at El Prado," I answered, remembering my

last trip to Madrid.

Sherlock looked pleased. *Maybe I'm not the gringa you thought I was!* "*Bueno*, let's sit down and chat." He motioned me into to the living room. Similar to my apartment, they had floor-to-ceiling windows facing the ocean. Maroon oriental carpets with blue, white, and gold detail accented their dark wood floors. Theirs was an old-world home in the land of pink flamingos. I sank into an up-holstered chair facing the ocean. Sherlock sat to my right on a bro-cade, rose-colored sofa custom-built to complement his father-in-law's work titled "Signorina Con Una Rosa" on the wall above it. Shilah put down a tray of biscotti, plates, and napkins.

Sherlock opened his laptop on the coffee table. "I found some-thing interesting. The Long Island Lothario has a business registered in Florida as an LLC—a limited liability corporation. It's called American Athletic Apparel. It sells exercise clothing for men."

"Is that right?" I asked, smirking. *Interesting choice.*

The irony did not escape Sherlock, but he was intent on his discovery. "Two years ago, American Athletic Apparel reported $25,000 in revenue—not profit, but revenue." He looked at me to make sure I was paying attention.

"I'm listening."

"Its fiscal year ended on March 31st. Do you know how much revenue it just reported?" Sherlock asked.

"How much?"

"One point four million dollars."

"What!" Biscotto fell out of my mouth. I grabbed a napkin.

"*Sí, señorita.* One point four million dollars!" Sherlock sat back on the couch, savoring my reaction. "And on what date was Con-doland's loan approved?"

"March 15th," I answered.

"And how much was that loan?" *We're playing 21 questions? I guess you earned it.*

"Eleven million dollars."

"Isn't that an interesting coincidence?"

"How do you know this?"

"I have my sources."

"You know everything before the rest of us. What's the secret?" I asked.

"My family was in the newspaper business."

"In Colombia?"

"Close." *More mystery.*

"But not anymore?"

"No. The new government gave us three choices: 1) sell our paper to the state, 2) print what the state told us to print, or 3) report the truth and be shut down. We went with option number one."

"How awful! I can't imagine how frustrating that was." *Actually . . . I can.* I leaned toward him. "Were you a reporter?"

"Among other things, but that was a long time ago." He crossed his legs, his arms spread across the sofa. "Now, I'm just a South Florida retiree."

"I'm going to pay you my highest compliment: You're an onion!"

He laughed. "That's your compliment? Do I need mouthwash?" He popped a mint from the candy dish into his mouth.

I shook my head. "You're full of layers!"

"Thank you, *Artista. Oye,* there's something else I want to discuss."

"Tell me."

"The Drektors made changes to the Club House without holding the vote required by the bylaws. This is not right. I am an owner. You are an owner. We did not give permission! That has me thinking about votes."

"What votes?" I asked.

"The vote to renovate the Club House and the vote for the $11 million loan," he said.

"What about them?"

"Why haven't we seen the election results? With the Champion's help, I submitted a request for information about the vote for the renovation months ago." *Is he paranoid?*

"You think they lost the vote and went ahead anyway?"

"Maybe," said Sherlock. "Then Shilah helped me write a letter in English to send to the board with all of my questions. Her Highness asked to meet to address my concerns. Shilah doesn't like conflict. If you would be willing, I'd appreciate your coming with me to be my translator."

"Of course I will!" *I wouldn't miss it for the world.*

I helped Shilah put away the dishes. "I need your help," she said.

"What can I do?"

She put down the plates and grabbed my hands. "My husband likes to be the cowboy, and his machismo can get him hurt. He's not from here. He doesn't see the fault lines. You understand?" I nodded, remembering the Mobster's $500 assassins. "Keep him calm at the meeting."

"I'll do my best. You have my word." Whatever Highness was up to, I'd be there to help.

I picked at my food that night. The Drektors were pressing all the wrong buttons. I was not one to look for a fight, but I had two triggers: bullies and cheaters. When I was 12, I went into my mom's shoe closet looking for shoelaces. I opened the drawer where she kept them and found something else: love letters from someone with the initial T, postmarked from Rome. After reading the first letter about a love that couldn't be, I looked at the date. It was written a year earlier.

My happy family was a lie. My mother took an oath to be faithful, and she broke it. Did she want me and my dad to be someone else? Is that why she always seemed angry, criticizing us for the most minute infractions against her world order? When I was 13, she told me how disappointed she was that my eyes weren't blue like hers. When I was 21, my parents and I went to Italy, and she challenged my dad to ask for the restaurant bill *in Italian*—a language he didn't speak—rolling her eyes as he did his best, trying to please her.

I remembered those letters from Rome. During that trip, I confronted her about them. Who wrote them? What was he to her? She wouldn't answer. "I don't want you to judge me," she said.

"Did you sleep with him?" I had to know.

She twisted the sapphire ring she wore on her right hand. "No. I couldn't do that to your father—or to you." It was cold comfort.

"Did he give you that ring?" I asked.

"We better get back to the hotel. Your father is waiting."

I never told my dad about the letters. It wasn't my place. More importantly, I couldn't bear to see him hurt. He deserved so much better, but I knew he loved her. *I* loved her, too—she was my mother—but I was never sure how she felt about me.

I couldn't get over the hypocrisy. She argued right v. wrong for a living. Her *hero* was Honest Abe. Lincoln's letters hung in her office.

I swore to myself that my conduct would always be beyond reproach. If I made a mistake, I would own it. And whether it was personal or business, I expected the same from others.

Sherlock knocked on my door the day of the meeting. "Who else will be there?" I asked.

"Just Her Highness. We're meeting in the Conference Room."

"Does she know I'm coming?"

"She doesn't need to know. You're my interpreter. And you're a unit owner. You have every right to be there."

I'm not so sure about that, but it's your call. "If you say so. May I ask you a favor?"

"It depends on the favor."

"I want you to promise me whatever she says to you, you'll remain calm."

"*Alambrito,* you think I won't behave myself?"

"No, I think you're a gentleman, but I also think she may upset you, and I don't want you to give her ammunition to discredit your request. Please, will you promise?"

Sherlock hmphed. It was not my place to tell him how to behave, but he was a practical man. "Don't worry, Alice. I stay calm."

"You promise?"

"I promise, *muchachita*! You sound like Shilah!" *Oops.* He shook his head. Restraining himself, he smiled. "*¡Vamos!*"

We walked into the Conference Room five minutes early—English time, thanks to Sherlock's junior year in London. Her Highness was seated, along with the Bulldog and the Long Island Lothario—three Drektors, not one. *This is an illegal board meeting!* Lothario was sitting uncomfortably close to a junior lawyer from Condoland's law firm. As we sat down, she got up, adjusted her mini skirt, and moved to the other side of the table to face us.

I addressed the Drektors. "You can't all be here. You represent a majority of the board, which makes this an illegal, unannounced board meeting." Including the lawyer, they were four to our two.

"I'm here as a unit owner," said the Long Island Lothario. "I just want to listen, that's all."

I turned to the lawyer. "You know that's a violation of the Florida Sunshine Law."

"Are you an attorney?" she asked me.

"No. I'm a law-abiding Floridian. How 'bout you?"

"Until you've passed the bar, I suggest you don't make accusations about laws you don't understand."

Fuck you! I wanted to scream it, but Sherlock had a better idea. He opened his phone and hit record. "Excuse me," said the lawyer in Spanish. "You can't record this meeting. Put away your phone." *You don't talk to him with that tone.*

"Why *she* have phone?" said Sherlock in English, pointing to Her Highness's phone on the table.

"I'm expecting a call from my husband's doctor," she said. "I have to keep it on. You don't have a reason, and I don't trust you. Turn it off!"

"I no trust you, neither!" said Sherlock. He spoke to the lawyer in Spanish. "Either we all turn off our phones, or none of us do." He turned to me. "Tell them." I did.

"It's not worth arguing." The lawyer sneered at Sherlock. "This should be a short meeting." *What's wrong with her?* "Let's all turn off our phones." I translated, and we cleared the first hurdle.

"Why is she here?" asked Highness, pointing at me.

"She my interpreter," said Sherlock. "She ees owner, too." He looked at the lawyer. "You leeve here?"

"No, I don't. I represent Condoland."

"Yes, I know. I pay you," said Sherlock. *Touché.*

I'd had enough. "Since you brought an attorney," I said to Her Highness, "maybe we should reschedule so Sr. Holmez can have his own representation." It was a semi-bluff. Sherlock and I exchanged looks. He wanted his answers, and he wanted them now.

"I'm only here as an interpreter," said the lawyer. *Bullshit! Two Spanish speakers are sitting in the Office. They'd translate for free. God knows how much this one charges.*

"She's just our interpreter, Alice," said Her Highness.

"Sr. Holmez," said the "interpreter" in Spanish, "I read your letter." She stood up, put both hands on the table, and leaned forward. "The vote tallies have already been announced. There's nothing else to provide. As for the room changes in the Club House, if you want to host an event, use one of the rooms upstairs. The reception space wasn't eliminated, it's serving a different purpose."

"I see," said Sherlock. He pointed at the Drektors. "And the board decides which public space can be used for what?"

"Correct," said the lawyer.

Sherlock folded his arms and sat back in his chair. "Allow me to make sure I understand correctly." He spoke in Spanish. "Let's say you decide to turn a tennis court into the kitchen, would that be an acceptable repurposing?" He paused for me to translate for the Drektors. "And speaking of the tennis courts," he placed photographs on the table, "does this court look usable to you?" One of the courts was filled with paint supplies, slabs of leftover wood, trash, and stacks of old Restaurant chairs.

"Let me see that." Highness grabbed a picture. She whispered to the Long Island Lothario, then turned to us. "I wasn't aware of this. It must have happened since the grand opening." She leaned toward Sherlock. "Mr. Lothario, the Bulldog, and their counterparts at Condolands II and III were in charge of the Club House renovation." *Right under the bus.* "We'll take care of this, Sr. Holmez." I didn't need to translate; Sherlock understood and nodded to her.

"I have more pictures," he said, laying them out like playing cards. "What happened to the Tiffany lamps in the Billiard Room? There was no flood damage there. These new lamps are lower quality. Where are the Tiffany lamps?" I translated. Nobody answered. *Check on eBay.*

Sherlock laid out more pictures. "The big screen TVs in the Kids Room are gone. No flood damage there, either. Where are they?" He waited for me to translate.

The junior lawyer asserted herself. "Sr. Holmez, if you're going to second-guess every decision the board makes, perhaps *you* should run. Assuming you were able to get elected, you could be part of the solution instead of wasting everyone's time with problems that don't exist." I glared at her. Her condescension was excruciating. She was less than half Sherlock's age and obviously raised by wolves. *This is NOT how a lawyer behaves.*

The Bulldog turned into his angry alter ego. "I'm working on multi-million-dollar projects for Condoland. I don't have time to worry about TVs and lamps!" He was shouting. *Did we hit a nerve?*

Sr. Holmez understood English better than he spoke it. So far, he'd kept his promise to me, but the disrespect shown him was more than anyone could bear. "Alice," he said sternly in English, "I want you translate exactly what I say." *Oh, boy.* He turned to the Long Island Lothario. "How is it that all of the flooding in Condoland comes from either your apartment or your friends' apartments? Isn't that an interesting coincidence?" Speaking to me, he said, "Tell him." I did.

"Are you accusing me of something?" asked Lothario.

"Jes."

"But my apartment was flooded, too!"

"Jes, and the insurance pay," Sherlock said in English. Lothario's cheeks swelled. Both hands gripped the table. *Oh, please, don't stand up!* Sherlock's lips pursed and his eyes narrowed. He sat straight in his chair. One false move and these two were going at it. *They're too old to fight!* I stared at my friend, reminding him of his promise. He sat back in his chair. So did Lothario. *Phew.*

The lawyer resumed her attack. "Sr. Holmez," she spoke in English so her clients would understand, "if you insist on pursuing trivial issues, your only remedy is to go to court." *Is that your "interpretation"?* She folded her arms. "Keep in mind board members are protected by errors and omissions insurance. They have no personal liability. Your odds of winning are one in a million, and even if you did, you'd probably get stuck paying your own legal fees *and* your portion of Condoland's legal fees." She scowled at Sherlock with contempt. "Do you think your neighbors would appreciate that?" *Even the law firm's complicit.* It was a disturbing revelation.

"We done here," said Sherlock. He stood up and tipped his cowboy hat, a gentleman to the end. We left the intimidation squad in the Conference Room.

I was fuming. "I'm so sorry. She had no right to talk to you that way."

"Is OK, Alice," said Sherlock. He switched to Spanish. "They know I'm right. Again, we rattled the snake. I'm not sorry, and I thank you for your help and support." He smiled, but there were tears in my eyes. It wasn't right.

The next day, the littered tennis court was cleaned and reopened. It was a minor victory, but to Sherlock Holmez, it was validation. He'd asked for and received an audience with the president of the board. She saw Sherlock as a worthy opponent and felt the need to bring reinforcements. The Drektors heard him. They took action to address one of his concerns. After years of being a stranger in his wife's land, he felt like he belonged.

Weekly voice lessons were a welcome escape from the stress of Condoland. With my teacher's direction in phrasing and intonation, my singing and voice acting were improving. Over time, I came to consider him a friend.

"Alice," he asked on a Friday afternoon, "what are you doing this weekend?"

"I have an old friend visiting, and I'm playing tour guide. Why?"

"One of my students is performing tonight at the Music Box in Hollywood. Peter Pan's my biggest success story, and I think you'd enjoy meeting him. He's from Boston!"

"I'll see if my friend wants to go. Thanks!"

This was a former New York colleague from BFC. He was in town for a conference and was happy to hear live music. The sign outside the Music Box announced Peter Pan's show. Inside, I was transported to a coffee house in Greenwich Village. The walls were covered in kitsch art, photos of The Beatles, Andy Warhol, Bob Dylan, and the like. Shelves jutting out from the walls housed papier-mâché dolphins and alligators.

The people in the Box were unpretentious. They wore jeans, T-shirts, sandals, and sneakers. In a state filled with frozen faces and boob jobs, this place was a refuge. Immediately, I felt at home. We pulled up two wooden chairs and sat at a small round table near the stage. The singer was tuning each of his three guitars in preparation for his performance.

I went up to introduce myself. "Hi, I'm Alice. We both study with the same voice teacher. He suggested I come hear you."

"I'm glad you did." He held out his hand. "I'm Peter." He had a warm, sultry voice.

"Nice to meet you."

As we shook hands, I felt a jolt in my solar plexus. He looked over my shoulder at the man he must have presumed was my date. "I appreciate the support!" he said. Peter was six feet tall with wavy brown hair and bright blue eyes. I usually went for guys with last names ending in vowels, but there was something about him . . .

For the next 90 minutes, he revealed a larger-than-life personality. He wrote his own songs and accompanied himself on guitar. My favorite was the story of a guy who moved to Florida seeking sunshine and a new life. What he occasionally lacked in pitch, he made up for with charisma. He shared the inspiration for each song. They were quirky, fun, and sometimes sad. He was warm and loud, and he made me laugh.

"What a cool place!" my friend said. "Why don't you sing here?"

"I don't know; I'm not a singer-songwriter. I sing jazz standards." He gave me a look. "I know, I'm making excuses. It's my first time here. I'll ask, but I'd like them to hear me first."

"It's your life. Just remember, nothing ventured, nothing gained!"

"You're right. I promise you; I'll ask."

"I'm gonna hold you to it!"

"Thanks. You're the best—"

"Alice! I just noticed the time. My conference starts at 8 a.m. I gotta go. You stay; I'll take an Uber."

"No, I'll take you back." We paid and I waved good-bye to Peter Pan. I pointed to my friend, then to my watch, and put my hands together to say thank you. He winked, and I gave him a thumbs up.

I hope he didn't think I was on a date . . . or is that a good thing? Either way, I was glad I went.

A few days later, I bumped into the Champion in front of the elevators. "How'd your meeting go with Sherlock and Her Highness?" she asked.

"It was awful! She brought two other Drektors and that *nasty* junior lawyer. The way she spoke to us was disgusting. No respect."

"Did they address his concerns?" she asked as the elevator opened.

We got inside and I hit close. I wanted privacy before I continued. The door didn't shut. I pounded the close button, waiting for the door to respond. She watched but said nothing. Finally, it closed. "They wouldn't show him the vote tallies. They ignored everything except for the tennis court, which they cleaned and opened the next day. The rest—the rule-breaking, the missing fixtures—they dared Sherlock to take them to court. I gotta tell you, I'm discouraged."

"In my experience," said the Champion, "it's the guilty who deny and deflect. You didn't expect them to say they violated the bylaws and stole from us, did you? The next election is in December, and I intend to do everything in my power to get them off this board. It's April. We have time. Chin up, and let's stay focused. We're on the right path!"

"Thanks for the pep talk. You're probably right."

Right or not, I remained discouraged. The Drektors flaunted their corruption in our faces. They had power, and they had no intention of playing by the rules.

14

Trials and Revelations

Narrating books was on my bucket list. When I saw a former BFC colleague on LinkedIn was now working for an audiobook company, I messaged her, asking how to audition. She put me in touch with a producer who scheduled an audition at the company's headquarters in Manhattan. *It can't be this easy.* I rehearsed the scripts with my voice teacher until I knew them by heart, then flew to New York.

I auditioned in a recording booth with Sarah Vaughan's name on the door. The producer listened on the other side of the opaque glass. He could see me, but I couldn't see him. Nervous and alone, I relied on muscle memory as I read.

"Very good," said the producer after I finished.

"Really?" *Don't say really. You amateur!*

"Yes. Your voice would be good for romance novels. Would you be comfortable narrating them?" he asked. "They have some explicit scenes."

"Do I get to keep my clothes on?"

"Definitely." He smiled.

"Then I'm good!" *I'd be happy to read the phone book!*

"How often are you in New York?"

"I come up all the time for work," I fibbed. If they had a book, I'd be on the next plane. I did have a client in the City and a friend with a pullout couch.

"All right. I'll be in touch when I have a book for you."

"Thank you so much!"

I floated out of the office and onto the train to Boston to spend a few days with my parents.

Toward the end of the visit, my father asked me to cut his toenails. "It's hahd for me to reach," he explained. Ever since his first quadruple bypass at 62, he'd been a model patient. He ate a meticulously heart-healthy diet and exercised each morning to the sound of marching music.

Like all the Millers, he looked younger than his years, even at 80. It irked my mother when friends asked about her "handsome husband." At five feet eight-and-a-half inches—emphasis on the half—he was short, dark, and handsome. "Why do they focus on his looks?" she'd ask me.

This visit, something was wrong. His ankles were swollen. The right side of his face sagged. He didn't look old; he looked unwell.

"Do you have to leave tomorrow?" My father never asked me for anything. I felt a lump in my throat.

"Daddy, I wish I could stay, but my flight's nonrefundable. Besides, I have meetings next week with clients and with the Finance Committee. But I'll be back soon!" We both tried to smile. His face was wan. *This is not like him.* He nodded in quiet disappointment.

He started describing me—how he saw me. He said I was "kind." I was a "good person" with a "good haht." I was "loving, caring," and a "wonderful daughter." I'd never heard these words before. Coming from *him*, they were overwhelming. My eyes welled, and a feeling of awe came over me. He saw my soul. I'd never been seen that way before and never will be again. It was pure, unconditional love.

I tried to normalize what was happening. *He's almost 81; he's just sentimental*—but I knew there was a reason he was telling me this now.

My parents drove me to the airport. We cried as I hugged them good-bye. We always cried, but that day, it felt different.

"I'll be back in four weeks!" I forced a smile. I'd need to visit more often now.

"That's wonderful," said my mother, regaining control of her emotions.

"Love you!" I said.

"Love you, too, sweethaht!" said my father, standing straighter. "See ya latah, alligatah!"

"After a while, crocodile!" I stayed and waved as they drove away. My heart was heavy, but I had to get back to South Florida.

The monthly Finance Committee meeting came a few days later. My mind was still in Newton, and staying busy helped. With the loan approved, I emphasized the unit owners' need to see how our money was being spent and how costs compared to budget for each project.

The Bulldog came up to me after the meeting. "Hey, Alice," he said. "The board wants transparency, too. I'd like to talk to you about the concerns you and your friends have raised." *You would?* His hands were relaxed against his sides.

"I appreciate that," I said.

"Have time for lunch?"

"Now?

"Why not?"

"All right." I headed in the direction of the Restaurant.

"No, no!" He motioned me toward him. "Let's go somewhere else." I looked at him skeptically. "You know, so we can have privacy." Under bushy eyebrows, his eyes darted frantically around the room. *Is he afraid to be seen with me? Am I the enemy?* "Everyone in this building talks."

Let 'em talk! I have nothing to hide. In the interest of rapprochement, I didn't challenge him. "Where do you want to go?"

"A little place not too far from here. I'll drive."

Oh, no. I am NOT getting in a car with you. "Thanks, but I have to run an errand after lunch. How 'bout I meet you there?"

"Of course," he said. "I understand." Whether he did or he didn't, he gave me the address. Fifteen minutes later, we met at a hole-in-the-wall Chinese restaurant. We sat in a corner booth and ordered.

"I heard you used to work at BFC."

We're making small talk? "Yep," I said. "First in New York and then here."

"What are you doing now?"

"Mostly, I work from home."

"I work from home, too," he said. "You can really practice law from anywhere these days."

"That's nice." *How much more of this?*

He flashed a conspiratorial smile. "I want you to know I appreciate your ideas about presenting the loan—even if we didn't use all of 'em."

All of them? How 'bout any *of them?* "Thanks for telling me." We paused while the waitress brought my Buddha's delight and his BBQ spareribs. Rolling up his sleeves to reveal Popeye forearms, he attacked a rib with both knotted hands. The blood-red sauce dripped on his plate.

"You look like you work out," I said.

He wiped his hands and put down his napkin. He clenched his fists, then extended his fingers, watching his forearm muscles flex and release. "Yeah, I used to."

"I heard you were a boxer. Is that true?"

He nodded. "I got into some trouble as a kid. My father had a temper, and I was angry because he was angry. Ironic, huh?"

You're still angry. "Yeah, it is."

His eyes were vacant. "I threw a rock at a classroom window on a dare. People were inside. No one was hurt, but I got expelled. My coach saved me, got me into boxing . . . it was a safe place to let off steam. I was good—wanted to go pro—but a kid lost an eye . . . It wasn't my fault!" He looked straight through me, remembering someone else. "I didn't box after that. My mother insisted on college . . . I went. Got a law degree." He was back. "Now, I'm on the board!" And now, I understood the clenched fists. I would proceed with caution. *At least we're in a public place.*

"Yes, you are! Is there something in particular you want to discuss?"

"I'm glad you asked. You help that Cuban guy with the cowboy hat—"

"He's Colombian." I smiled. No need to antagonize.

"Sorry, that Colombian guy, Mr. Holmez . . . How do you know him? Is he a relative or something?"

"He's my neighbor. And my *friend.*"

"Of course. Of course. I—I didn't mean anything by it. Just curious, 'cause . . . well . . . you two seem different."

"Really?" *Smile, Alice!* "How so?"

He coughed and took a sip of water. "I don't mean to offend you . . ." He rolled down his sleeves and leaned forward with the ask. "Because you're his friend—and his translator," he chuckled nervously, "I want to discuss something with you, and I hope you'll mention it to him."

"What's that?"

"Well," he looked around. "When we met in the Conference Room, the junior attorney—she was only there as a translator, you know—but she mentioned something about going to court."

Ah. There it is. "I remember."

"She spoke out of turn. I want you and Mr. Holmez to know that. She was trying to protect the board, but she got carried away." He picked up another sparerib. "You know, it's politics—like any election." He laughed at his joke, his mouth smeared with sauce.

Stay calm. "No. It's not!" I said, my face expressionless. "It's an unpaid volunteer job. What's the connection between pro bono work and politics?"

"Alice, you misunderstand me!" He dropped the rib on his plate and wiped his sticky hands. He was trying to read me. "The board wants the same things you do!"

Smile. "What things?"

"What's best for Condoland! You know," he leaned against the table, "sometimes we may—I may—overreact." *No argument.* "Old habits die hard—but I'm workin' on it! Between us, I see a therapist, and it's helping."

Why do they confide in me? "Good for you." I meant it.

"We work very hard on the board. It's not like we get paid!" He giggled. *It isn't?* "When people attack us, it hurts our feelings!"

"I can't help but wonder, given all the aggravation, why do it?"

"I'm not looking for sympathy. We ran for the board, and we're all happy to do the work. We're on the same team, Alice! I hope you'll ask your friend Mr.—I mean *Sr.*—Holmez to give us a chance. We're working with a professional decorator. The changes we made to our common areas will boost our property values." *Or your bank accounts.* "You have to see the big picture. Why waste money on lawyers," he said, chuckling again, "to argue over every fixture or TV set?"

The bill came, and the Bulldog grabbed it. *Oh, no you don't! I'm not gonna owe you anything.* "It's so nice of you to want to treat," I said. "You work so hard for Condoland, I should be treating *you*!" I smiled. "On second thought, with this legal talk, maybe it's best if we each pay for ourselves. You know, perceptions."

Hearing the word "legal," he released the check. "You're an independent woman." I nodded. "I respect that. I was just trying to be a gentleman."

"Thank you. It was nice chatting with you. Please excuse me, though, I've got to get going." I slid out of my seat and stood. "I'll relay your message to Sr. Holmez." At the entrance, I reached for my phone. *Shoot! It must be in the booth.*

I returned to the table. The Bulldog was on his phone. "She'll talk to him. Don't worry, I've got this under cont—"

"Hi there."

He spoke abruptly into the receiver. "I'll call you back."

"Sorry to interrupt. I think I left my phone." I looked under the booth. "Got it!" It was on the floor. "Were you talking about me?"

"No, no. It's . . . another matter." He blushed as I stood, studying him. "You forget anything else?"

You're fucking with the wrong Jew, buddy. "I did. It's a little advice." I leaned on the table. "Next time you meet with your neighbors, don't bring your lawyer. That way, no one gets the wrong idea." I left the restaurant and stepped into the Florida heat. *Sherlock was right. They are scared. We really have rattled that snake.*

15

1 Corinthians 13:4-7

After my lunch with the Bulldog, my mother called. "Your father went to the doctor. He has excess fluid, and they have to drain—"

"Can I talk to him?"

"He's not home. He's in the hospital." *NO!* "They're taking good care of him. Do you want his number?"

"Please." She gave it to me.

"He thinks he'll come home in a few days. You know your father; his glass is always half full. I hope he's right."

"Me, too, Mommy. How are *you*?"

"I'm fine. Of course, I miss your father. And I had to cook my own dinner tonight." She was half-joking and half-serious. "But I'm managing."

"I'll come home," I said.

"No. Absolutely not! Focus on your work. We'll see you as scheduled."

"But—"

"Alice, do as I say!" My mother used her resolute voice. It

157

scared me then as much as it did as a child.

"OK," I said. "If anything changes, you promise you'll tell me?"

"Yes, but we're fine, and we look forward to seeing you *as planned*."

I called my dad. He fumbled with the receiver. "Hello?" His voice was muffled. He sounded confused.

"Daddy?"

"Hi sweethaht!" he brightened.

"How are you?"

"I'm fine. They're taking good care of me. Honest, sweethaht. There's no reason to wuhree."

"I'd like to come home and see you." I scanned for flights on my laptop, expecting him to be the good cop.

"No. You were just here, and you're coming back in a few weeks. I'm *fine*. I'm going home in a few days." His tone became firm. "OK?"

"OK, Daddy."

I called every day he was in the hospital. To distract him, I described the goings-on at Condoland. Growing up, he told me stories of corruption in Boston, and I wanted him to know it existed far beyond the Bay State. The crazy characters made him laugh; he was glad I had friends I could trust.

"You have a good head on your shouldahs. You keep doing what yah doing—and document everything. I'm glad yah working with yah neighbahs on this."

"Thanks, Daddy. I will."

In my early years, my dad worked 18-hour days. I didn't see him during the week. Over time, he willed his robotics business to success.

"Only a third of small businesses succeed. What kept you going? Didn't you worry you'd fail?"

"I don't think you understand, Alice. Failyah was not an option. No mattah how tough things got, I nevah gave up. I worked hahdah and hahdah until it paid off."

"Hmm." *He did it for us, and now he's in the hospital.*

"I think they're gonna dischaj me soon."

"Oh, I'm so glad!"

"Me, too! Thank you," he said, talking to someone in his room. "They brought my lunch."

"Whaddayou having?"

"Lemme see." I heard him lift the metal cover from his plate. "It's a piece of white fish, broccoli, and a baked potato. Pretty good fah hospital food."

"Want to hang up so you can enjoy your lunch?"

"No, you keep me company. Hey, I haven't eaten that yet!" He was talking to the person in the room again.

"Daddy, what happened?"

"I don't know. They took away my lunch. Maybe they're gonna bring me something else."

My mom called an hour later. "The doctor's worried your father could aspirate. If he eats, he might choke. They can't give him food."

"What do you mean, can't give him food? For how long? He's so thin! He can't stop eating!"

I heard her swallow. "The doctor says we have to decide . . . whether or not to insert a feeding tube . . . I'm not sure it's worth living like that."

What's wrong with you? "Well, that's not your call." Legally, it was her call, but that wasn't going to stop me. "May I have the doctor's number please?"

I called and left a message. He called me back a few minutes later. "Doctor, if we give him a feeding tube, could he go back to eating normally?" *Please!*

"He could. If he regains the strength to swallow, he can go back to eating regular food. But Alice, either way, your father is dying."

"Wha? What do you mean?"

"His heart is failing. I'm so sorry."

I wasn't ready. I remember leaning over my kitchen counter. "How much time does he have?"

"Six months max."

I reached for a tissue. "If he were your father, what would you do?"

"I'd give him the feeding tube. Not giving it to him would be cruel."

"Thank you for telling me. Please go ahead." I called my mom to explain my decision. She had my dad's healthcare proxy, but without saying it, she'd let me decide.

I dropped everything and boarded the next flight to Boston. As the doors were shutting, I saw a text from Peter Pan. *Not now.* I'd respond later. I shut off my phone.

My dad was discharged to a convalescent home five minutes from our house. It was an award-winning facility, but he hated it. So did I. He wanted to go home, but he'd become messy. He had a feeding tube. My Brooks Brothers, wingtips, weekend jeans with a collared shirt and pullover sweater with sneakers father was incontinent. My mother couldn't handle messy. She needed order and control always, in all ways.

I went back and forth between Massachusetts and South Florida for the next four months. Each trip home, I spent most of the day with my dad. "All that mattahs to me in this world," he told me one afternoon, "is ah family. Family is everything, sweethaht. Remembah that." I called my aunts and uncles so they could visit with him by phone. Each conversation was emotional. While he slept, I worked.

He opened his eyes, startled. "I'm here, Daddy."

"I was afraid you left."

We talked. We watched the news and discussed politics. Anything to take his mind off the tube in his stomach and his windowless room.

"When you or yah mothah aren't heah, I cry," he told me. My heart broke. "I probably shouldn't have told you that." I couldn't stand to see him suffer! *How could she leave him here?*

A woman poked her head in the doorway. "Are you Alice?"

"Yes."

"Can we speak for a moment?" she asked softly.

I put my hand over my father's and spoke loudly. "Daddy, I'll be right back."

"All right, sweethaht. I'm not going anywheah." He managed a wan smile, and I followed the woman into the hall.

"I'm a therapist. I've been speaking with your dad." She hesitated.

"What is it?"

"He's depressed." I nodded. *Who wouldn't be?*

"Did he say anything specific?"

"He wants to go home . . . he feels his wife should be taking care of him." She watched me closely. *What can I say?* He was right, but my mom was neither willing nor capable.

I started to cry, and she handed me a tissue. *She came prepared.* "I'm sorry."

"Don't be. I wouldn't normally repeat a client confidence, but I thought you should know." Was she hoping I'd speak to my mother? I did over dinner that night.

"Your father needs 24/7 care," she said. "I'm not capable of that!"

"We could get nurses."

"He can't take the stairs. Where would he sleep? He needs a hospital bed!"

"We could put him in the living room."

"That's out of the question. Your father needs to stay where he is. You're not being realistic!"

I'd never seen her so frail and stressed, and I knew she was at her limit. If I pushed too hard, I might lose them both. I dropped it, but my dad's sadness gnawed at me.

"Daddy, would you like to come with me to Florida?" I asked the next day.

"Florida!"

"Well, I know you don't like it here. You could stay with me and be near the ocean. I'll get nurses." *Anything to get him out of here.*

"I can't leave yah mothah." *If you only knew about those letters.* "Thank you, sweethaht, but I can't." They had their own life and relationship apart from me. I had to accept their choices.

Visits with my mom were . . . constipating. Literally. A sock left on the floor was the first step on the road to anarchy. I walked on eggshells, unable to relax. The tension impeded the function of my lower intestines.

I did my best to help her. I offered to cook. One night, I made her favorite—veal marsala with polenta, zucchini, and a salad. I timed everything perfectly, cleaning up as I cooked to avoid the wrath of Attila, as my uncle called her. "Dinner's ready!" I rinsed two wine glasses and dried them quickly as I put them on the kitchen table.

She walked into the kitchen and smiled. "It smells delicious!" I pulled out her chair. Glancing down, she saw her worst nightmare. "There's water on the floor!" *Call the cops!*

It must have dripped from the wine glasses. "No worries," I said, dropping a paper towel on the floor and moving it around with my foot.

"You're missing the spots!" She grabbed a *shmata*[19] from under the sink and dropped to her hands and knees, searching for moisture. *No wonder I can't have bowel movements here.* "If you're not going to take care of my things the way I do," she said looking up from the floor, "then I don't want you cooking in my kitchen!" It was her fear talking, but it still hurt. From then on, we ate out or got delivery.

I called my parents daily in between visits. At the end of July, my mom called *me*. "Your father pulled out his tubes."

"What do you mean? What happened?"

"He asked me if he was going to get better." All this time, he hadn't asked, and we didn't tell. None of us were ready to face the music.

"What did you say?"

"I told him the truth." It was the right thing to do.

"What did he say?"

"That he had to take care of me. I asked him how he could in his condition. He really can't, Alice. I think he understood, because this morning, he pulled out the IV and the feeding tube."

"Mommy, I'm coming home tomorrow night. PLEASE tell Daddy to wait for me!"

---

[19] Shmata — Yiddish for rag

I arrived at Logan in the rush of my life. Everything and everyone took too long. In the taxi to my parents' house, I silently shrieked at each red light. I got home, dropped my bags, and drove with my mom to the convalescent home. He was lying in bed, his eyes closed. He looked peaceful. *Free at last.*

"Daddy, it's Alice! I'm here!"

He opened his eyes and lifted thin arms, hugging me to him with every last ounce of strength. We stayed like that for a long time. I was in the land of the living. I still didn't understand. Didn't want to understand. Eventually, I pulled up to a sitting position and held his hand. "I'll be back in the morning, Daddy. I love you!"

"I love you, too, sweethaht. See you latah, alligatah!" His lips were dry.

"After a while, crocodile."

At 8 a.m. the next morning, the Ceevil Engineer called. "Alice, do you have a moment?"

"This isn't a good time."

"It's urgent!" he said.

"I have five minutes. What's wrong?" *Daddy's waiting.*

"There are termites een the Restaurant—een the new beams installed during the renovation. They must tent the Restaurant and replace the beams. I told them to check for termites *before* the installation. They deedn't leesten!"

"How can I help?" It was 8:03.

"Thees mistake could cost $100,000. Please, tell the treasurer to call the wood supplier. Thee wood should be termite resistant with a one-year guarantee. Eet should be covered!"

"Forgive me," I said. It was 8:05. "This is really not a good time. Would you do me a favor and call the Champion?"

"Can you do eet later today? Eet's a financial matter, and you are the Commeettee chair!" It was 8:06.

"I can't! I gotta go. I'll text you her number." I'd never hung up on a responsibility before. Six precious minutes were gone.

I got to my father's room at 8:11. My mom got there at 10. By noon, he was barely responding. I called the synagogue to ask our rabbi to come and give last rites.

"Judaism doesn't have last rites," the rabbi's assistant said gently.

"Can't the rabbi come? PLEASE!" I wailed. "He needs a prayer from the rabbi. PLEASE!"

"Yes, there is a prayer. I'll ask him to go right away."

"Thank you. Bless you. I'm sorry, I'm scared."

"I understand. I'll get the rabbi."

Thirty minutes later, he was in the room. He said a prayer over my dad, who was receding into another place.

"Ben!" my mom yelled. "The rabbi is here!" He didn't open his eyes, but they moved under his lids as the rabbi recited the prayer. *Daddy knows. God is with him. He knows.*

The facility called hospice. A hospice nurse entered the room with a wave of calming energy. She knew how to talk to my dad, how to explain the morphine she was giving him. Everything foreign and excruciating to me was natural to her. Somehow, I relaxed. So did he.

The Condoland Office called with "urgent" business.

"Hello?"

It was the Manager. "Miss Miller, you haven't scheduled the Finance Committee meeting for August. Three members called me this week. They're making travel plans, and if the meeting isn't on their calendars today, they may not be available!"

My dad reached out to hold my hand. I felt guilty about everything. I hesitated to say the words, not wanting to share something so private, but he couldn't wait, and he was all that mattered. "My father's in hospice. He wants to hold my hand. I'm sorry; I have to go." The Manager understood. The meeting *could* wait. Or someone else could run it. I didn't care.

"Hearing is the last sense to go," said the hospice nurse. "Talk to your dad, he'll hear you."

"Thank you." She left us alone. I didn't have to tell him how much I loved him. He knew, and I knew how much he loved me. I played music for him on my phone. His music: Nat King Cole, Bobby Darin, Sinatra. I played songs I'd recorded so he'd hear my voice: "Come Rain or Come Shine," "I'm Beginning to See the Light," and "Fly Me to the Moon." I played the last one a lot. It was my parents' song.

He drifted off to sleep, and my mom and I went to the kosher supermarket to arrange food for the *shiva*.[20] We ordered a fish platter, bagels, cream cheese, coleslaw, potato salad, rugelach, hermit cookies, fresh fruit, coffee, juice, water, soda. All to honor the man who wouldn't—couldn't—attend. It was surreal.

On the way home, I realized I left my book in my dad's room. *I have to go back.* We drove to his facility and I ran in.

"Hi, Daddy. I left my book. I'll see you in the morning. I love you!" I kissed him on his forehead.

He roused. With effort, he spoke. "Fahgive yah mothah. Look aftah hah. Will you do that for me?" Summoning his remaining strength, he opened his eyes. He was past tears and fast approaching Truth.

Still on this plane with many lessons left to learn, my eyes

---

[20] **Shiva** — a period of seven days' mourning for the dead, beginning immediately after the funeral

welled with sadness, resentment, and love. *Forgive her for leaving him in this place when he needed her most? Forgive her for carrying a torch for someone else?* I wasn't prepared. *But how can I refuse him?* I nodded. "I will, Daddy." He continued to stare. "I promise!" He closed his eyes.

"See you latah, alligatah!" It was barely a whisper.

"After a while crocodile!" That was the last time we said it out loud.

My phone rang later that night. I did not want to answer, but I did. He was gone.

A week later, my mom drove me to the airport and parked in front of the departures gate. "I adored my father, too," she told me. "It doesn't seem fair when the parent you love more leaves first. I understand that."

"I love you both," I said. What else could I say?

"It's all right, Alice."

"But—"

"Let me finish. I've been hard on you, and you should understand why: Much is expected of those who have much to give. We both know I've made mistakes, but I've always wanted what I thought was best for you. You're my little girl!" She smiled through tears. We were both crying. "Your father loved out loud. For me, actions speak louder than words, but I want you to know that I love you very much."

I moved past my resentment. It was what my father wanted. "I love you, too!" We hugged until the policeman blew the whistle telling her to leave the drop-off area.

"We're unloading, Officer," she said.

We walked to the back of the car, and I pulled my bag out of the trunk. *Show her, don't tell her.* "I'll be up soon to see you."

"Oh, that would be wonderful."

"Wanna have Thanksgiving in Florida this year? I'll do the cooking." I smiled. "Maybe stay the week?"

She nodded, trying to compose herself. "Call me when you get home."

"I will." I stayed and waved until she was out of sight.

After my grandfather died, my father told me, "I feel like he's sitting on my shouldah. He's always with me."

On the flight back to Florida, I thought about my dad sitting on my shouldah and what he'd expect of me now. Everything I learned from him was with me. My father was the finest human being I'll ever know. If I could be half the person he was, I'd be grateful. With his help, I was going to try.

16

Back to Condoland

I couldn't talk about my dad after he passed. It was too painful. When I returned to Condoland at the beginning of August, my friends and neighbors tried to console me. They wanted to know the details of his departure.

"I appreciate your concern," I said over and over and over again, "but I'm not ready to talk about it. If we don't change the subject, I'm gonna cry." That usually did the trick.

The Oracle knew better than to pour salt on an open wound. "How are you?" she asked, handing me a towel at the spa desk.

"I'm OK." Her expression said she didn't believe me. "Really, I'm fine." I took a deep breath and exhaled. "I know I was loved, and I am grateful I had the father I did."

"You know he's still with you." She'd met my dad at the gym, and she liked him, but who wouldn't?

"He is?"

"Yes."

"Wait, do you see him?"

"I do. He'll be with you for a while. You're going to be all right."

"What do you mean 'for a while'? How long?"

"Until you have a partner—a husband." She had a Sphynx-like smile when revealing just what one needed to hear. Enough to give hope or guidance without influencing an outcome. "But before that can happen, you have to resolve an internal struggle. You have to forgive." *How does she know?*

"I've known for a while, Alice," she said, reading my mind. "I see it in your aura."

"It's my mom."

She nodded. "When you let go, you will have peace." *I'm trying!* "By the way, have you had issues with your laptop?"

That's an odd segue. "Yeah! My mouse didn't work last night. Why do you ask?" I was dreading the expense of a new laptop.

She gave me the smile again. "That was your father. He was having fun with you."

I got goosebumps. "When I was in high school, he hid the mouse sometimes to see if I was actually doing my homework."

"See?" said the Oracle. "One more thing. He wants me to tell you about alligators. Do you know what that means?"

"I do. Thank you!" I walked toward the treadmill, wiping my eyes with the towel. He was watching, and he would know whether or not I kept my promise. *I gave you my word, Daddy. After a while, crocodile!*

While I was away, there'd been some unsettling developments in the lobby. The Drektors were spending like drunken sailors. A new display of African art—spears, masks, and a zebra print—hung on the wall. It was a beautiful collection, but beauty is in the eye of the beholder, and I knew my people. This wasn't art Condoland unit owners were equipped to appreciate.

"What's with the sticks?" I heard a woman say to her friend on the way to the Card Room.

"Never mind the sticks—do you see that *shmata* on the wall? It's not going to dust itself, you know!"

A man walked by with his granddaughter. She ran to the exhibit. "Halloween!" she said, trying to pull a mask from the display. *What was the Drekorator thinking?*

Kitty-corner from the collection, a funhouse mirror hung over new couches replacing our perfectly good old couches. Cones of reflective glass jutted from the wall. Facing it, I saw my distorted reflection. *I'm embarrassed to live here.*

At the elevator bank, construction workers lay black marble on the two-story wall where our peaceful, cascading waterfall had been. It was unsubtle.

An elevator door opened and out came Joanna Rivers. "What's with the circus in the lobby?" I asked.

She walked over, and we stared at the erection. "Is it hideous, or what!" she said. "If my Edguh was still president, this nevuh would have happened. This was Lothario's idea." She pointed toward the workers. "You know what we're paying for this *farkakteh* wall?"

"Too much? I'm afraid to guess."

"A hundred thousand dolluhs!" I shook my head. *That's $20,000 for Lothario, Mr. 20 Percent. Of course he insisted.* "That's how he's spending the insurance money. It looks like a fucking mausoleum!" I laughed, because it did. The wall had gold-trimmed marble pockets—perfect for remains.

"Maybe Lothario's planning ahead?"

"I'll help him use it now." Steam was coming out of Joanna's ears. "I gotta meet my friends in the Cawd Room."

"I'll walk with you," I said. "I've been distracted lately."

"Alice, I'm so sorry—"

"Thanks, but let's not go there. What's going on with the Re-sistance?"

"Not too much," she said. "The Champion sent a lettuh to the Drektuhs for maw infuhmation. Beyond that, I dunno. We stopped meetin' while you were going back and fawth—ya know." She looked at me with motherly eyes.

"I appreciate your concern. I just can't talk about it."

"I wanna tell you something." She pulled me to the new couches under the funhouse mirror. "I don't usually tawk about this, but you need to understand grief. If you try to bottle it, it explodes."

"Why are you saying that?" I asked.

"It happened to me," she said.

"*What* happened?"

She took a deep breath. "You remember how I said Edgah came down heuh far a case and nevuh left?" I nodded. *I knew she'd tell me when she was ready.*

"You know we have two daughters."

"Mm-hmm."

"We have *four* children: two daughters on earth, and two sons—twin boys—in heaven." *OMG.*

"Oh, Joanna!"

She bit her lip, blinking back tears. I put my hand on her shoul-der. "Lemme finish." I put my hands in my lap, and she looked away. "When they turned 12, their uncle—Edgah's brothuh—in-vites them on a ski trip with theyuh cousins. They begged and begged until we let them go. They were beginnuhs. They swore they'd stay on the easy trails, but 12-year-old boys don't listen. They snuck into a restricted area . . . and . . ." She closed her eyes. "There was an avalanche."

"I'm so sorry!"

"So am I, but I'm telling you this for a reason. We couldn't stand to be in aw house. We came here to start ovuh. I didn't tawk about my boys fuh years. The girls stopped mentioning them in front of me, because . . . I'd fall apawt." She faced me. "But that was wrong! I was angry. Do you know I nevuh used to curse?"

"I don't believe it."

"Hand to Gawd! I was a real goody two-shoes." *Says the lady who bared her breasts to the Red Hats.*

"Well, you certainly made up for lost time!" We laughed.

"What I'm telling you is tawk about yaw fathuh. It's OK to cry. Trust me, you'll thank me latuh. Now I gotta go."

I walked with her to the Card Room. "Would you be up for a meeting on Saturday?" I asked as she opened the door.

"You bet, honey!"

"Good. I'll organize it. We've got work to do!"

"Commeer." She gave me a hug.

"You would have loved my father." Tears flowed down my cheeks and onto her shoulder. She patted my back.

"I know, because I love his dawtuh!"

Since all roads led to the Champion, I called her next. "I understand the Resistance slacked off while I was gone."

"It did. You ready to get going? We have four months 'til the election." She knew I'd talk about my dad when I was ready.

"I am. Are you free Saturday for a meeting with the larger group?" I asked.

"You bet. What time?"

"Two?"

"Two p.m. Who do you want to include?"

"Maybe the same folks who went to the penthouse meeting?"

"Sounds good," she said. "Before the meeting, I think it's time to see the lawyer. Do you want to come?"

I was honored to be included. "You bet I would!"

"Good. We can update everyone on Saturday." She paused. "Alice, I wonder if . . ."

"What do you need?"

"I have to work late tonight. Can you walk Cookie this afternoon?"

There's no therapy like dog therapy. "I'd love to."

"You're a lifesaver! I'll let you know when I get the appointment with the lawyer."

According to the heat index, it was 100°F that afternoon. Cookie was panting, so as soon as he finished his peemails, we went to the garage, where he could exercise in the shade. As we walked, four Drektors—everyone except the Corpse—entered the garage from a door I'd never seen before. Their backs were to us. I picked Cookie up and we hid behind a rectangular column. *Please, please don't bark!*

The Drektors didn't see us. They looked in every direction to make sure the coast was clear—*ha!*—then split up to exit the garage. Two went out the front entrance, one walked back into the building through the door to the lobby, and one made haste toward the basement exit to the street. *That's how the board meets illegally!* Four of the five Drektors was more than a voting majority. *What's behind that secret door?*

"*¡Buenas tardes, Señorita Alambrito!*" said Sherlock, answering the phone. "Have you been eat—"

"I'm eating, I swear!"

"Eat more! A little meat on the bone is a good thing."

"I know, I know. I haven't had much appetite. I called for something else."

"*Estoy tomando el pelo* [I'm teasing you]," said Sherlock. He kept things light. "What's on your mind, Alice?"

"I saw the Drektors walk out of an unmarked side door with no doorknob."

"Where was this?" *There's more than one?*

"In the garage on the main level. Do you know what's behind that door?"

"The Manager's office. He has a door that looks like a panel. It opens to the garage. *¿Artista?*"

The Manager's in on it. "I'm here."

"Want me to investigate?"

"Would you?"

"*A la orden, Alicia,*" said Sherlock. I told him about the meeting on Saturday. He'd be there, and he'd invite his kosher friends from the penthouse meeting.

The Champion and I went to see the lawyer Friday afternoon. We pulled into the parking lot in front of a tall glass office building. "The Good Firm's founder would love to stick it to his ex-partner—my words, not his," said the Champion.

"Works for me!" I said.

A lawyer met us in a professional yet modest conference room. She was four foot eleven and wore a navy-blue pants suit with sensible heels. When she spoke, it was clear what she lacked in height, she made up for in brains. Someone brought us coffee as we got down to business.

"What brings you here?" she asked.

"We represent a group of people," said the Champion. "We're concerned that our board is running Condoland's Association against the interests of unit owners. For example, money disappears from projects. Costs far exceed estimates—sometimes double—and allegedly, the Drektors—that's what we call them—" The lawyer laughed. Apparently, she understood the Yiddish. "They're allegedly getting kickbacks from vendors."

"I'm sorry to hear it," said the attorney. "What would you like to accomplish today?"

"First," said the Champion, "we need to know what information to gather if we decide to pursue legal action against individual Drektors. You can't imagine the corruption we're seeing."

"Oh, I can imagine," said the attorney. It felt good to be believed.

"The second issue," said the Champion, "concerns the next board election in December. Our goal is to replace a majority of Drektors to restore normal order. How can we ensure votes are accurately counted?"

"Let's start with the corruption," said the lawyer. "Sadly, it's very common in South Florida. Probably because it's hard to prove. Are there vendors or employees who would testify if you went to trial?"

I shook my head. "If employees speak up, they'll be fired. My friend works in the gym. They threatened to sack her if she says a word." The Champion looked at me. I nodded.

"That's pretty typical, Alice," said the Good Firm lawyer.

So, the crooks get away with it? I got up and started pacing. "There has to be something we can do!" I said.

"Would you consider a forensic audit?" asked the lawyer. "Unless you already have proof, you'll need one if you want me to prosecute financial crimes." She turned to the Champion. "You mentioned you represent a group of unit owners. Do you think they'd pay for one?"

"A forensic audit can cost $65,000, $75,000," I said. "We had to talk our people into paying for *this* meeting!"

"Cost is usually a hurdle," said the Good Firm lawyer. "Assuming the audit turned up evidence, you'd also have to factor in court costs and legal fees. As much as we want to help, we need to be compensated for our time. And there's no guarantee you'll win." She looked sympathetic. "I don't mean to discourage you, but you should know it's an uphill battle."

I looked at the Champion. "I don't see how we do it. Do you?" *The audit alone would cost the Resistance $5,000–7,000 each.* We shook our heads. *Fuck!*

"Is there another option?" asked the Champion.

"To win in court, we need evidentiary documents," said the lawyer. "Supporting witnesses will boost your case, but in my experience, they're afraid to come forward."

"It's so unfair!" I said.

"It is," said the lawyer. "I suggest you focus on the election. If you can get at least 15 percent of the unit owners to sign a petition, you can secure an election monitor from the State of Florida to oversee the counting and tabulation of votes. It's your best bet."

I perked up and stopped pacing. "What does that cost?"

"A few hundred dollars. Your condo association pays for it."

The Champion saw me nod violently. "That we can do!" she said. We had a plan! "When do we need the signatures?"

"At least 60 days before the election," said the lawyer. "That's when your request is due to the State." *That's October 15th.*

"Assuming we get them, would you notify Condoland about the election monitor?" the Champion asked the lawyer. "We think the Bad Firm would 'appreciate' your involvement." She winked. *Oh, this is good.*

"My pleasure," said the Good Firm lawyer. "And I'll have my partner sign the letter."

"Wonderful," said the Champion. "What do we owe you for today?"

"No charge for the first consultation."

We've been here for two hours! "Really?" *Alice, stop talking. You want her to change her mind?*

"Really. Should you win your election," she said shaking our hands, "Good Firm would love to bid on representing Condoland under new management."

"Count on it," said the Champion.

"It kills me we won't see these fuckers behind bars," said the Champion on the drive home.

"Agreed." I pictured Mrs. Lothario's new kitchen. "But on the upside, imagine their faces when the election monitor walks into the voting room. Whatever they pull between now and December— and you know they'll try—their ballot-stealing days are numbered."

I went to the gym Saturday morning before the Resistance meeting. I was working the leg machine when the Oracle came to talk to me.

"Alice, do you need help adjusting the settings?" she asked, loudly.

"Yes, I do. Thanks!" I said, matching her volume. Barbies were watching us through the mirror. "What's up?" I asked quietly.

"I was told not to talk to you," whispered the Oracle. "After the meeting you and Sherlock had with the Drektors, somebody threatened my boss. The Drektors know we're friends, and Her Highness hates you."

"*Damn!*" I felt the force of that animus throughout my body. *But Her Highness is contemptible. Do I care?* It took me a moment to recalibrate. I took a deep breath. "I think I'll take that as a compliment."

"You should." She looked around. The Barbies were watching us. "Do you ladies need help?" she asked. They dispersed, and the door closed when they left the equipment room. The Oracle whispered, "I have to talk fast. The Drektors padded the cost of gym equipment. And they know about your Resistance meetings. Look into it. Also, and I don't know if you can prove this, they took the loan without a majority vote." I stopped lifting. "Keep exercising."

"Can you help me move the seat?" I asked in a raised voice.

"Sure!"

Back to whispering. "Do you know for certain, or is it your intuition?"

"Both." *Sherlock was right about the votes!* The Barbies returned with free coffee. One of them called the Oracle for help. "I gotta go."

The Daredevil opened the equipment room door and swaggered toward me. "Hey, Alice, how are you? I haven't seen you in a while."

"I've been out of town a lot. My dad passed."

"Ooh! I didn't realize." He put his hand on my shoulder. "May his memory be a blessing to you." That was the Jewish expression of sympathy.

"Thank you."

"What happened?" he asked.

"I can't talk about it." Sharing my grief with him didn't feel right.

"Of course. I understand. I've been away, too—in Uruguay. *My* father's ill."

"Oh, no! I'm so sorry." The Oracle told me he had a difficult relationship with his dad. He seemed troubled, and I hoped he'd have time to make things right between them.

"Thanks. Me, too." He went to the shoulder press. "While I was home, I qualified as a tandem skydiving instructor." *Didn't you just say your father's sick?*

"That's nice."

"Yeah. I taught this married couple. The wife was super cute. I gave her my phone number, and we went out a few times." *You are disturbed.* He looked me over, head to toe. "*Oye*, Alice, you look good!" I caught his eye and held it. "What?"

Whoever hurt him, this is not my battle. "We have different values." I wasn't going to fix him, and I didn't want the heartache of trying. I needed someone to meet me halfway.

Slowly, he nodded. "You're right . . . we do." He got on a treadmill and started running. *How ironic. The first time he reaches a mature conclusion, we're done.*

17

Resolve

I went overboard on refreshments for the Resistance meeting. I served crudités and dip, meatballs with toothpicks, fresh fruit salad, cranberry muffins, lox and cream cheese, bagels, and a plate with tomato, red onion slices, and capers. To drink, I had coffee, mimosas, orange juice, and water. Our group's mission was a welcome distraction from grieving my dad.

The core team was coming—the same people who met at the penthouse. The men helped me bring dining room chairs into the living room, and we sat in our usual circle.

"Thanks for coming, everyone," I said. "It's been too long since we got together! I'm so glad you're here—"

"Edguh!" said Joanna, "Bring the cawfee to the living room." The judge's cognitive capabilities were diminishing, but as a former board president, his experience was still valuable. "Sorry, Alice."

"For what? I'll keep this short. We have two topics. First, oversight of the Drektors between now and the election. We need to scrutinize their every move and let them know we're doing it. It's our best chance to keep them 'honest,'" I said using air quotes. People nodded.

"What's the second topic?" asked Florence Nightingale.

"The election," said the Champion.

"Right," I said. "Do you want to explain what the lawyer told us?" She had the room's attention.

"We spent two hours yesterday with a Good Firm lawyer," said the Champion. She explained the connection to Condoland's Bad Firm.

"*Excelente*," said Sherlock.

"Condoland's lawyuhs will shit their pants!" said Joanna. It was our first chance to stick it to the Drektors.

"Two hours?" asked the Ceevil Engineer. He was calculating.

"No charge for the first consultation," said the Champion.

"Really?" He grinned.

"When he was a lawyuh, Edguh didn't charge for the first meeting, eithuh," said Joanna.

"I didn't," said Edgar.

"Guys, we're off topic," I said.

"We are," said the Champion. "Back to the election. Most unit owners go to the Office and hand their sealed ballots to the receptionist. She's supposed to put them in the ballot box behind her desk, but we have no way of knowing how many ballots make it into that box."

"Or stay theyuh," said Joanna.

"You think they tamper with the ballots?" I asked.

"I wouldn't put it past them," said the Champion.

"What do we do?" asked Joanna.

"The lawyer recommended we petition for an election monitor," said the Champion. "We need at least 15 percent of unit owners to sign. That's—"

"Sixty people!" I said.

"That's it, smarty-pants," said the Champion. "We need 60 signatures to get the monitor. I suggest 80 in case there are signatures we can't verify."

"What does it cost?" asked the Ceevil Engineer. *Oy. Again?*

"A few hundred dollars," said the Champion. "And you'll like this: The Association pays for it!"

"It may be a good idea," said Harvard. Coffee spewed out of my mouth.

"Jes, I agree," said the Ceevil Engineer.

"Let's do it!" said Joanna. "I'll help." She had a lot of friends in the building.

"Me, too," I said.

"May I help?" asked the Connector.

"Of course!" I said. She knew the international owners.

"Do the rest of you agree?" The Champion surveyed the room. No arguments.

"What's not to like?" said Edgar.

The Champion got up and perused my buffet table. Others followed her. *Yes! They're eating.*

"You know . . . some people . . . won't sign your petition," said Harvard. He stabbed and dragged an enormous portion of smoked salmon onto his plate, "but . . . you might as well try." *Don't you dare ask me for a Ziploc.*

"Gee, thanks!" I couldn't help myself. My dining room was too small for the group, so I opened tray tables in the living room. "Guys, we can eat in here and keep talking."

"OK then. We have our canvassers," said the Champion, picking at her fruit salad. She was an on-again, off-again dieter. She pointed to me, Joanna, and the Connector. "I'll email you three a copy of the petition, and you're good to go. Try not to ask anyone who might be loyal to the Drektors."

"We got this," said Joanna.

"Yep. So that's the election," I said. "Now, let's talk about oversight."

The Champion reached for a folder beneath her seat and gave us each a copy of her second letter to the Drektors. She'd requested copies of all bids, proposals, invoices, and payments for projects funded by the loan between March—when the loan was approved—through July. "The Sunshine Law gives each unit owner the right to access all records related to condominium business. *This* is how we hold the Drektors accountable."

"That's good," said Edgar. "The law applies to everything except legal and human resource records. If Condoland's attorneys were involved, the board can't share that information. It's privileged."

I pictured the Office filling boxes with evidence they didn't want to share. "Humpty Dumpty's not going to like this!"

"None of them'll like it," said Joanna. "Let 'em squirm!"

"Oh, we'll make 'em squirm," said the Champion. "I sent the letter in July and got a boxful of documents two weeks later. I want a different unit owner to request the *same* information at the end of each following month, using the *same* letter, until the election—people the Drektors would never associate with us. I call it shock and awe; the Drektors will see the Resistance everywhere!"

"I'll ask a woman from my cawd game," said Joanna.

"Good," said the Champion. This deliciously annoying PSYOP made us all smile.

A few days later, when the Condoland Office and the Board of Drektors received a second request for information identical to the

Champion's letter, something snapped in Humpty Dumpty's head. She couldn't deny the request, but she *could* make the records harder to access.

I was making dinner when the Champion called. "I forwarded you an email. Take a look," she said. "I received it this morning."

"Hold on." I washed my hands and opened my laptop. "I'm looking." Attached was a letter addressed to the Champion on Condoland letterhead. It was emailed from the Office, and all the Drektors were copied. "Who wrote it?"

"Keep reading." She clipped her words, seething. Nobody likes to be called a laughingstock, even by a laughingstock.

I laughed. "Forgive me. This is something!"

Here's Humpty Dumpty's letter, typos and all:

August 15th

Ms. Champion,

Your request for information is ridiculous. We know what you're up to! Instead of wasting our time, why don't you attend some meetings and keep your acusations to yourself? You don't seem to understand how the Board does business. You make eroneus allegations in your letters to the Board. I find them insulting.

Where do you get your information from?
How many architectural meetings have you attended?
How many financial meetings?
How many sports meetings?
How many decoration meetings?
How many Board meetings? (You attended very few Board meetings).
How many times have you called our maneger to find out what-is-happening?

It seems that your information comes from gossip and heresay. I remember when you were on the board. Unit owners laugh you off the dayis, after you talked down to them and enraged them.

I was elected to the Board. I am the Treasurer. We have an extremely competent bookeeper and a prestigus accounting firm that produces a detailed annual audit - every year!

If you or any other unit owner want financial information, make an appointment and come to the Office Monday thru Friday, 9 to 5. You can have all the information you want for 25 cents a copy.

I resent that you, without proper knowledge, have the chutzpah to tell me and my Co-Board members how and when to spend unit owner's monies....and....how and when to assess them.

Please, do not answer this e-mail. My time is very valuable. I have many responsibilities. I will not take time to defend myself from someone who does not check her facts.

Humpty Dumpty
Condoland Treasurer

"Are you going to respond?"

"She told me not to. She's very busy."

"You're letting it go?" *That doesn't sound like her.*

"Are you kidding? It's a good thing I worked from home today. As soon as I got the letter, I went to the Office. The Bulldog was in with the Manager. I barged in and asked the Manager who sent the letter. Bulldog wouldn't look at me."

"Why?"

"He's a lawyer. He knows why I asked."

"Sorry. Keep going." I heard a pot rattling in the kitchen. I ran to the stove to lower the heat.

"The Manager admitted he sent it. He said Humpty Dumpty

instructed him to cc the Drektors. I knew he sent it; I wanted him to say it in front of two lawyers. Bulldog was my witness. I told them I was considering filing a lawsuit for libel. I asked the Manager if he'd testify under subpoena that he emailed the letter, or if he'd lie about it. I had him dead to rights."

"And?"

"He said he'd tell the truth. What else could he say? On my way out of his office, I said my attorney would be in touch if I decide to move forward."

I hope I never get on her bad side. "Are you going to sue?" I asked.

"I don't know yet. Wait, there's more. I wanted to scare them, and apparently, I did. My phone was ringing when I got to my apartment. It was Bad Firm's senior lawyer. He'd been 'authorized' to talk to me." I heard her pour something. "He said what we're doing—the Resistance—is 'hideous and wrong, because we have no idea how wonderful our board members are. Other condos would be lucky to have them!'"

"What did you say?"

"I said, 'Please transfer them immediately to those buildings.' I tried to discuss the Drektors' behavior with him, but he was on his way to a meeting. He didn't have time. Speaking of time, he let me know he was billing the Association for the call." *I need to review our legal expenses.*

By the end of her second glass of wine, the Champion had found the humor in it all. The Drektors played dirty to hold onto power, but they weren't the brightest bulbs.

"Whatever happens between now and December," I said, "we've got to take the high road. I mean 100 percent above board, even if it costs us."

"Agreed. We'll do everything by the book."

Sunday afternoon, I met my BFC friends for lunch in Wellington, just north of Palm Beach. We ate on a large, shaded patio in a friend's backyard. This was horse country, and neighbors lived out of sight from each other. It was a welcome relief from the prying eyes at Condoland.

"Alice, what's new with you?" These women lived in single-family homes. I told them about the Drektors and the Resistance.

"Sounds like a movie!"

"It really does."

Our hostess's husband manned the pizza oven a few yards away. He took a break from the pie he was assembling and came over to us. "I don't mean to interrupt you ladies—"

"Don't be silly," said his wife. "You're one of the girls!" *That came out wrong.* He wiped his hands on his apron, self-conscious. "I didn't mean it that way, honey," she said, smiling sweetly.

"We enjoy your company," I said. "Have a seat!"

"Just for a minute," he said. "I have a pineapple pie in the oven." *Gross.* He sat next to me. "Alice, I have a water restoration business, and I work in condos all over South Florida. In fact, I did a job for your building a few years back."

"Really!" I looked around at the sloping lawn and the horse stables. *Water restoration must be a good business.*

"Yep. Corruption is very common on condo boards. They have floods; they submit claims. My guys repair the damage, and the boards use the rest of the insurance money to redecorate, buy a car, whatever. It's a business model."

"I had no idea," I said. "Why do the insurance companies keep paying?"

"Cuz it's hard to prove. With a fire, you can do forensics. But if a pipe bursts, it bursts. I'm curious, how much have you spent on water restoration? Do you know?"

"Last year, it was $450,000. This year, it'll be closer to $600,000."

His eyes widened. "That's a lot. Have you considered *buying* the water sucking machines? If you have another flood, maintenance just puts them in the hallway."

"How much are they?"

"Hmm . . . $10,000, $15,000 max. For a building your size, you'd be fine with six fans."

"So, $90,000. We paid five times that last year!" *I wonder what a cat jungle gym costs.* "Could you give me something in writing to show what the fans cost? It'll sound more credible coming from you."

"Sure. I'll get an estimate from my supplier. Is that good?"

"That's great! Thank you so—"

"Do you smell smoke?" asked a friend. We did.

"The pizza's burning!" He ran back to the oven and pulled out the pineapple pie.

"Sorry, ladies. We've got to 86 the pineapple." *Phew.* "Give me five minutes for arugula and goat cheese." *Thanks, Daddy.*

"I appreciate your help," I said. "I'm glad I'm not imagining things. Sorry about your pizza." He waved his hand, making nothing of it.

"Alice," said a friend, "it sounds like you're smack in the middle of this."

"It does!" said another.

"I guess I am. I know Florida's famous for fraud, but it's hard to believe when your neighbors are the ones stealing from you." I nodded in the chef's direction. "At least we're not the only building with the problem."

"What are you gonna do?" asked a friend.

I shook my head. "The Drektors hold the power, so getting rid of them is a long shot. We have an election in December. I don't know how, but . . . ." I felt my father on my shoulder. "Failure is not an option!"

18

Petition

Four months before the election, it was time to engage our like-minded neighbors. I got my first signature waiting for the elevator—Gladys Kravitz approached.

"Why you holding a clipboard?" She shook her head. "I know, you can't tell me."

When my friends and I began investigating, we tried not to attract attention. I found Gladys's questions intrusive. But wasn't I just as curious? I took a leap of faith, starting with my nosiest neighbor.

"It's about time you people shared your plans!" she said.

"Loose lips sink ships, Gladys." She tilted her head, thinking. Then she nodded. "Remember, not a word to the Drektors or anyone you think supports them."

"Don't worry! I have NO intention of telling THEM!" She looked aghast. "If you need more signatures, lemme know," she said.

"I do!" The elevator door opened. The car was full of ears.

"We'll take the next one," said Gladys. *She's learning!* "Wait here. I'm gonna make a list." She marched toward her apartment.

"I'll be right back!" Right back turned into 10 minutes, then 15. *"Inch Worm, inch worm . . ."* A door slammed at the end of the hall, followed by slow, heavy footsteps and the swishing sound of pant legs rubbing against each other. "Aaa-lice! You there?" She trudged down the hall as fast as her legs would take her, waving a piece of paper.

"I'm here!"

"Take this!" She handed me the paper, bending over to catch her breath. It was a list of names, apartment numbers, and phone numbers. *Jackpot!* "There's 20." She was flushed, panting. "I'm not as young as I think." *Or as fit.*

"These are people for the petition, right?"

"That's right." She stood up, breathing easier, her cheeks still rosy. "You aren't the only ones fed up with the board!"

"This is fantastic! Thank you! Please understand, we've been careful because—"

"Don't tell me. Just get 'em off the board. A lot of us are rooting for you." *I had no idea.* It felt like a hug.

Some on Gladys's list were snowbirds; the rest were in the building and happy to sign. A few gave me more names, bringing me to 21 signatures.

I kept going. The elevator afforded me a captive audience, but I had to move fast. It was easy to recognize prospects, and I never left home without my clipboard.

"Hi, how are you?"

"Fine. How are you, Alice?" My role in the Resistance was common knowledge, so friendly responders were leads. Non-responders—awkward—were Drektor loyalists, and we rode in silence.

My pitch was simple. "I'm collecting signatures for an election monitor to make sure everything's kosher at the next board election." I'd hold out my clipboard. "Would you like——"

"I'll sign!" Maybe we had a chance.

I bumped into Joanna on the elevator. "How's it going?"

"Like shootin' fish in a barrel. I gawt half the ladies in the Cawd Room, including two friends of Huh Highness. They came up to *me!*"

"How many names do you have?"

"So far, 31," said Joanna. "You?"

"Thirty-four . . . that's 65. Plus the Connector's, we may have the 80."

"She was in the mailroom. You just missed huh. She ran upstairs mumbling something about cocks and vans." *Huh?*

I went home and called the Connector. "Alice, how nice to hear from you!" She was chopping. "Have you had lunch?"

"Not yet. I called about the petition. Do you have a minute?"

"I don't like to talk on the phone when I'm cutting. Why don't you stop by? We'll talk, and you'll eat. You need to eat, Alice."

I know. "That sounds tempting . . ."

"¿Y [And]?"

"I'm on my way."

The elevator opened to the smell of roasted chicken and banana bread. The door was ajar, and I walked in.

"*¡Alicia, ven, ven!*" She kissed me on the cheek, closing the door behind me.

"It smells wonderful. Chicken?" I inhaled.

"It's coq au vin."

Cocks and vans.

"Come, sit down. I'll make you a plate." I sat at the kitchen island where a place setting was waiting for me.

"Salad?"

"Thanks." The coq au vin was getting its finishing touches in a cast iron pot on the stovetop. It smelled divine.

"Leg?"

"Yes, please!" I didn't realize how hungry I was. It was the aromas. She watched me, waiting for the verdict.

"It melts in my mouth." She put her hands together in a single clap. "Where did you learn to cook like this?"

"When we were first married, my husband and I spent two years in Paris while he earned hees master's degree. He studied engineering; I took cooking classes."

"You could *teach* them now!"

"Thank you," she said. "I'm glad you like it."

"Is your husband home?"

"No, he's at lunch with Sherlock and the others."

"Ah, that's right. It's Wednesday."

She leaned over the counter. "You want to talk about the petition?" I nodded and she waited for me to finish a bite.

"How are you doing with signatures?"

"Well," said the Connector in her perfect but accented English, "a lot of my eenternational friends are away now." It was August and offseason.

"Don't worry. Joanna and I have 65. We'll keep going. We're almost there."

"Wait! I deed not feenish," she said. "I focused instead on thee Latin people leeving full-time in Condoland. You know, because of problems in their kone-trees."

I nodded. "So, how'd you do?" I asked.

"I have 30 names. They are fed up, Alice. They come to America to get away from corruption. Now eet's een our building. To them, eet's like cancer, and eet—the board—needs to be removed."

"I understand." But I didn't understand. I couldn't understand.

I'd worked in Latin America, but I never lived there. I only knew democracy, and I assumed the rules applied—more or less—to everyone. Until now. "We have 95 names. We're done!"

"I can get more," said the Connector.

"No, let's stop. We don't want the Drektors to find out."

"*Vale.* I agree."

I left the penthouse with a container of salad, two slices of banana bread, and two dinners' worth of chicken and vegetables in wine sauce.

I put everything in the fridge and called the Champion. "We have 95 signatures!"

"Wow! I didn't think you'd get 80. People like to complain, but don't want to go on record."

"It's too expensive not to!" I said. "So, what's next?"

"Bring me the signatures; I'll send them to Tallahassee."

"You got it."

I stopped by the Champion's apartment that evening. I rang the bell and squatted outside the front door. Cookie ran out as soon as she opened it and gave me a face full of kisses.

"Come in!" We sat on her large, curved sofa. I gave her the signature pages, and she turned off the news. Cookie went back and forth between us, demanding belly rubs.

"How was it?" asked the Champion.

"Easier than I thought. A lot of unit owners are fed up."

"Glad to hear it, but don't get your hopes up. It won't be easy to win this election."

"I know," I said. "Let's keep working! What's next?"

"We need to find five candidates to run against the Drektors."

"Five? We only need three for a voting majority." Cookie sat in my lap, and I scratched behind his ears. *One day, when I stop traveling,*

I'm getting a dog.

"True, but we don't know which three will win. There are five slots. I want to run on a slate of five solid candidates. I don't see any downside. Do you?"

"*You* want to run?"

"I'm thinking about it," said the Champion.

Yes! "You should do it!"

"I'm not sure I want the aggravation. What if my husband's in town and I have a board meeting? We have so little time together." She hesitated. "Would you—"

"Want me to ask the Oracle?" She nodded.

"You got it."

I asked the next night at the gym. The Oracle thought for a while. "She can do it for one year."

"Why one year?"

"Because it's stressful," she said. "More than that will strain her marriage."

"Should she do it at all?" It wasn't worth putting the Champion in harm's way.

"Yes, she should. She'll get things done, and you'll all need her courage. But after the first year, like I said, she has to step down." The Oracle didn't sugarcoat her opinions. The advice made sense.

"Does that mean we're gonna win? That's what you're saying?"

"I can't tell you that. You asked if she should run, and the answer is yes." *Can't blame me for trying!*

I called the Champion as I left the gym. "Thanks," she said. "I'll think about it."

"Do we need another meeting?"

"Yes. We'll need to expand our circle to find the right candidates. I've got a few people in mind. If you think of anyone, invite them."

"I will."

I invited Florence Nightingale, my kind friend from the gym. We needed a big room, and the Connector offered her penthouse. We scheduled it at the beginning of September, right after the next Finance Committee meeting.

I walked into the Conference Room three minutes late for the Finance Committee meeting.

"Nice of you to join us!" said Humpty Dumpty.

Some of us work. "Hi, everybody. I see we have a full house!" The room was packed. I placed my laptop in front of me on the new conference table—another unnecessary purchase. I sat facing the audience. Her Highness sat at the head of the table. *Why is she here?* "Are you joining us today?"

"I am," she said. "We want to discuss the new payment system for the Restaurant." *We?* It was on our agenda, and I'd prepared an analysis for the Committee that argued against the change.

The Long Island Lothario was sitting in the front row. He and Her Highness plus Humpty Dumpty and the Bulldog made four Drektors. *They're hijacking my Committee to hold an illegal board meeting. How dare they!*

"No worries, it's on our agenda," I said with a snide smile. "But we can't have four board members here. That's a violation of the Sunshine Law."

I thought I had her. The Bulldog whispered in her ear. "I'm here as a unit owner, not a board member," she said. "So is he." She pointed to the Long Island Lothario. *Bullshit!*

There must have been 50 people in the audience. I knew she wouldn't budge, and there was no point in making a scene. I added this violation to the list on my laptop. Maybe we could deal with it later. "I don't think it works that way," I said, "but let's get started." If looks could kill, Her Highness would have ended me. I turned to the Manager. "We have a full agenda. How 'bout we focus on the biggest variances from budget to save time. All right with you?" The Manager looked at Highness for his cue. She was stone-faced. "All right?"

"Sure, Alice." He spent 10 minutes on a $2,000 savings in natural gas and a $4,000 overage in water use. *Did you not hear me?*

"Manager," I said, "do you know why our legal expenses spiked? They're hundreds of thousands of dollars over budget." I spoke to my colleagues around the table. "If we can't offset this, we'll need to increase the maintenance."

"You raised our maintenance 10 percent this year!" said an observer.

"What the hell are you people doing?"

"Money doesn't grow on trees, you know! *Do* you know?"

"Be quiet!" said Humpty Dumpty. "Only Committee members may speak. If you can't be quiet, then please leave!" *But Her Highness can talk? And sit at our table?*

The Manager leaned his head left and right trying to catch Her Highness's eye. Her face was burning. I continued. "Do we have legal exposure? Did—"

"Shut up! Shut up! Nobody wants to hear from you!" Her Highness shouted. "Just sit there and behave yourself!" I. Saw. Red. Demeaned. In front of my neighbors. For doing my job.

Humpty Dumpty didn't tell Her Highness not to interrupt, so I did. "As our treasurer just reminded us, only Committee members may speak." I tried for calm, but I was trembling.

"I am the president of the board of directors," she said, pulling her baseball cap down over her thinning hair. "I'll speak at any meeting I please! If you don't like it, Alice, you can leave!"

Despite the lies, the theft, and the hypocrisy, the Board of Drektors was Condoland's governing body, and Her Highness was its president. I felt powerless. *Fuck this Committee! I can't stay here. I won't!*

It wasn't in me to yell back—not yet—but I had no intention of sitting there and behaving myself. I gathered my things, stood up, and put one foot in front of the other. My eyes welled. *Hold it! Don't blink.* I looked straight ahead until I found the door.

The Bulldog called the next morning. "I'm calling about the meeting yesterday."

"What about it?" I emptied my yogurt down the drain and ran the disposal in his ear. I'd lost my appetite.

"Alice, what's that noise?"

"Nothing. How can I help you?"

"What happened wasn't right." *Why didn't you say something?* "Both Humpty Dumpty and I told Her Highness she was wrong to speak to you like that."

"The president of the board told the Committee and the unit owners watching that she doesn't value my contribution. I can't be effective in my role anymore. I have to resign." I wasn't bluffing.

"Please, don't do that."

"I have no choice."

"What if she called you to apologize?"

"She can do whatever she wants."

"Leave it with me." *Now he's my ally?*

"OK. Thanks for your call."

"Thank *you* for your work on the Committee. You're doing a

great job. Please know that." *What gives?*

When Her Highness called, I was ready. Her voice quavered. She hated apologizing even more than she hated *me*. "Hello, Alice?"

"Yes?"

"I heard you want to resign from the Finance Committee. I hope you'll stay . . . I . . . didn't mean to yell at you. I'm under a lot of pressure." She waited for me to react. I didn't. "My husband isn't well. He's disoriented in the nursing home. He doesn't even recognize me! It's rough, and I snapped. Please forgive me." She started to "cry." Joanna had told me Highness nagged her husband out of his mind and into that facility. These were crocodile tears.

"Thank you. I appreciate your apology, and I'm so sorry about your husband. The problem is everyone heard your vote of no confidence yesterday, and I can't serve Condoland when the board president doesn't respect me."

"I do . . . respect you!" *Ha!* "We want you to stay on the Finance Committee." *Why?* "What can I do to fix this?"

"Well . . . I suppose you could apologize at the next meeting." *She won't do it.*

She hesitated. "OK . . . I will."

I learned later that unit owners were angry with her after I left. The election was three months away, and her apology was entirely self-serving, but I relented. The Finance Committee gave me a forum to challenge the Drektors' spending.

Peter Pan texted Friday afternoon. "U back?"

"Yes."

"Going 2 Box tonight. U shld come."

Why doesn't he call? "What time?"

"9-ish"

"K. See u there!"

I dressed casually—jeans, espadrilles, and a purple cotton top. I got there fashionably late. Peter was unfashionably late, so I waited at the bar by myself. The owner remembered me, and we chatted. Some of the musicians also remembered me, and they kept me company. This was a neighborhood bar. People knew each other, and the vibe was friendly. Nobody asked what I did, what I drove, or where I went to school. I felt comfortable being there alone.

Peter walked through the door 40 minutes later. He wore jeans, a gray sweatshirt, and sneakers. *Unpretentious.* I loved that. He left a seat between us at the bar. Discreetly, I smelled my armpits. All good. *I don't get it.* We spoke over the music about our favorite bands, and I told him about my audiobook audition. We both grew up in Newton! *What are the odds!* He made me laugh, and I wanted to sit closer. This arm's length thing was unnatural. Something about the way we sat, facing each other, talking, must have told people not to sit between us. The guy on the other side spoke to me, and I turned to respond. Glancing back at Peter, I saw him turn away quickly. *He's watching me. So, why's he holding back?*

Peter and I spoke over the music until the owner said, "Shh! Keep it down. Wait for the break."

By the time the break came at 11 p.m., I'd had enough of the seating arrangement. *Why invite me here?* "I'm gonna get going," I said.

"Oh!" *He's surprised?* He signaled for the bill and paid for my drink. "I'll walk you to your car."

We passed a store with Judaica in the window. "Look, beanies!" he pointed to a display of yarmulkes through the glass.

"I'm Jewish." I said it before he said something he couldn't take back.

"Me, too." *Interesting.* "You ever been married?" he asked.

"No. Engaged, not married. You?"

"No. Do you want to be married?"

Talk about mixed signals! "If I found the right guy." He was quiet. His eyes were extraordinarily blue. "This is my car." We stopped.

"Thanks for hangin' out!" he said.

"It was fun." *Was it?* "Thanks for the drink."

He stood close as I opened my door. After seven years in South Florida, I expected hello and good-bye kisses, but he was stiff. *Do I kiss him on the cheek?* I couldn't read him. I got in the car and waved through the window. On the drive home, I replayed the evening. *Why wouldn't he sit next to me?* I was attracted to him and pretty sure he felt something, too. Why was he blocking?

I found the Oracle at the gym the next morning. It was pouring outside. "Nobody's here today," she said. "It's the rain."

"Good! Can you talk?"

"Yes. I'll meet you at the elliptical machine." *How does she know I'm going to—of course she knows.* "What's on your mind?" she asked as I pedaled.

"I met Peter Pan last night at the Music Box."

"How did it go?" she had that smile.

"I don't know. I don't get him."

"Mixed signals?"

I nodded. "He didn't want to sit next to me."

"I know." By now, I accepted her visions and advice as gospel.

"I felt something, but the way he acted, I don't know what to do."

"There's nothing for you *to* do. He looks at you and sees his future. That scares him. Also, you intimidate him."

"I'm five foot three. How can I intimidate him?"

"You're smart, and you don't play games. You talk about books and the news." *Guilty.* "He's used to pushovers. He's afraid to say the wrong thing and blow his chance." *Never crossed my mind.* "Also," said the Oracle, "he has some growing up to do."

"Even *he* knows that——he calls himself Peter Pan!" We laughed. It was ridiculous. "So, I let it go?"

"Yes."

"You mean, I forget about him."

"No," said the Oracle. "You throw it out to the Universe and live your life. When the time is right, love will find you."

I loved the metaphysics, but the suspense was killing me. "Is he the one?"

"I can't tell you that. All I can say is your story isn't over."

19

The Fab Five

Joanna called two days before our candidate-recruitment meeting. "Tokyo Rosenberg wants to come." Her kimonos earned her that name. "Whaddaya think?"

"Do you trust her?" I asked.

"Yeah. I know huh fuh years."

"Then it's fine by me."

The Champion invited Paul Revere. A retired business executive, he was a shirtsleeves kind of guy who remembered everything you told him and inquired with genuine interest the next time he saw you. His wife was even nicer. When their only daughter moved to South Florida to marry an Orthodox Jew—a rich Orthodox Jew, the only kind anyone converts for—the Reveres sold their house in Marblehead, Massachusetts, and moved to Condoland, 10 minutes from their daughter, son-in-law, and four grandchildren.

Saturday mornings, they sat with their grandkids in temple. Mrs. Revere taught her granddaughters how to make scones and Irish stew, and Mr. Revere played basketball with the boys at the Club House. Paul's character and work experience made him a shoo-in—*if* we could get him to run.

The day of the meeting, we gathered again in the Connector and Ceevil Engineer's penthouse. As soon as Paul Revere opened the door, Joanna ran up to him. "I'm so glad yaw heuh! Pawl, you gotta run. Please say you'll run!"

"I'm not sure," said Paul. "I'm heah ta listen."

"What's to listen?" asked Joanna. "You know what these Drektuhs aw doing. Poo poo poo!" She fake-spit, ridding her mouth of their names. "Yaw the perfect candidate!" Mrs. Revere smiled. Her husband blushed. "Will ya do it?"

"Like I said, I'm heah ta listen . . . I'll think about it."

"Aright, aright, I'll leave you alone—fuh *now*." The Reveres took their seats in the circle. We were 20, maybe 25 people.

Sherlock invited the Panamanian Prince and Princess. Like Paul, the Prince was undecided. His wife chaired the Condoland Decorating Committee and represented our building on the Club House Decorating Committee. She obsessed over tile, fabrics, and wallpaper textures as only the privileged could, and I got the impression the Prince felt his wife's activities beneath him. I hoped he wouldn't view all condo governance that way.

Tokyo Rosenberg came with her three-pound "service dog" in a mesh bag. She placed him on the seat next to her.

"Let's get started," said the Champion. I sat across from her in the circle, between Joanna and Sherlock. "Thank you for coming today, and thanks to the Connector and Ceevil Engineer for opening their beautiful home to us once again."

"Eeet's my pleh-zure," said the Connector, hand to chest, smiling. Thanks to the Resistance, she'd become our Argentine Martha Stewart.

The Champion had us each take an oath of secrecy before she

got down to business. "We have two things to accomplish today," she said. "We need to agree on a campaign strategy for the election, and we need to convince some people in this room to run." She flashed her Candice Bergen smile at Paul Revere and the Panamanian Prince.

"Let's start with the campaign strategy," she continued. "We *need* a voting majority. As long as we elect three new directors, they can vote down anything that goes against the unit owners' interests."

"Why three?" someone asked. "There are five directors. Why not replace them all?" Unit owners could vote for zero to five candidates. There was no minimum, only the maximum.

"That's the question," said the Champion. "How many candidates should we ask the unit owners to support?"

Florence Nightingale raised her hand. *Are we in school?*

"Florence?" said the Champion.

"Thank you," she said in her little-girl voice. Her Ferragamo feet dangled above the polished marble floor. "Hi, everybody. I'm Florence Nightingale." A few people smirked when they heard her speak. "In my experience—"

"She's a therapist," I said. *She needs a boost—in more ways than one!*

"Thank you, Alice," said Florence. "In my experience, people want a choice. If we ask them to vote against all five of the current board members, they may disregard our recommendations altogether. We certainly don't want that!" She giggled apologetically.

"Whaddayou suggest?" asked the Champion.

"I think we offer five candidates but let the owners choose," she squeaked. "Explain that we need a voting majority—three or more *new* directors—to make prudent decisions for our property. Then we let the unit owners decide." *Logical.*

"I agree with Florence," said the Champion. "Some of the

Drektors *will* get re-elected. We can't expect to get rid of them all, and we don't need to."

"Should we take a vote?" I asked.

"Let's do that," said the Champion. "How many people want three candidates?" Two hands went up. "That's out. And how many people want five?" Sixteen hands went up. "That's settled. We'll have a slate of five *fabulous* candidates." She smiled at Paul and the Prince.

"I have a question," I said. "People will need information on the candidates."

"What's your question?" asked the Champion.

"Would you like me to help the candidates put their info together?"

She thought a second. "Nothing in writing. It gives the Drektors ammunition. We should talk to people."

There's careful, and there's shooting yourself in the foot. "You can't talk to everybody," I said. "What about the snowbirds? We need something in writing—English *and* Spanish—explaining our candidates' priorities for the building." Spanish speakers nodded.

"You're wrong!" said the Champion, her voice like a foghorn cutting across the room. "We don't put anything in writing!"

Lawyer! Stick to word of mouth, and we lose. "No. I'm not wrong," I said calmly. The Champion scared a lot of people, but she didn't scare me. "People won't vote because we say so. We have to make our case."

"I think Alice has a point," said Florence. "I'm sure we have to be careful about what we put in writing, but having information about our five *will* help the unit owners. Maybe we can beef up the candidate bios the Office sends out and use those. Would that work?"

"Yes!" I said. "Great idea, Florence!" *I think I underestimated her.*

"Knock, knock!" The door opened and the Bulldog walked into the living room. We froze. "Hi, everybody!" He waved. *What's he doing here?*

"Hi!" said the Champion. She walked over to him and put her hand on his back. "Everyone, you know the Bulldog. Yes, he's currently on the board, but he's interested in joining us." *Is he wired?* I suppressed a twisted laugh. The tension was palpable. "We decided to recommend a slate of five candidates," she told him. "Have a seat." Tokyo Rosenberg's dog was parked on the only available chair. She left him there. No one made room for this Drektor.

"That's OK, I'll sit on the sofa."

I zipped to the coffee station behind the Champion and whispered in her ear, "Break."

"Guys, let's take a five-minute break," she said.

"Are you crazy?" I murmured.

"Calm down. We spoke this week. Since the incident in the Manager's office, Bulldog's had second thoughts about the other Drektors. He says he wants to break from them, and he asked to come to the meeting." I was unconvinced. "He's an attorney; he's different from the others. Relax."

Sucker. "It's your call, but I don't like it." Bulldog sat alone on the couch, outside the circle. "Look! Nobody wants to get near him."

People were vying for her attention. "Talk to you later," she said. "It'll be fine!"

The Champion resumed the meeting. "Everyone, I have good news. Thanks to these three ladies," she pointed to me, Joanna, and the Connector, "we're going to have a state-appointed election monitor overseeing our vote count."

Tokyo Rosenberg shook her head, grabbed her dog, and walked out of the penthouse as fast as her kimono allowed, slamming the door behind her. *Uh-oh.* I looked at Joanna. "What was that?" I mouthed.

She flicked her right wrist. "Don' worry about it. I'll tawk to huh." Joanna stood and strode across the room. She leaned her hands on the back of the Champion's chair. "So, who's gonna run?" she asked. "What about you and you and you?" She pointed to the Prince and Paul, then put her hands on the Champion's shoulders. "Whaddayou say?"

"I've served on the board before," said the Champion, "and I'm willing to run, but only if you two join me." She pointed at Paul and the Prince. *Yes!* She could be a pain in the neck, but we needed her courage. Besides, she had the green light from the Oracle.

"I'm thinkin' about it," said Paul. "I don't like what's going on heah any mah than you guys do."

"Let's not preshah him," said his wife. "Trust me, it nevah works. He has to come to it in his own time."

"*¿Y tú?*" Sherlock asked the Panamanian Prince.

"I don't like the decisions made by this board," said the Prince, "but today, I, too, am here to listen."

"Am I the only one stepping up?" asked the Champion.

Sherlock elbowed me. I shook my head. Leading a committee was one thing, but being on the board was a huge, thankless commitment. More importantly, the Oracle advised against it. Whatever was in store for me, being on the board would interfere.

"Anyone?" asked the Champion. Florence raised her hand again. "Florence?"

"Thank you, Champion. I've watched the erosion of decorum in our building with great sadness. If my training can help to bring us together, I'll run for the board, too." She was a dark horse. *I'll work with her.*

"Wonderful!" said the Champion. "That's two candidates. We need three more . . ." She stood and faced Paul Revere and the Panamanian Prince. "I know you guys need to think about it. Can you let us know by September 15th? Submissions are due on October 15th. If you decide *not* to run, we'll need time to find other people," she said, mock crying.

"Yah," said Paul. "No problem."

"Is OK for me," said the Prince.

"Thank you," she said. "That's it, everybody! Thanks for coming, and remember not to share anything yet about our election strategy. Enjoy what's left of your Sunday!" She turned to me. "Alice, can you stay for a minute? Let's discuss what you want to put in writing."

"May I join you?" asked the Connector.

"Sure," I said.

"Anything else?" asked Harvard. He was tapping his foot, not realizing the meeting was over. *You're 93. Where do you have to go?*

The Champion ignored him. *This thick skin, I could learn from her.*

I stopped Joanna on her way out. "Why did Tokyo leave?"

"I dunno. She's does that sometimes. Maybe her dog had to pee."

"I don't think that was it. And I can't believe the Champion invited the Bulldog!" He hadn't said a word during the meeting. He sat, listening to our plans. *Is the Champion considering him as our fifth candidate?*

"I wondered about that, too," said Joanna. "But it's done. No point worrying about it." Maybe, but goose bumps on my forearms told me otherwise.

I caught up with Florence. "I'm so happy you're going to run!"

"Thank you!" she chirped. "To tell you the truth, I'm a little nervous about it."

"Maybe I can help. You're relatively new to the building, and some people don't know you." *How do I say this?* "You're very nice . . ." *You have to be cruel to be kind.* "Maybe a little too nice. You know, you're—"

She put her hand on my forearm and smiled. "Don't worry about my feelings. I'm accustomed to being underestimated, and I enjoy exceeding expectations. You're the marketer. What do you suggest?"

I felt myself blush. *She's so gracious!* "Thanks for makin' it easy. I think we do an open house so people can get to know you. I can have it—"

"No, let's use my apartment. In fact, let's include the other four candidates once we have them."

"I love that idea," I said.

"Well, I have you to thank, don't I?"

"No, but you're kind to say so. How can I help?"

She thought a moment. "Would you go over Condoland's finances with me? I'm not a numbers person, but I need to understand where things stand."

"Sure. My pleasure—"

"Florence!" It was her husband.

"Go, go, go!" she told me. "We can talk later. Thanks, Alice!" *It goes to show you don't judge a book by its cover. She's a steel magnolia!*

I joined the Champion and the Connector in the living room. "Ladies," said the Connector. "I have friends een the building who leeve in o-ther kone-trees."

The Champion looked at me. "Countries," I said.

"Jes," said the Connector. "They are here only a few months a year. In the past, I don't think they voted. If I can get those votes, we weell have an advantage."

"We sure will," said the Champion.

"Also, I think we need—*Alicia, como se dice campaña de base?*"

"Grassroots campaigning."

"*Gracias.* I think we need to do grassroots campaigning." *Has she done this before?*

"What do you have in mind?" asked the Champion.

"Een Buenos Aires, we had a similar situation. I made a leest of the people I thought would agree to change the board. My friends helped me. First we called, then we knocked on doors the week of the election. What do you theenk?"

"It's a great idea! Would you organize it?"

"I would love to," said the Connector. This campaign would complete her crossover into the English-speaking world of Condoland.

"Can I help?" I asked. The Connector nodded. I turned to the Champion. "And I can work with the candidates on their bios."

"All right," she said.

"There's a board meeting this Thursday," I said. "Are you guys going?"

"I am," said the Champion. "Today was a good start, but those Drektors will do anything—and I mean anything—to win." *Like send a Trojan Bulldog to our meeting?*

"I am from Argentina," the Connector said with a knowing smile. "I understand."

I heard "Nobody Knows the Trouble I've Seen" in my head. "See you Thursday!" I left quickly before the Connector tried to give me the leftover hummus. *We need three more candidates . . .*

The vast majority of Condoland unit owners were not civic-minded. When things ran smoothly, only Sherlock and a handful of

others attended meetings. Thursday's board meeting was packed—
not a good sign for the Drektors. Sherlock saved me a seat. As I
sidestroked to him through people clasping hot coffee and cookies,
I flashed back to weaving through the crowded sidewalk on that
rainy day when I decide to leave New York. *At least there aren't um-*
brellas aimed at my head! Strangers greeted me by name. *How do they*
know me?

I sat with Sherlock's friends. Accomplished, retired professionals. We laughed about the Drektors—in Spanish. We didn't do it
to be mean. We were frustrated, and humor was an outlet.

"*¡Oye,* Sherlock, *mira!*" I said. The Long Island Lothario was
staring at us.

"He knows we're talking about him," said one of the men. Like
a moth to a flame, the object of our derision shambled toward us,
making small talk. He smiled, the nerdy boy at the popular lunch
table.

"Is he pouting?" I asked.

"He doesn't understand a word we're saying," said one of the
men. "I'm glad he knows how it feels." For years, the Drektors
snubbed Condoland's Spanish speakers. Now, the Drektors needed
their votes.

A white baseball cap floated through the noisy crowd and
stopped at the dais. "Order! Order!" yelled Her Highness, banging
her gavel. "Please take your seats! Order! Order!" The talking continued. "Order!" she pounded. "Order! Order!" *Class, class, class,*
SHUT UP!

The Drektors lumbered like zombies to the front of the room.
They know it won't be pretty. The Panamanian Princess was ending an
intense conversation with her husband. He scowled as his wife sat
slumped beside him.

The Bulldog read last month's minutes, and Her Highness moved on to new business. "Condoland III requested a change in representation on the Club House Decorating Committee," she said. "The Panamanian Princess will be stepping down." *Huh?* "The Corpse will replace her. His casino design experience will be useful for this role." *The house always wins? That was back when he had a pulse!*

"What just happened?" I asked Sherlock.

"The Princess asked too many questions," he said. "Why put shade plants in full sun? Why buy residential-grade equipment for a commercial kitchen?" Sherlock lowered his voice as much as he was capable. "The president from Condoland III hired his brother-in-law to renovate the Club House kitchen. *Artista,* are you catching flies?" I shut my mouth. *They have Drektors, too!* "She drives everyone crazy," he said, "but she asks the right questions, which to some people are the wrong questions, which is why they replaced her." He partially covered his mouth. "Her Highness and Lothario have an arrangement with Condoland III's board president. He's just as dirty as they are, but he's meaner and smarter, and they're afraid of him." *This election can't come soon enough.*

The Prince's wife wiped her eyes, her head bowed. She annoyed me, too, but kicking her off the Committee was a bridge too far. The Prince raised his hand. "I would like to speak." He was eerily calm.

Audience questions normally came at the end of these meetings. Perhaps it was his bearing, or perhaps she was having a senior moment. Whatever the reason, Her Highness called on him. "Yes? Do you have a question?"

He got up, and all eyes turned to him. "I have an observation. I am an architect. There are other architects and engineers here tonight." He swept his hand across the room. The Ceevil Engineer—

chair of the Architectural Committee—got up from his seat in the back and stood against the wall next to the Prince. "In 35 years," said the Prince, "I have never, NEVER seen a project go 100 percent over budget. It's just not possible." *Oh, boy.* "Naturally, BECAUSE SHE'S DOING HER JOB, my wife asks questions to understand what went wrong with the Club House renovation. After spending twice the money you assured us it would cost, you are about to close the Club House while you tent the Restaurant for termites. Is this correct?" He looked at Ceevil, who nodded.

"Well, yes," said the Long Island Lothario. "We installed a beam in the Restaurant, and, umm . . . it had termites. Unfortunately, they spread." Lothario played with his chains. "It wasn't something we could anticipate. In fact—"

"Thees is not true!" interrupted the Ceevil Engineer. "We had termites in the Club House *before* the renovation. Mold, too! I showed the Manager! I have peectures!" He scrolled through his phone. The Manager looked into space. The other Drektors were silent. They knew.

"Remember Lothario had guaranteed bids for $1.3 million?" Sherlock asked me in Spanish. I nodded. "He told the contractors to exclude mold remediation and to do that separately—later. Same for termites. They lied by omission to get the project approved. That's how we got here."

I whispered, "How do you know this?"

"Arepas." I remembered the stuffed cornmeal cakes Sherlock brought to the contractors during the renovation and smiled. *A wise investment.*

"So, what do we know?" continued the Prince. "We know the costs of this project are out of control. We know even with these costs, the work is not done. We know many mistakes were made.

"And what don't we know? I will speak for myself. I don't know why you allow Condoland III to make decisions for our board and our building. I don't know why YOU," he pointed at the Drektors, "are not asking the questions my wife is asking. Why YOU would remove her from the Club House Decorating Committee for doing her JOB!" The Prince took a deep breath. He took off his glasses and lowered his voice. "That is my observation." He sat down. His wife reached for his hand, and he held hers between both of his. There was a pause as people absorbed his words, followed by thunderous applause.

The rest of the meeting was as contentious as meetings in Condoland had become.

"Sherlock," I said, "something's wrong with the Corpse!"

"How can you tell?"

It was a fair question; the Corpse never moved during meetings. But he looked different. A friend of my parents was a gerontologist. He used to categorize his patients as O's and Q's. "The O's," he'd say, referring to those who were open-mouthed, "can be cared for in assisted living. They sleep a lot, but their condition is generally chronic, not critical. It's the Q's I worry about. If the patient's tongue hangs out of his mouth, I call an ambulance."

"Look! His mouth—he's a Q!" Sherlock looked at me quizzically. The Corpse's head hit the dais with a thud. The Drektors shrank back in horror. *Do something!*

Sherlock yelled, "*¡Nueve, once!* Nine, one, one!" Someone from Security dialed, and in minutes, paramedics arrived and took the Corpse to the hospital.

"You see what you people did! This meeting is adjourned!" screamed Her Highness as she banged her gavel.

Sherlock and I sat and watched. As the room cleared, I saw the

Prince talking to Paul Revere. They walked over to the Champion, and I ran to hear their conversation.

"I have made up my mind," said the Panamanian Prince. "I will run."

"So will I," said Paul Revere. "That's no way to treat a lady!" He put his hand on the Prince's shoulder. "Let's pray fah the Corpse, but we gotta turn this ship around."

"Excuse me." We turned. It was Harvard. "I am here to answer the call of duty. I salute you!" he said to the Prince. Literally. He saluted.

I walked out with the Champion. "I guess beggars can't be choosers."

"Don't start," she said. "I can manage him."

"Better you than me! On the bright side, he's better than the Bulldog. And now we can submit all five names to the Office."

"No way!" she said. "We'll wait until October 15th. We need to keep the Drektors in suspense for as long as possible."

20

Unexpected Developments

I'd been away from music for 15 years. Nobody was banging down my door to sing; I had to go after it. Before I reached the age of second-guessing, I loved being the center of musical attention. Singing was pure joy. Now that I sang professionally, the stakes were higher. It was impossible not to imagine all the things that could go wrong. But putting myself out there was the only way to get gigs and meet musicians who could lead to more gigs.

The Music Box held open mic jazz jams on Monday nights. Monday morning, I put the Box on my to-do list so I wouldn't chicken out. No matter what excuses the day brought, I was going. At 8 p.m., I put one foot in front of the other, got into my car and drove toward trial by fire. I sat at the bar with the other solo patrons. *Does Peter Pan come on Monday nights? Stay focused!* I kept tabs on the door, just in case.

Talented musicians jammed on stage. Everyone was friendly. A familiar couple walked in and sat near the bar. I remembered their photo hanging at a recording studio. The wife was a talent agent, and her husband a saxophone player. "You should meet them,"

218

the studio owner had said. *What are the odds?* I swigged the rest of my sauvignon blanc and walked over.

"Hi. Rick from Rick's Recording Studio speaks very highly of you guys. I'm Alice. I'm a singer." *Fake it 'til you make it!*

"Rick's a great guy," said the husband, motioning me to take a seat at their table. "You work with him?"

"For voiceovers."

"What do you sing?" asked his wife.

"Mostly standards. The American Songbook and some Spanish and Italian songs."

"Do you sing bossa nova?" asked the horn player.

"Mm-hmm, but in English."

"As long as you know the tune!" He smiled. "I'm in the mood for 'Ipanema.' When I'm up, I'll call you to join me." *Just like that?* "It's Alice, right?"

A flash of nausea. *Do you want this or not!* "Yes. And thank you!"

I watched the musicians play. They were improvising, immersed in the music. They worked in a feedback loop, playing off each other. A nod from the piano player to the bass meant it was her turn to solo. If one player riffed, the others responded. It was a musical conversation.

"How long has the band been together?" I asked the talent agent.

"It's not a band," she said. "I mean, they know each other, but they're just jamming. Anyone can join." *Duh! What do you think open mic means?* I was feeling underqualified when the sax player called me up to sing. *My mouth is dry.* I popped a Ricola and stepped up on the stage.

"Key?" asked the piano player.

"Db." *Sounds professional.*

"Db everybody."

"Tempo?" asked the drummer. I snapped my fingers to the speed I wanted. "And a one, and a two, and a three, and a four." He played a samba rhythm, and I nodded, confirming the beat. I kept my eyes on the piano player as he played "The Girl from Ipanema" intro until he turned and nodded at me—my cue. I sang and neurotic thoughts danced in my head. *Was I flat? What's the next line? Don't forget! You're gonna forget! That's OK, just scat. You can't scat! Do they like it? Am I loud enough?* I closed my eyes. *Alice, SHUT UP!*

When I opened them, a couple was smiling at a table in front of me, moving their heads to the rhythm. The Box owner stopped loading glasses into an overhead rack, resting her arms on the bar counter as she listened.

After my first pass through the song, the piano player cued each instrumentalist for their solo. I had time to listen. *People are watching me. Do you want them to ignore you? You're on stage!* Uncomfortable, I moved around to look like I had rhythm. Eventually, the pianist cued me for my next pass through the song, ending my interpretive dance interlude. This time, it was easier. I made eye contact with the audience. I smiled and swayed to the beat. *They're happy! I'M making them happy!* I held up two fingers, indicating to the pianist how many times I'd sing the last line of the song—a signal I'd learned. When we finished, the room filled with applause.

"Let's hear it for Alice!" said the sax player. *God bless you.*

I put my hands together in namaste, bowing slightly. "Let's hear it for this terrific band!" I extended my arm backward. Walking to my seat, two people spoke to me as I passed their table.

"That was really nice! Are you a professional singer?"

You sang at the Alice Hotel. And the Condoland Restaurant, and you got paid. That makes you "professional." "Yes."

"Where can we hear you perform?"

Uh-oh. "Ahh—"

"Right here!" It was the Music Box owner. "When can we get you on the calendar?"

I need time to practice. Shit or get off the pot. "How's October?" I asked. *Let her think my calendar's full.*

She booked me for the third Friday night in October with the musicians of my choosing.

"I'm so glad I came tonight!" I told her.

"So are we!" Her expression shifted slightly, like she was up to something. "You're a friend of Peter Pan's, right?"

He considers me a friend? "Yeah, I know him."

"He's a regular. He speaks highly of you."

He does? "That's nice." I smiled. *Don't get her involved.*

I drove home pleased with myself—going there alone, meeting the musicians, and singing through cottonmouth. The way things fell into place, it felt otherworldly. "Thank you, Daddy!" I said it instinctively, but as the words moved from my unconscious to my conscious mind, I knew I had a guardian angel—and a gig at the Music Box!

Late one afternoon near the end of September, the Champion called. "Are you home tonight?"

"Yep. I'm practicing. Why?"

"The Bulldog called. He wants to talk to us."

"Us, meaning you and me?"

"That's what he said."

"Why?"

"That, he didn't say, but I'm pretty sure it's about the election. Remember he came to our last meeting." *Oh, I remember.* "Maybe he's seen the light." *Wishful thinking.*

"You trust him?" I asked.

"Well, he's an attorney, and—"

"And what? Does he speak up when the Drektors break the Sunshine Law? When they lie to us? Steal from us? Anything? I know you like him, but I think he's complicit."

"Let's just hear him out," said the Champion. "I know him professionally, and I owe him that much."

"OK, fine. Let's meet at my place."

"Eight o'clock?"

"Sure.

They arrived together. *I'll be civil.* "Hi, guys! Come on in." The Bulldog smiled politely. He looked awkward.

"Can I get you something to drink?"

He perked up. "I'd love a coffee."

"How do you drink it?"

"Black, please." I led them into the kitchen.

"Want some?" I asked the Champion.

"No, thanks. I'm good."

I handed him a full mug and we sat at the kitchen table. "To what do I owe the honor?" I asked.

"Thank you." He took a sip and had an ah-hah tasting moment. "This is excellent!"

"I'm glad you like it."

"Alice," said the Champion, "the Bulldog is interested in joining our slate of candidates."

"Well, I'm thinking about it," he said.

"Why?" I asked.

He thought for a moment. "I don't agree with some decisions made by the other board members." *Vague.*

"Such as?"

"Can I have another napkin?" he asked.

Yes, sir! "Of course."

"Thanks," said the Bulldog. "Do you have anything to dunk? Crackers or maybe a cookie?" *Answer the question!* The Champion saw my expression when I placed a napkin, a plate, and several biscotti in front of this *schnorer*.[21] *She owes me!* She tried not to laugh.

The Bulldog dunked a biscotto in his coffee and chewed it slowly. "That hit the spot."

"I'm so glad," I said, turning to the Champion and raising my eyebrows. *Why is he here?*

"What specific decisions give you pause?" she asked.

"Oh, yes," said the Bulldog. "Well . . . such as . . . for example . . . the decision-makers on the board should have let everyone know the Club House renovation was over budget before last year's election." *Dissemble after the fact and blame your friends. Nice.*

"We agree. I wonder," I leaned toward him, "why didn't *you* speak up before the election?"

He tried to look sincere. "I've asked myself the same question. I guess I assumed they had good reason to wait. He shrugged as fine crumbs settled like dandruff on his shirt. "After all, the renovation was boosting our property values! But if the decision-makers came clean on the full cost from the beginning—or even right before last year's election—unit owners would have tried to shut everything down—you know how cheap they can be." He leaned toward me in an *entre nous* posture. "That would be a mistake for everyone."

"So, you agree with the board," I said.

"No. That's not what I mean. As I look back on it, I think they

---

[21] Schnorer — Yiddish for beggar—one who wheedles others into supplying his or her wants

made a mistake." *They?* "The board should always be transparent with unit owners because that's who we serve. I like the ideas your group—the Resistance, you call it, right?" I nodded. "I like the transparency you've discussed, and I agree an election monitor is a good thing."

"How can we help?" asked the Champion. *Thank you.*

He shifted to face her. "You're going to recommend a slate of candidates. Do you have your five yet?"

"We do," she said.

"I see . . . Would you consider recommending a sixth? Florence Nightingale is an unknown. I bring name recognition. What good is a candidate if no one votes for her?" *You ARE a Trojan Bulldog!*

"We're keeping Florence. That said, if you want us to recommend you," said the Champion, "you need to publicly commit to full transparency in all board decisions—including spending. You have to prioritize health and safety repairs over cosmetic projects, and you'll need to denounce what's gone on in previous years under your watch. Are you comfortable with that?"

He nodded. "We need a board people can trust, and I want to be a part of that."

"All right. Alice and I will talk to the others, and I'll get back to you."

He stood up, his mission accomplished. "I really appreciate your listening to me. And thanks for the refreshments, Alice. Top notch." I smiled politely. "Would you mind if I took a couple of those cookies home? Can you spare them?"

Is there a hidden camera somewhere? "Here you go," I said. I didn't speak again until I heard the elevator door shut. "Anyone else you want to invite for refreshments before the kitchen closes?"

"Sorry. I know he's a bit much," said the Champion.

"You know he tried to get the Oracle fired to eliminate her salary?" She shook her head. "I'm underwhelmed. You?"

"I don't know," said the Champion. "We have our Fab Five. What harm can he do?"

"He'll compete against our candidates," I said. "He needs our endorsement. That's what's in it for him. What's in it for us? The more votes for other candidates, the more votes our five need to win. It's a risk."

"It's a good point. Let's think about it," she said.

The Champion called the next morning. "You're not going to believe this."

"What?" I squinted at my nightstand. 9:30 a.m.

"Did I wake you?"

"Yes," I groaned. "It's not 10 yet." Now that I worked for myself, I indulged my night owl inclinations.

"Sorry. I'll call you back."

"No, I'm up now. Tell me."

"The Drektors know about our petition for the election monitor. The Manager called. He told me we don't need to go forward with it."

I sat up. "What!"

"They're willing to get an election monitor, and he said we won't need to worry about the petition and paperwork."

"I don't get it."

"They know someone. They want *their* person to monitor."

"It never ends!"

"Don't worry," she said. "I called the State of Florida's Condominium Ombudsman and explained the situation. He called our

Office and then called me. Apparently, he told the Manager he hoped Condoland hadn't spent money for its own monitor, because the State of Florida would be choosing our election supervisor."

"You rock!"

"Sometimes," she said. "Can you picture the look on Her Highness's face when she finds out?" I sure could.

That afternoon, I went to the gym. "Who told the Drektors about the election monitor?" I asked the Oracle. "Think it was the Bulldog?"

"No," she said. "It was Tokyo Rosenberg. Why was she at your meeting?"

"She's Joanna's friend."

"You've got to be really careful. From now on, only trust your inner circle."

"Does that include the Fab Five?"

"Your inner circle," said the Oracle. "Think about who that is."

"Did we blow it? Do we have a chance?" I asked.

"We can't tell you that. Just be careful whom you trust, and be aware."

"'We' means my spirit guides?" I got the Sphinx smile. "Thank you! I really appreciate it . . . . I'll figure it out."

"I know you will," said the Oracle.

I stayed on the treadmill for another two miles, thinking. Circle of Trust . . . I saw Sherlock, the Champion, Joanna, the Connector and Ceevil Engineer, and the other four board candidates—Paul Revere, the Panamanian Prince, Florence Nightingale, and yes, Harvard. Ten people.

I called Joanna, the Champion, and Sherlock—my inner, inner circle. "We gotta be super careful. From now on, beyond our Circle of Trust, we only share information on a need-to-know basis."

"Why?" each friend asked.

"Because the Oracle said so." They understood.

21

The Home Stretch

It was early October, and Sherlock called me after dinner.
"*¡Buenas tardes, Artista!*"

"*¡Guapísimo!*" I said. "*¿Todo bien?*" It was 9:00, and he was an early bird. "Isn't it past your bedtime?"

"I'm making an exception. *Oye*, I learned something interesting about the valet company." His complaints to the Manager fell on deaf ears. The Drektors kept using the valets for unpaid side jobs during their shifts. "You know who owns the company?" *Here we go.*

"Who?"

"The Mobster's bastard son."

"The Mobster's dead!"

"I know. This is why I tell you. Our valet contract ends December 31st. You have a Finance Committee meeting tomorrow, yes?"

"Yes. I'll bring it up. Thank you!"

"*No hay de que, Artista.*"

I strode into the Finance Committee meeting, resignation letter in hand. Either Her Highness apologized publicly, or I resigned.

She could ill afford blowback two months before the election. *My, how the tables have turned.*

"Good morning, everyone." She sat at the head of the conference table, her voice scratchy. *It must be the humility.* "Before you start your meeting, I . . . um . . . hmm-hmm." She cleared her throat. "I want to apologize for the way I spoke to Alice last month." She looked in my general direction. "I hope you'll continue as chair of the Committee. I . . . value . . ."—she looked me in the eye—". . . your contribution." *Bingo.*

The room was packed when she demeaned me. Now, only a handful of unit owners were present, but a deal was a deal. I swallowed my pride. "Thank you, and yes, I will."

"Good." She bolted to the door. "I'll let you get on with your meeting."

With Highness gone, only two Drektors were left—Board Treasurer Humpty Dumpty and Finance Committee Member Bulldog. Both had legitimate reasons to be in the room. *Maybe they heard what I said about the Sunshine Law.*

"Expenses are growing because the building is aging," said the Manager. "Let's be realistic. We may have to raise the budget again next year."

"Again?" I asked. "Hold on! Before we ask unit owners for *more* money, shouldn't we *try* to spend less?" I took out my exhibits. "I have some ideas."

"Go ahead." He opened his laptop, answering emails, not even pretending to care. *Isn't this your job?*

"We spend half a million annually for valet service," I said. "That contract expires at the end of this year, correct?"

The Manager stopped typing. No eye contact. "Correct."

"How do the other bids compare? Can we save money here?"

"What do you mean?" *What do I mean? Did he just ask me that?*

I took a deep breath. "It's Condoland's policy to get three bids before awarding contracts. That's how we get the best deal *and*," I leaned toward him, "avoid the perception of impropriety." No answer. *Enough!* I banged both hands on the table and willed him to look at me. "Manager!" He looked up. "Are you going to help us or not?" Every Committee member was staring at him.

"Thank you, Alice." Humpty Dumpty spoke rapidly. She was sitting next to me, nearer to the Manager. "I'll share that suggestion with the Bawd."

"I'd like to let the Manager answer my ques——"

"Thank you, Alice. You made yuh point!" said Humpty.

A unit owner I called Rage Man jumped up and yelled at the Manager. "We're not printing blank checks here! If you won't do your job, then quit!" He pointed toward me, turning to Humpty. "She made a good suggestion. Don't just share it, DO IT!" I appreciated the support, but I wanted nothing to do with him. Two years ago, *I* was on the receiving end. He shrieked at me in the gym, eyes bulging, for using a weight machine he intended to use next. When the Resistance got into full swing, he tried apologizing to me through Joanna. I told her to thank him but never invite him to a meeting. He was unstable.

Rage Man was frightening, but effective. The Drektors had ignored angry unit owners all year, but an outspoken, erratic owner like Rage Man put their power in peril. Humpty Dumpty bit her nails watching Rage Man take his seat.

An awful noise outside made us all look out the window. Two turkey vultures were hissing at each other over a dead squirrel. Humpty saw them, too. She swallowed. The Manager closed the blinds.

"What's your second idea, Alice?" she asked, her voice saccharine. *She just asked for my idea?* To get re-elected, the Drektors had to play nice. It was insincere and self-serving, yet this temporary civility was a welcome reprieve.

"It's to reduce what we spend on water restoration—assuming we continue to have floods." I answered, making eye contact around the table and then with the audience. "This year, we'll spend $600,000 on Water Pro. Maybe more."

"We have to dry the water, Alice, or we'll have mold," said the Bulldog.

Thanks, Captain Obvious! "Yes, I understand. I did some homework. We can *buy* the same fans Water Pro rents to us. According to this estimate, a fan costs $14,000." I passed copies around the table.

"I want to see that!" shouted Rage Man. Nobody told *him* to be quiet.

I handed the secretary a stack to pass to the rest of the room. "A friend of mine owns a water restoration company," I said. "He's done work here at Condoland. For a building our size, he thinks we need six fans. That's a one-time, $90,000 investment. We have to get two more estimates, but already, you can see it's a big savings."

"Lemme see that!" said Humpty Dumpty, grabbing the paper out of my hand. *There's a copy right in front of you.*

"This is interesting," said the Bulldog. "Thanks!"

"It's just a start," I said. "I'm sure we can find—we *have* to find—more savings, cuz we can't increase the maintenance again. A neighbor told me she can't afford to live here, and she can't sell her condo, either. Know why? Our maintenance fees are the highest in the area. She's trapped. We're *all* trapped. All this spending has actually *lowered* our property values!"

The Manager looked at Humpty Dumpty, who tapped her watch. *We see your hand signals!* "Thank you, Miss Miller," said the Manager. "I have another meeting. We're going to have to cut this short. Great ideas. Thanks, everybody!"

"Wait! When do we discuss next year's budget?" I asked. Each year, the Finance Committee worked with the Manager to propose an operating budget to the board for the coming year.

"Not sure," said the Manager. He grabbed his laptop and rushed to the door, pushing it open. "We'll let you know. Bye, everybody! See you next month!"

"He just leaves?" snarled Rage Man.

"It must be an urgent mattuh," said Humpty Dumpty. "Running a lawge propuhty's a 24/7 job." With a straight face, she added, "Without the Manuguh here, there's not much maw we can do today. Someone make a motion to adjourn." *Excuse me?* It was almost noon, and these folks ate early.

"I so move," said the Bulldog. *You phony!*

"Second," said Gassy. There was nothing I could do. By a four-to-three vote, we were adjourned.

The next week, I helped the Fab Five put their bios together. Once they submitted them to the Office, their candidacies would be official. These weren't the cutesy, I'm-your-neighbor-I-love-the-building-and-please-vote-for-me kind of bios. Each candidate presented credentials, priorities, and actionable strategies to deliver results. Sherlock translated everything to Spanish, and we printed one language on each side.

I worked on the Champion's bio last. We sat in front of her home office computer as she read the others. "The Drektors won't have anything close to these," she said.

I smiled. "Good. Tomorrow's October 11th. You sure you don't wanna submit them now?"

She shook her head. "We wait 'til the last minute. The longer we keep them guessing, the less time they have to copy us. You know the Manager will show them. Didn't you tell me Her Highness parks herself in his office?" I nodded.

"You have a point," I said. It was two months before the election. "Do you realize we've been at this for almost two years? Now that it's so close, it doesn't seem real."

"I know. But things are about to heat up."

"You ran before. What's next?"

She smiled. "Two glasses of wine."

We walked through the living room into the kitchen. Her apartment was modern and sleek. I prefer cozy and comfy—but it was right for her and her husband—and Cookie.

She poured two glasses, then took a thick stick out of a cabinet drawer. "Here, give this to him. He'll be your best friend."

I made a face from the smell. "What is this?"

"You don't want to know. Just give it to him." Cookie followed us back to the living room. He jumped up to grab it, returned to the floor and chewed voraciously. "It's puppy crack," said the Champion. "I give it to him when I need to concentrate. They're good for his teeth." Later, I learned it was dried bull penis.

"You were saying?" I asked.

". . . What's next: The Office mails the candidate bios and a ballot to each unit owner the first business day of November. That's when we'll start telling people about the Fab Five. Florence still hosting the open house?"

"Yep. When should it be?"

"The week before Thanksgiving, when the snowbirds return."

"OK. What else?"

She pulled her legs up sideways on the couch. "We need to organize. Who's calling whom? Do we go door-to-door? Collect ballots? It's legal if the owner designates one of us as proxy, but imagine the Drektors if we show up with a bag of ballots. They'll flip. Should out-of-towners mail their ballots to us? It's a lot of moving pieces."

I took a sip, thinking. "Let's get the Circle together and define roles. It'll be you, me, Sherlock, Joanna, the Connector and Ceevil Engineer, and the other four candidates. Nobody else."

"I agree," said the Champion.

"You around this weekend?"

"Yes."

"I'll find out what works for everyone." We chatted for a while. When I got up to go, Cookie followed me to the door. "Good-bye, Cookie Monster!" I said, squatting to pet him one more time. "I'll keep you posted."

Since the Oracle advised we circle the wagons, I conducted Resistance business in person or by phone. If I reached voicemail, I left a message asking for a callback, nothing more. It took a lot more time, but I left nothing to be overheard by the wrong people.

The Fab Five submitted their bios on October 15th at 4:59 p.m. Two days later, we met in Joanna's apartment. We had from noon to 1:45 p.m., because Paul Revere was shooting hoops with his grandsons at two sharp. On my way to the meeting, I shared an elevator with my neighbor, Gladys Kravitz. Though an ally, she was outside the Circle of Trust.

"Are you on your way to one of those secret meetings?" She

sounded like she'd inhaled helium. *"We represent the lollipop guild . . ."*

I smiled. "How are you, Gladys?"

"When you gonna share the whole plan?" I rode down to the lobby with her so she wouldn't see where I was going.

"Soon, Gladys. Nice to see you—and thanks again for your help with the petition." The doors opened and she got out. "Enjoy your Sunday. Oh, I forgot something!" I hit the "close door" button until the door shut. We couldn't be too careful.

I knocked on the Rivers' apartment door and the Champion let me in. Sherlock, Florence, and Harvard were in the living room. Sherlock wasn't wearing his cowboy hat. *We've made the cut!*

"Aaalice!" called a nasal Bronx voice from the kitchen. "How aw you, honey? Come in! Would you like cawfee?"

"Yes, please. Thanks!"

"Howdayou like it?"

"Milk and stevia, if you have it."

"Of caws we have it!" Joanna had one of the larger units— 2,500 square feet, with three bedrooms. Her dining room seated 12 and opened to the living room. Her furniture was big and comfortable. She had a corner unit with spectacular views. We could see the nearby towns on one end and the ocean at the other. Joanna was pouring at a coffee station set up in her dining room bar.

"I could have done that!" I said.

"Don't be silly."

"That's a beautiful bar. Oak?"

She nodded. "Thanks. We had it custom built. Edguh and I used to entertain a lot—when he felt bettuh. She pointed to an open area between the two rooms. "It's a perfect space. We used to dance. Anyway, let's change the subject. Heuh's yaw cawfee, honey." Joanna once told me I reminded her of one of her daughters. She was nothing like my mother, but she did feel like family.

"Thank you!" I kissed her cheek. "Where's Edgar?" I asked quietly.

"He's resting." I left it at that and joined the others in the living room. Ten minutes later, the full Circle was there.

"Let's toast to the Fab five!" I said, raising my mug as the others raised theirs. "Here's to a fair fight!"

"Heah, heah!" said Paul Revere.

"Speaking of fights," said Joanna, "what's the plan?"

"I have notes." I pulled a spiral notebook from my bag. "We do everything old school until the election. Nothing electronic. Agreed?" Everyone agreed. "Good. Today's topics are campaigning and voting. Connector, do you want to lead the grassroots campaign?"

She sat up, shoulders back, smiling. "I do. Yes!"

"Fantastic. This includes get-out-the-vote calls starting the first week in November—two weeks from now. We go door-to-door the week after Thanksgiving." I looked at the Champion. "Right?"

"Right."

"Done," said the Connector.

"Sherlock." I turned to him.

"*Sí, señorita.*" He saluted me, and I laughed.

"You have influence with the Latin owners in the building." He raised his eyebrows. "You know you do. You're the mayor!"

Sherlock smiled. "As mayor, do I get a salary?"

"No, but if we win, you won't get robbed!" The Champion gave me a look. "What? We're among friends!"

"I know," she said. "Just don't get in the habit of making aspersions. If you say the wrong thing to the wrong person, the Drektors could sue you."

Lawyer! "For telling the truth?" I asked.

Sherlock tapped me on the shoulder. "*Artista*, what are my orders?"

Many of the Spanish-speaking unit owners at Condoland turned to Sherlock for advice. At 150 units, it was a critical voting bloc. "When people ask you about the candidates, tell them about our slate of five. Ideally, they shouldn't vote for anyone else."

Sherlock nodded. "Consider it done," he said in English.

"What about Bulldog?" asked the Champion. She looked at the others. "He split with the Drektors, and he wants us to recommend him. He claims to support our priorities."

"Can we afford to?" I asked, scanning the group. "The more votes other candidates get, the more our five need to win."

"I stick with the five," said Sherlock. I smiled. Neither of us trusted the Bulldog.

"Can't argue," I said. "Sr. Holmez, would you coordinate with the Connector? You both have international contacts, and they may overlap."

"Yes," said the Connector. "We'll work together."

"Excuse me!" said Harvard.

You're not excused. "Yes?" I asked.

"I . . . can talk to the . . . veterans. I'm holding my annual Veterans Day dinner."

"That's a great idea." His, but still great. I glanced at my watch. It was 12:45. We had an hour. "Now let's talk campaigning."

The doorbell rang. "Did you invite someone else?" I asked Joanna.

"That's the Restaurant. I ordered food." She put one hand on her knee, pushing hard on the arm of her chair to stand up. "I don't have the patience to cook anymaw."

"We didn't expect food!" I said.

"Nevuh mind. I'm using up my minimum." Each unit owner had an annual Condoland Restaurant assessment. It was use it or lose it.

"Guys," I said, "maybe I'm paranoid, but let's move out of sight. Everyone knows we meet, and Her Highness grills the Restaurant employees. Better safe than sorry."

"Go into the kitchen!" said Joanna. "I'll tell him to put the food on the doyning room table. Go!" We crowded into the galley kitchen. I laughed silently, like my dad. I could hear the men breathing heavily. As ridiculous as we looked, this was fun!

Joanna spoke to the waiter. "Thank you. No, no, just leave it on the doyning room table. My friends aw coming to play cawds. Heuh, this is fuh you." The door shut.

"You can come out now!" said Joanna, laughing. "Theyuh's sandwiches, salads, fruit, and chocolate chip cookies. Come. Let's sit at the table and eat."

"Paul has a hard stop in 50 minutes," I said.

"Keep talking, Alice," said Paul Revere. "What else ya got?"

I opened my notebook. "You each give two-minute speeches on meet-the-candidates night in the Party Room. I'm happy to help you with 'em."

"Yes, please," said Paul.

"That would be great, Alice," said Florence Nightingale.

"You can proof it," said Harvard.

"Proofing costs extra!" His face cracked into a smile.

The Panamanian Prince was quiet, and I didn't push. Big ego. The Champion had my help whether she wanted it or not. "Oh, Florence, I almost forgot!" I said. "You still want the open house at your place?"

"I do!"

"Excellent. The Champion says the best time is the weekend before Thanksgiving, so the snowbirds are here."

"Fine with me," she said.

I talked while they ate. "Guys, it's super important we invite supporters only. Don't assume; try to probe before you mention the gathering. Tokyo Rosenberg asked to come to the last meeting, and she turned out to be a double agent. She's the one who snitched to the Drektors about our election monitor!" Joanna's face fell. I reached out to her. "You had no way of knowing. I just want everyone to be careful."

"Whaddayou suggest?" asked Joanna.

Someone's phone rang. *I know that ring tone. Peter covers that song . . . he thinks I'm his good friend . . . I wonder if he'll come to my gig.*

"Earth to Alice!" said the Champion.

"Sorry. Where were we?" I asked.

"Alice, may I?" asked Florence. I nodded. "The best way to learn how people feel is to ask for advice. You know, 'Which candidates do you like this year?' Say you need help deciding. If they're happy with the Drektors, don't invite them."

"Ees good," said Sherlock.

Joanna's doorbell rang again. "Dessert?" I asked, smiling. She wiped her palms on her pants, uncomfortable. My smile faded. "Who is that?"

"Somebody wants to apologize to you. Face to face," said Joanna.

"No way." Rage Man was the kind of guy who could pull out a gun and shoot people. You can't fix bad people. I'd always avoided them. It's why I left BFC. I searched for a place to hide.

"Alice," said Joanna. "Listen to me!" I looked up. "He's sorry about what he said in the gym. I tawked to him. He's not just saying it. He means it."

"He means it *today*. Right now," I said. "He's erratic. He goes off on people. I don't want anything to do with him!" My underarms were wet.

Joanna grabbed my shoulders. "Listen 'ta me!" Her voice was firm. "You can't live yah life being afraid o' people. Don't give him that powuh ovuh you!" *I never thought of it that way.* "This is about all of us. He's on aw side, and we need him. He gets the unit ownuhs riled up, and right now, that's a good thing. *¿Comprendes?*" She smiled at Sherlock. He was standing next to me, my bodyguard. *I'm with my friends. What's this guy gonna do to me?*

Rage Man knocked on the door. "One minute. Coming!" Joanna said to the door, then turned back to me. "Alice, you gotta let it go. People screw up!" She stood back, looking me over. "You think yaw poyfect? Everyone deserves a second chance." Her comment struck a nerve. I thought of those goddamned Italian love letters in my mother's closet. *Why did Joanna say that? Am I judgmental?* "Do you heuh me?"

"I hear you." I took a deep breath. My heartbeat slowed. "It's all right. Let him in."

Rage Man entered our Circle of Trust. "Hello, everybody," he said, face flushed, his hands interlocked in front of him. "You people are doin' great work. I want you to know . . . I'm here to help."

"We need all the help we can get," said Joanna.

Rage Man stepped toward me and stopped, keeping a respectful distance. "Alice, I really admire the work you've been doing on the Finance Committee."

"That's nice of you to say."

"No, seriously. You're asking the right questions, and you're coming up with good ideas. I—I—I'm sorry I blew up at you that day in the gym. It had nothing to do with the machine or even with you." He looked at his feet. "My daughter was diagnosed with MS." *Oy. Now I'm the asshole. You never considered that something might be going on with him, did you?* "I'm not good at handling my emotions. That's what my wife tells me." He flashed an apologetic smile. "Will you forgive me?"

I held out my hand and shook his. "Consider it ancient history. I hope your daughter is doing all right, and I really appreciate your coming here today. We can use your help when the campaigning starts." A weight lifted. No need to avoid him anymore.

"Just say the word," said Rage Man. "Bye everybody!" He waved.

"Thanks fah coming!" said Paul Revere.

"I'll walk you out," said Joanna. She came over to me after he left. "Ya did good, kid!" I gave her a hug, then looked at my watch. It was 1:15. "Guys, we have 30 minutes left. We have to talk about the ballots."

"This'll be quick," said the Champion. "Here's our golden rule: Assume the Drektors will change or add votes if we give them the chance."

"That's terrible!" said Paul.

"I like to plan for the worst and hope for the best," said the Champion.

"So, what we do?" asked Sherlock.

The Champion turned to him. "We ask unit owners to hold on to their ballots until the day of the election, then drop them in the ballot box—in front of the monitor—on election night."

"What about eenternational owners who won't be here?" asked the Connector. "If they vote, they usually mail their ballots to the Office."

"Assume the Office will change their votes," said the Champion.

"And when they do, how will we know?"

"You really are skeptical," I said.

"Twenty-five years practicing law, my friend. I've seen it all."

"I get it. Better safe than sorry. So, how? Should they mail their ballots to her?" I pointed to the Connector.

"I think so," said the Champion. "Along with their proxies."

"I'll explain to them," said the Connector. "Ees OK."

"And the people in the building," I said, "what if they can't be here on election night?"

"Then they give their ballot to one of us," said the Champion. "We can't vote in advance. Period," said the Champion.

"Ahrighty then!" said Paul. "Fahgive me; I gotta meet my grand-sons."

"Of course," I said. "I think we've covered everything. We're good until the first week of November, when the ballots go out."

"I love the team effuht," said Paul. "See yuh latah!"

See you later, Alligator! I looked around the room. How unlikely it was that we found each other, liked each other, and were working together. We were equally determined to succeed. I knew my father was watching. I wouldn't let him down.

22

Letting Go

J oanna was right. People *do* screw up, including me. I wrestled with resenting my mother, realizing my own hypocrisy. El Innombrable was separated when I first met him; swore he was nearly divorced. I heard what I wanted to hear. It's just a technicality, right? The relationship was long over—except it wasn't—not legally, anyway. I should have waited until the papers were signed. It was my guilty secret. I loved him, and we weren't hurting anybody, right?

When I was a little girl, my mom told me our feelings aren't good or bad, they're just our feelings; it's our actions that count. She loved the Italian who wrote those letters, but she didn't sleep with him. She kept that love a secret to protect her family. In choosing *us,* she buried a part of herself. That took strength—more strength than I'd had.

Do I call her? But what do I say? She already knew I preferred my father. Was I going to hold her imperfections against her for the rest of her life? Who would that make *me? "Family is everything, sweet-haht. Remembah that."* My mom was my closet living relative, and

243

breaking through this impasse was up to me. Before I could talk myself out of it, I dialed.

"Hi, sweetie," she said.

"Hi, Mommy. You sound sad."

"The house is so empty . . . but I'm looking forward to Thanksgiving," she said. "It's my first trip since . . ." She lost control. *Since when does she get emotional?* The Oracle said my mother was struggling with guilt. Her grief was complicated.

"I'm looking forward to it, too! But that's not why I called."

"Oh?" she asked, snapping out of it.

Just say it. "I need to apologize to you."

"Really?" she said. "Why's that?"

"People who live in glass houses shouldn't throw stones. I've been angry with you since I found those letters, and looking back as an adult, I don't think it was fair." There was a long silence. "Are you there?"

I heard her exhale. "Yes," she said.

"Mommy, *I've* made mistakes, too, and I can't hold you to a standard to which I didn't hold myself—even if you are my mother."

"I'm glad to hear it," she said. "I know those letters hurt you. I'm not going to justify them. I loved your father . . . yet it's possible to love more than one person. But I married your father, and I don't regret that choice." I didn't respond. I wanted to mend our differences. "Life is so short," she continued. "I want to enjoy the time we have together."

"I do, too. We'll have fun when you come to Florida next month. Wanna take a cruise to the Bahamas?"

"Oh, I'd love that!" she said.

"Good! I'll book it. I love you, Mommy."

"I love you, too, sweetheart—so much." When she called me

"sweetheart," I knew my father was there. *Thank you for your wisdom, Daddy.*

My resentment didn't magically disappear after that phone call, but I decided not to dwell on it, and so did she. She was never going to be the mother I wanted her to be. I wasn't the daughter she wanted, either. I was too much like my father. But anger was a poison, and I needed to flush it from my system. To love and be loved, I had to accept—and forgive. Maybe one day, someone would do the same for me. I let go.

23

Tuning

The day of my Music Box gig started with Alka-Seltzer. All my Florida friends were coming, and the possibilities of screwing up in front of them were *endless*. For the past month, I practiced two solid hours a day, but no amount of practice would ever be enough. I was raised by a mother who demanded perfection, and that pressure was too ingrained to disappear after one conversation. When I performed, the sword of Damocles hung over my head.

After "breakfast," the Champion went through my closet and helped me pick an outfit—a black, sleeveless A-line dress, mid-length. Then I jewelry shopped in her apartment. She suggested the real stuff; I went with costume. If I lost or broke it, at least I could afford to replace it.

Around noon, I went to the gym to work off some steam and see what the Oracle had to say.

"Peter Pan will be there," she told me. "He'll sit at the outer curve of the U-shaped bar, facing you."

"Have you been there?" I asked.

"No, but I'm going tonight, and I'll show you who I think he

246

is." She smiled. *Who you "think" he is? You know everything!*

"That's so nice of you!" I felt better knowing she'd be there. I managed two poached eggs in the afternoon. *At least my stomach is flat.*

I arrived at the Box 40 minutes early to set up and do the sound check. The piano player and drummer got there 10 minutes later. By 8 p.m., the room was full. My voice teacher was there, and my friends had a table in front of the stage. They smiled as we began. *So far, so good.*

Peter sat exactly where the Oracle predicted. I felt his eyes on me, but when I looked at him, he turned away. I told stories of the songs and songwriters, looking at my iPad more than I should have. I knew the material, but I was nervous. It was my security blanket.

I remember a man holding his wife's hand during "Embraceable You." Feet tapped to "Fascinating Rhythm." At some point, Peter Pan yodeled, "Woo-hoo! Go, Alice!" All in all, I thought it was . . . good enough.

My teacher approached me after the first set. "You exceeded my expectations," he said. *Ouch!* "I'm talking about showmanship, not your voice." *Fair enough.*

During the break, I went to each table and thanked people for coming. I saved the Oracle for last because I knew she'd tell me the truth in a way I could hear it. I sat across from her at a small, round table. "You sound good," she said. "Now, don't make faces."

"I'm making faces?"

"Alice—"

"OK, maybe I make faces."

"Nobody knows there's a mistake unless you tell them!"

"What if I'm off-key?"

"Let it go. Have fun. If you're enjoying yourself, so will the audience. Understand?"

I nodded. "Thanks." I scrunched my face remembering how I'd scrunched my face.

"Let's talk about Peter Pan," she said. "He's sitting over there, right?" She leaned her head toward the exact place she said he'd be, facing the stage.

"Damn!"

She laughed and flicked back her dreadlock ponytail. "He asked people on either side of him, 'Isn't she great? Doesn't she have a beautiful voice?'"

"He did?"

"Yes, ma'am! He's loud. It's hard not to hear him."

Peter Pan was ambling our way. "Hmm-hmm," I said.

The Oracle whispered, "He wants to invite you somewhere. Say yes!" She tapped my arm. "I loved 'Someone to Watch Over Me.' I think that's my favorite song from this set."

"Thanks! I love that song, too."

I felt strong hands on my shoulders. "Nice job, Alice!" The Oracle raised her eyebrows when she heard his voice. It was like hot cocoa with a shot of brandy.

"Thank you. I appreciate your coming!" I introduced him to the Oracle.

"Hi, there," said Peter.

"Have a seat," I said.

"How ya doing?"

"I'm nervous. I haven't sung on a stage since school. It's weird to have everyone focus on me."

"Well, you sound great. Just one thing . . ." He hesitated.

"Tell me."

"You're looking at your iPad." When Peter performed, I noticed he memorized everything cold. It gave him freedom to have fun with his audience.

"I know." I leaned toward him, my arms folded at my waist. "I'm *nervous!*" Speaking at a business conference or to unit owners was easy because it wasn't about me, but singing was personal, like reading my diary out loud.

"Don't worry about it. The more you sing, the easier it'll be."

"Thanks." *Maybe the Oracle was right. Something about him—his warmth—felt . . . familiar.* I saw the clock on the wall behind him. "Oh! I gotta get back on stage!" His sleeves were pushed back. I touched his forearm. "I'm so glad you came."

The piano player was outside smoking and talking to the drummer. I opened the door. "Guys, it's time." The pianist took a few more puffs and threw the butt on the sidewalk, grinding it out with his heel. They grabbed beers before coming onstage. Musicians drove me crazy. I never drank until the gig was over. I was hired to perform, not get drunk. I showed up on time and gave it my best. *How can they be so unprofessional?*

The second set went faster than the first. I was elated when it was over. *I did it!* Now that the pressure was off, I could enjoy myself. My friends came over.

"Who's that guy?"

"Which one?" *I know which one.*

"The guy you were talking to." *Too soon. Keep it to yourself.*

"Oh. He's a regular here," I said.

"Sister, those eyes! He is *cute!*"

"Yep."

"And?"

"I don't know. We're friends."

"He's watching you!" I smiled. Didn't want to get my hopes up.

"Work on that!"

"We'll see. Thanks so much for coming, you guys!"

I felt "those eyes" on me again as I gathered my equipment. Peter left his seat at the bar to help me put a 25-pound monitor in its box.

"Don't worry about the iPad," he said, picking up where we left off. "You did a great job."

The chemistry was undeniable. "Thanks again for coming."

"I wouldna missed it! Listen, I have a gig next month—Thanksgiving weekend. Can you be there?"

"He wants to invite you somewhere. Say yes!" Thank you, Oracle! "Sure. Which day?"

"I'll text you." He kissed my cheek. The Box owner leaned over the counter, watching. I thanked her for booking me. Peter left, and the drummer helped me load the monitor into my trunk.

"When you need a drummer, please keep me in mind."

"I definitely will. Thanks!"

My mind raced all the way home. Whatever this was with Peter, I wasn't imagining it. "Something's Coming" from *West Side Story* played in my head.

The phone woke me up on Saturday morning.

"Is this the star?" asked the Champion.

"What time is it?"

"Were you sleeping? It's 11:30, missy! I've been up since 7:00."

"That's cuz you have to walk Cookie. I couldn't fall asleep," I told her. "I had to unwind." The Champion came to my gig, but she left after the first set. She was a morning person.

"I'll give you a pass *this* time! What are you doing today?"

I stretched, cracking the bones in my neck. "I'm relaxing."

"Do you have a minute? I have news."

"What?"

"The Bulldog called."

"And?"

"He doesn't want to align with us anymore."

I'm shocked! Shocked, I say! "He's running with the Drektors?" I asked.

"He wants to run independently."

He's hedging his bets. "Even better!" I rolled out of bed and put her on mute while I went to the bathroom, then shuffled to the kitchen. "I never trusted him."

"I know," she said. "And you were right. Anyway, I agree, it's for the best. He hopes we'll recommend him if anyone asks, even if he's not part of our slate."

Not gonna happen. "Why should we?" I asked. "He's playing both sides!" I spooned coffee into the brewer and flipped the switch to "On." "I'm committed to the Fab Five. If anyone brings *him* up, I'll let them know he won't denounce the Drektors."

"I get it. So, you're relaxing today."

"Why?" I asked.

"The Office put out the candidate list. Can we discuss it tomorrow?"

"Today's good," I said. Now that the gig was over, I felt liberated. "Want me to invite Joanna and Sherlock?" The four of us formed an innermost circle within the Circle of Trust. We were family.

"I'll do it. You take it easy."

"Thanks." It was ages since I read a book, and a best seller was beckoning on my nightstand.

We met at 4 p.m. at the Champion's apartment. "Hi, everybody!"

said the Champion. "Come in. Alice'll be here any minute."

"I'm here!" I was squatting behind the others. Cookie ran out of the apartment and kissed my face. "Hi, Cookie Monster!" I stood up. "First the dog, then the humans."

"You're nuts," said the Champion. "But that's why we love ya! Come in."

"Here's your jewelry," I said. "Thank you."

"Sure. Any time you want it, you know where it is." *When we first met, she didn't trust me with her dog.*

We sat on her deep, curved sofa. A bowl of almonds and cashews sat on the table with cocktail napkins. To drink, there was white wine or water. The Champion was an amazing cook when so inclined, but those inclinations were few and far between. Like many Jewish women I knew, she preferred making reservations. She kept so little food in her fridge that I used it for storage when I entertained.

"So, let's see the list!" said Joanna. The Champion gave us each a copy.

"It's better than I expected," said the Champion. "Just the Drektors and our five."

"Wait, the Corpse is running?" I asked. "Didn't he just have a heart attack?"

"He's breathing," said the Champion, "and even *less* likely to ask questions." I shook my head.

"You sure about Harvard?" I asked. "I know he's trying, but—"

"I can handle him," said the Champion. "He doesn't bother me the way he does you."

"Yet," I said. "He doesn't bother you *yet!*"

"He gawt kicked off bawds at two othuh buildings!" said Joanna.

"You're kidding!" I said.

"Noope," said Joanna.

"Where'd you hear that?" asked the Champion.

"My friend lives in one of the buildings. He was such a pain in the ass, they asked him to resoyn."

"Can they do that?" I asked.

"I dunno, but they did," said Joanna. "That know-it-all bullshit o' his drove them craaazy. He's lucky nobody hurt 'im. My friend says he got kicked off the bawd at his *next* building, too. That's why he came heuh."

I gave the Champion an I-told-you-so look. "I hear you," she said, "but he's the least of our problems. I'm telling you, I can handle him." I shook my head. "Besides, what's the alternative? There are five directors. Who do you want to fill the other two slots? The Drektors?"

"You have a point," I said.

"Alice, we gotta work with what we've got," said the Champion. "These are the candidates—unless *you* want to run."

Touché. I shook my head. *I'm not running. The Finance Committee is more than enough for me.* "Maybe this isn't so bad," I said. "There are 10 candidates, and five of them are new. If by some miracle a majority of unit owners votes for the *new* candidates, we'll get rid of the Drektors!"

"Exactly," said the Champion. "It's a long shot, but not impossible."

"Huh," said Joanna, slowly nodding her head. "So whadda we do?"

"I need a bio break. Would you excuse me?" I asked.

"Sure," said the Champion. She walked toward the kitchen. "Anyone want more wine?"

"*Sí, por favor,*" said Sherlock.

His wife worried he drank too much. As I walked away, I placed my index and middle fingers under my eyes, pointed them at Sherlock, and back to my face. "I'm watching you!"

"I in prison," he told the others. "Shilah and Alice ees the wardens!"

"That's right!" When I left the bathroom, Cookie was sitting on the door sill, waiting for me. I picked him up and we sat together on the sofa. "So where were we?"

"I'm waiting to heuh the plan," said Joanna.

"*I* think we tell people to vote against the Drektors. Period," said the Champion. "We have five new candidates, and our message is 'change.'"

"We'd *like* a full change, but we *need* a voting majority. I think *that's* the priority," I said.

"What do you suggest?" asked the Champion.

Cookie started fidgeting, wanting off my lap. I grabbed a tennis ball from the floor and threw it against the front door. He jumped off the couch and ran after it. "We ask people to vote for our five, but if they like some of the Drektors, we don't argue with them. We ask them to read the bios carefully and come to the open house to ask questions. We emphasize that if we don't elect at least three new directors, we can expect more of the same—higher maintenance fees and lower property values." Cookie brought the ball back to me, and I threw it again. "Make sense?" I asked.

"It does," said the Champion.

"And you guys?" I asked. They nodded. "Then that's that. What else?"

"One more thing," said the Champion. "The Drektors play dirty—"

"Of caws!" said Joanna.

"And?" I asked.

"And no matter what they do—even if it means losing . . ." said the Champion. *We won't lose. We can't.* I heard my father's voice again. *Failyah is not an option!* "Alice, are you with us?"

"Yes." I shrugged it off. Memories of him came in waves. I forced myself to focus.

"No matter what they do," said the Champion, "no matter what the Office does, we're going to run this campaign by the book. Agreed?" We did. "Let's toast."

"To honesty!" I said.

We clicked our glasses. "To honesty!"

24

Campaigning

F ive weeks before the election, the Office issued our election packets, and our campaign began in earnest. The Connector asked me to arrange a meeting with Condoland's influencers, aka the "popular people." We needed their help to get out the vote. Florence held the meeting in her apartment. She grew on people, and we wanted to maximize her exposure.

I called Joanna. "Hi, honey. How aw you? What's doin'?"

"I'm great. I'm calling about the meeting at Florence's."

"I'll be thayuh. Can I help with anything?" she asked.

"Yes. We need volunteers to contact people before the election. I was wonder—"

"You want me to invite my friends?" Between her husband's time on the board and her canasta game, Joanna knew everybody.

"You read my mind!"

"Yeah? Maybe I'm an oracle, too!"

"OK, then. Who you gonna invite?" I asked.

"You want people on our side who know lots of othuh people, right?"

256

"Exactly. How'd you know?"

"Street smarts, honey. See you Sunday!"

I got to Florence's a few minutes early. "How can I help?" I asked.

"Everything's ready—I hope." She seemed uneasy. She picked up her beagle. "I'm putting Lucy in my husband's office. I don't want her barking at the guests."

I followed them into the office to pet Lucy before the door shut. "How are you feeling about today?"

She looked at her shoes. "I'm trying not to think about it."

"Florence!" She looked up. "These ladies are nice. I promise! They want to replace the Drektors as much as we do." She cracked her knuckles. "They're guests in your home. It'll be fine! They're gonna love you." Florence's big brown eyes were moist. "Just be yourself. What's not to like?" She didn't answer. "Right?"

She nodded slightly. "Right." *Whoever did a job on her, I'd like to have a word.* The doorbell rang. "I forgot the bagels!" She scurried away from the door.

Oh, no you don't! "*You* answer it. *I'll* get the bagels."

"OK." She turned and marched to the front door, then stopped. She took a deep breath, held it, exhaled slowly, then threw the door wide open. "Hi, everyone! Welcome!" she squealed with her small voice and big smile.

"Here come the yentas!" said Joanna, bursting in with five of her friends. These were the ladies who lunch.

"Oh, Florence, what a nice apartment!" said a yenta, brushing by her.

"Yeah, look at these views!" said another. Like Joanna, Florence had a three-bedroom, one of the larger apartments in Condoland. She joined the women in the living room.

"So, what does yuh husband do?" asked a yenta, fingering her diamond necklace.

Florence hunched her shoulders. "He's a coroner."

"You mean he looks at dead people?" asked a yenta. Florence nodded, biting her lip. *Uh-oh.*

"Is that a doctuh?" asked an excited bleached blond. *That's it . . .*

"Ooh, a doctuh! Where's he practice?" asked another.

Florence's smile returned. "At Famous Hospital."

"Really!"

"Very niiice!"

"Florence is a therapist," I said. "She has a PhD from FU—Fancy University."

"Is that where you met yaw husband?" *Deep breaths. Deeeep breaths.*

"It is."

The women nodded in approval. They blew by her achievements, but Florence didn't care. She'd passed inspection! She relaxed her shoulders and looked over at me. I was arranging a platter with bagels, lox, cream cheese, and capers in the dining room. I nodded and gave her a reassuring smile.

The doorbell rang again. This time, she ran to open the door. It was the Connector. "Am I late?" she asked.

"Not at all," I said. "Your timing is perfect. Shall we begin?"

We sat around the dining room table. While the yentas *noshed*,[22] Florence went to the kitchen. She returned wheeling a tea cart. "Ladies, here's coffee, water, and orange juice if anyone would like some. What may I get for you?" She asked the yenta closest to her.

"Sit down with us," said the woman. She was Joanna's decorator—the legitimate kind. "Anyone who wants a beverage can help

---

[22] Nosh — Yiddish for eating enthusiastically

herself." *I didn't see that coming.*

"Oh, all right," said Florence softly. She took the empty seat next to me.

The Connector pulled a thick folder from her briefcase and gave us packets of stapled papers. "Good morning, everyone," she said, slowly. "You each have a leest with uneet owner names and phone numbers. Half the people leeve here fool time."

The women looked puzzled. I translated. "She's giving each of us a list of unit owners' names and numbers. Half the people live here full-time."

"Thank you, Alice." The Connector blushed.

"I wish we spoke Spanish like you speak English!" said a yenta with reading glasses hanging from a gold chain around her neck. *Nice.*

"How do we reach the out-of-towners?" asked Joanna.

"I'll get to that," said the Connector. She was a linear thinker. "We start by calling people on our floors. Don't call anyone you think ees a Drektor supporter." The women listened as they ate, growing accustomed to her accent.

Lucy whined from behind the office door. Seconds later, a trim, gray-haired man in a suit with tortoise shell glasses walked into the apartment and saw nine women sitting at his dining room table.

"Hi, honey." Florence jumped up and kissed his cheek. "We're working on the campaign." She motioned to us. "These ladies are going to dial for votes."

"Hello, Dr. Nightingale!" said a brunette.

"Thanks for having us!" said the bleached blond.

He forced a wan smile. "Carry on." He strode to his office, and Lucy stopped barking. A few moments later, he walked out wearing jeans and a golf shirt with Lucy on her leash, pulling him to leave. "Ladies," he nodded.

"He's a bit of an introvert," explained Florence after the door shut.

"But handsome!"

"I read introverts have very high IQs."

"That's right!" Among Jewish women of a certain age, a doctor could do no wrong.

"Where were we?" I asked.

"The leest," said the Connector. "Now we decide who ees calling . . . whom." She looked at me after saying "whom." It was a question. Her choice was correct, and I nodded. *She must have a language headache. I know I would.* She turned to Florence. "You won't call. Seence you are a candidate, eet ees more conveencing that your neighbors recommend you." Florence seemed relieved.

The list included a dossier on each owner, providing all addresses and phone numbers for owners with multiple residences. Condos owned by a business—it was a popular tax shelter—were indicated along with the names of voting agents.

"Were you in politics?" I asked.

Her eyes flashed with surprise. "Sometheeng like that. A long time ago." *CIA?*

As we went through the names, she skipped over apartments. "Should we go in order?" I asked. "We're missing people."

"Don't worry," said the Connector. "Those owners leeve in Europe or South America. Sherlock or I weel call them."

"Fine by me," said a yenta. She turned to a friend. "I wonder if we need maw helpuhs."

"I was thinking the same thing," said the friend. *Don't wanna miss Wheel of Fortune?*

We finished lunch and moved into the living room to discuss our message. The front door opened, and Dr. Nightingale returned carrying a panting Lucy. "Still here," he observed.

"Can Lucy sit with us?" I asked.

"Sure." He put her down, removing her leash. "Please excuse me, I've got case notes to review."

"Of caws!" said a yenta as his office door shut behind him.

I held out my arms, and Lucy came to me.

"You spoke with the Champion, yes?" the Connector asked me.

"Yes." Throughout this campaign, people came to me with questions they were afraid to ask the Champion directly. It happened so often, I began calling myself Tell-the-Champion. Just using her name in a sentence gave it gravitas. "The *Champion* says we start by explaining why we need a change in leadership. Then, we emphasize the Fab Five and invite everyone to the open house here in two weeks."

"What about the ballots?" asked the Connector.

"Getting there—"

"I gotta cawl Margie," the blond said to the decorator, fishing her phone from her Fendi bag. "Maybe she'll split the list with me."

"Who's Margie?" I asked Joanna.

"Who?" She was a little hard of hearing.

"MAR-GIE!"

"Mawgie?" I nodded. "She's a blabbuhmouth. Why?" I pointed to the dialing blond.

"Hi, Mawgie" said the blond. "I'm here at this—"

"Gimme that!" Joanna grabbed the phone. "Mawgie? How ya doin'? It's Joanna . . . Yeuh, I'm tawking on huh phone . . . we had lunch." *Technically true.* "How's Harry? . . . Oy. So . . . aw you playing cawds on Tuesday? . . . Good. I won't keep you . . . Tell

Harry to lay off the cawned beef. Bye, doll."

"Whadja do that for?" asked the blond.

"Cuz she's gawt a big mouth! Listen, girls, NO ONE can know what we're doin' heuh. Unduhstand?" Joanna wasn't making the Tokyo Rosenberg mistake twice. "Swear on yaw CHILDREN, nothing leaves this room!"

"What about my husband?" said the brunette. "He gets jealous when I'm on the phone. He'll ask who I'm tawkin' to."

"Just yaw husbands—but tell them it's confidential," said Joanna. "Now swear ta me!" She stared down each of them until they took her oath. "Glad that's settled. We're too close to blow it now." She looked at me. "Excuse the intuhrruption. Where were we?"

"I forgot," I said.

"I asked about the ballots," said the Connector, ignoring the amateurs.

"That's right. Thanks," I said. "The *Champion* says we offer to walk people through the ballot to make sure they check the right boxes." *One hanging chad incident in Florida is more than enough.* "Stress that we need a totally new board. If they like any of the Drektors, don't argue. Tell them to come to the open house. Say they owe it to themselves to make an informed choice. Say without a change in control, we can expect higher maintenance fees and lower property values. Make sense?"

"Yep."

"Got it."

Normally, I would never socialize with these women, but we were united by an urgent goal. As the meeting went on, they grew on me.

"Last thing," I said, putting Lucy down. "This is super important: No one brings a ballot to the Office. They can bring it to the Party Room on election night, or they can list you as their proxy, and you'll bring it. Any questions?"

"It's cleeuh," said Joanna. "Change in leaduhship, Fab Five, open house, explain how to vote, don't bring ballots to the Office, and," she glared at her friends, "we keep aw fuckin' mouths shut!" They nodded. Joanna turned to me. "We got this."

"When can we start?" asked the woman with the diamond necklace.

"As soon as we feenish here," said the Connector.

"It's a good plan," said diamond necklace, cracking her knuckles. "I'm gonna enjoy this. And don't worry," she said to Joanna. "We won't tell a soul."

"Anything else?" I asked.

"No," said the Connector. "Let's get to work!"

"Ladies," said the decorator, "let's clean up before we leave." The women brought everything on the dining room table into the kitchen.

"No, no!" said Florence, racing past them before a dairy dish touched the meat section of her divided sink. It's a kosher sink!"

"I know. I got it," said glasses yenta. "I grew up with a double sink." She turned to the blond yenta holding a dish cloth. "Leave the dried dishes on the kitchen table so Florence can put 'em in the right place."

Joanna saw the surprise on my face. "Whadja think, they'd be assholes?" *Yes!*

On the way out, brunette yenta pulled Florence aside. "My daughtuh's interested in the psychiatric program at Fancy. Would you tawk to huh?"

"Of course!" said Florence. As I was leaving, she grabbed my hands. "Thank you, Alice. I couldn't have done this without you."

"Yes, you could," I said. "You rehabilitate schizophrenics! You can do *anything,* Florence! You'll knock 'em dead at the open house—you'll see."

She smiled. "I hope these ladies can get out the vote."

"If *anybody* can do it," I said, "they can."

I started calling Monday afternoon. Mostly, I reached voicemail. This was going to take time. The conversations I did have were straightforward, except for the unit owner at the end of my hall.

"May I speak with Mrs. X?" I asked.

"She's not able to come to the phone. Who's calling?"

"This is Alice. I'm her neighbor. I'm calling about the board election next month. It's important I speak with her. When would it—"

"Hi, Alice. I'm her grandson. This is not a good time. She's not well."

"I'm so sorry to hear that. It's just, we need everyone to vote. Maybe you can help her. I'll tell you which candidates to—"

"The hospice nurse is visiting. Like I said, it's not a good time."

"It'll be super quick. Voting will protect your property value—"

"Alice, she's dying!"

"I'm so sorry." But I couldn't stop. "It's just, this election *is really* important! Did she get a ballot? If you help her pick the candidates, she could just sign the—" *Did he just hang up on me?* I put the phone down and stared at the wall.

I had the same interruptions when my dad was passing. *How could I be so insensitive?* The election was consuming me, and I wasn't thinking straight. When I first started working at BFC, the same thing happened. I kept late hours. We all did. It was an unspoken competition. One night, I was stuck on a marketing plan when my dad called. It was 9 p.m.

"Go home and get yah mind off it," he'd said. "The answah will come to you in the mahning. Remembah, yah careeah is not a sprint; it's a marathon." I took his advice, and the next day, the solution was obvious.

Heeding that advice again, I went for a walk, then showered and went to the Music Box. Condoland could wait until the morning.

The next two weeks flew by. The day of the open house, we had no idea how many people would show. Every vote was critical. I prayed for a big turnout.

Joanna, the Champion, and I offered to bring refreshments, but Florence politely insisted on handling them herself. She was Modern Orthodox, and none of us were kosher. She did, however, let me replenish the hors d'oeuvres and clean up during the meeting.

The event ran from 2:00 to 5:00 p.m. At 2:30, we had 15 people. *Respectable.* By 3:00, there were 30 people—hungry, thirsty people, judging by the wine cups I tossed and the hermit cookies and whitefish salad trays I replaced. *If we feed them, they will come!* Unit owners continued to arrive. They crowded around each candidate, which told me they were serious about the election. By 3:30 p.m., there were so many prospective voters in Florence's apartment, I struggled to reach the door to take out the garbage. *This is worse than a New York sidewalk.* Someone tapped me on the shoulder.

"Aaalice!" That pinched, nasal voice scratched like nails on a chalkboard.

"Hi, Gladys."

"It's about time you people let us in!" said Mrs. Kravitz.

"I'm glad you're here."

"So am I," she said. *Do you not see the 20 pounds of garbage I'm holding?* I tried to edge toward the door, but she wasn't finished. "Ya know, I've been hearing things, and I hope they're not true. It's good so many people came today."

I stopped moving and turned to her, ignoring my arms. "What did you hear?"

"A lot of stuff."

"For example?"

"Well, that Paul wants to make the gym kids-only on Sunday mornings. That's when he's there with his grandsons. Oh, and the Champion's stuffing the ballot box . . . the Panamanian Prince wants to shut down the Restaurant, and——"

"Who's saying these things?" I put the garbage down, guarding it so nobody stepped on the bag.

"I think it's people on the board . . ."

"The Drektors?" I asked. She nodded. "Gladys, you're a smart lady." She looked startled. No one had accused her of being smart before. "You don't even *like* the Drektors. Do you think they might want to make their competition look bad?"

Her job dropped, and she inhaled quickly. "I'm so confused. How do we know what's true and what isn't? What if your candidates are just as bad as the Drektors?"

"That's why they're here. Why don't you ask them?"

She nodded. "Thanks, Alice."

I yelled to her as she shuffled toward Paul Revere. "Gladys!"

She turned around. "Yeah?"

"When you leave, tell your friends the truth!"

"I will. Don't worry. Now take out that garbage!"

First I had to find the Champion. "Why are you carrying that around?" she asked.

"I'm trying to take it to the trash room. Listen, the Drektors are lying about you and the other candidates!"

"Are you surprised?"

"Yes! Well, maybe not, but the point is they're sabotaging us. We have to do something!"

"What do you want to do?" She scanned the room. "Look at this crowd. These unit owners came to find out for themselves." She was right. "The Drektors play dirty. I know that, and you know that. It's why we're having the open house." A plastic fork poked through the bag. "Speaking of dirty, my advice to you is to get to the trash room ASAP!"

"Oh, shit. Thanks." I placed my hand around the burgeoning hole and squeezed through the packed hallway. I turned the dead-bolt to keep the door open for my return. Nobody would hear the bell ring with this noise. My arms were killing me, and the bag obstructed my view as I walked down the hall.

"Careful! Coming through!" I heard a Long Island accent and a forced laugh. *What's Lothario doing on this floor?*

"Hello," I said, looking at the designer sneakers in front of me.

"Need any help?" He took the bag and carried it to the trash room. "Do you live on this flaw?" *He's asking ME?*

"No, I'm visiting friends."

"Oh, reeeally? I heard there's an open house on this flaw. You mean *those* friends?"

You really have no shame, do you? Alice, don't antagonize him. "Yes."

We reached the trash room. "Would you open the daw?" he said. I did, and he dropped the garbage down the chute. Lothario was six foot two and big. *How can I tell him where he's allowed to go? But if he walks in, he'll ruin it!* A childhood memory flashed in my head.

When I was seven, my mom had to pick me up from the

babysitter at 6 p.m. *sharp*. One rainy day, she ran out of her office and got to the bus stop with a minute to spare. As the 5:30 p.m. bus drove around the corner, she stood near the curb waiting for the door to open. The driver didn't stop. She ran after him, catching up to him at a red light. She banged on the door. He shook his head no. The light stayed red, so she ran to the front of the bus, stood with her legs apart and her arms raised, briefcase in one hand, umbrella in the other. A court photographer recognized her and snapped a photo. It appeared on the front of the *Boston Herald*'s metro section the next day: "Lady Lawyer Stops Bus!" She was horrified by the publicity, but she did pick me up on time.

I sped ahead to Florence's door, turned around, and faced the Long Island Lothario with both hands outstretched. "Mr. Lothario, I'm sorry, but this is a private party, and you are not on the guest list."

He stepped back as if I'd stabbed him in the gut. I saw him recalculating. Making a scene would not work in his favor. "*Oh, is this 709?*" he asked. "I'm looking for 609. I must have gotten off on the wrong flaw!" He slinked away toward the elevator. I opened the door feeling like David defeating Goliath.

25

Getting Close

The week of Thanksgiving, my mom and I took a three-day cruise to the Caribbean. The change of scenery gave us neutral ground to forget and have some fun. I was grateful not to be in Newton. Thanksgiving had always been our favorite holiday. My father and I cooked, and we hosted six to eight people. His memory loomed large; it would have been unbearable.

Mercifully, a dear Florida friend invited us to her house. She was Italian and entertained with *abbondanza*. Her family and friends went out of their way to make my mom feel at home. One guest, a Labrador retriever, spent much of the meal with his head on my leg, waiting for turkey. He knew a pushover when he saw one.

During the meal, I got a text from Peter Pan. "Happy T-day! Gig Sat @ 8 at Max's Pavilion. CU there!"

"Happy T-day to U2," I wrote. "See u then. ☺"

"Why are you smiling, Alice?" asked my friend.

"Just happy to be here."

My mom was content to stay home Saturday night. She hated loud

269

music, and she wanted me to "socialize." I dragged a client/friend and her husband to the gig. We saw Peter tuning his guitars and we walked over to say hello.

He kissed my cheek and shook my friends' hands. "Are these your parents?" My friend was 48 to my 36. *Awkward!* I introduced them, hoping they didn't hear his question.

There were 10 performances, each with a half-hour slot from 8 p.m. to 1 a.m. Folk musicians, angry musicians, rock, salsa, it was soup to nuts, and it was LOUD. My friend's husband looked miserable. Peter went on at 9:30. His acoustic set was a relief.

"I've had a headache all night," the husband said when Peter finished.

"Is it OK if we leave now?" asked my friend. "I'm up at 5:30 for Pilates, and he's ready to pass out."

"Of course. Thanks for keeping me company." *Now what do I do?* After they left, I found Peter and paid my respects, wondering if I should stay or go. "It was nice seeing you. You sounded great!"

"Thanks!" he said. I started to walk away. "Hey, can you stay for a drink?"

My stomach flipped. "Sure." We ordered a Rolling Rock and some kind of white wine and talked. When my drink came, I took my wallet out of my purse.

"Oh, no. I got this!"

"Are you sure?" I asked.

"Are you kidding? If I let a woman pay, my mom would have my head on a platter."

So would mine. "Hey, can I ask you a question?"

"Shoot," he said.

"Last month, when we met at the Box . . ."

"Yeah . . ."

"Why didn't you want to sit next to me?" *You invited me!*

He searched for words, blushing. "I guess . . . I didn't want to cramp your style." *The Oracle was right. I am intimidating! All five feet three inches of me.*

"You'd never do that." I put my hand on his. It was warm. So was mine. This was bold for me. We were both blushing. *You need to hear it.* He ordered another round.

He drank faster than I did, though I lost track. He talked about his childhood. His parents split up when he was two. Clearly, it still hurt. His mom was a software executive. Never home. His grandmother moved in, raised him. His older brother left for college when Peter was in kindergarten. No pets. He partied in college, graduated, and coached tennis until his Achilles heel forced him to stop. *Was it your ankle or the partying?* He started a business running tennis tournaments and loved being his own boss.

"What about you?" he asked.

"I left corporate, and I've been figuring it out."

"What have you figured so far?"

"Well, consulting pays the bills . . ."

"But?"

"It's not my passion. I do voiceovers, and I love to sing."

"Is singing your passion?" He moved his chair closer. I looked into his electric blue eyes.

Who has eyes like that? I have to stop drinking. "One of them." He stretched his arm out on the bar, palm open, and I put my hand in his. My face felt warm. My stomach fluttered. I was giddy times tipsy. My whole body reacted to him.

In my altered state, I heard the astrologer's voice. "When you see that color again, you'll know." *Butterflies!* I looked into those eyes. Too intense. I looked up. "Hey, it's a full moon." I pointed toward it. A distraction. This close to the equator, full moons were intensely bright—and big.

"It's a blue moon," he said, still holding my hand.

I looked again. "Wow. I almost missed it." *Once in a blue moon . . . it's a sign.* The astrologer said when I saw that color again, I'd know what it meant. Peter's eyes were the same electric blue as that butterfly! My legs went cold. *Is he the one? Am I crazy?*

He pulled his hand away. *Yep. I'm crazy.* "Here. You do it—this time." *What?* He handed me a stack of napkins, his mouth curving mischievously. He looked straight at my lap. *Did I just get my—?*

"Oh my God!" I was wearing the house white. "Good thing I wore black pants," I said, patting the spill.

"Do I make you nervous?" he said in his sultry baritone. I bit my lip. "Tell me about your voiceovers."

My head spinning, I was determined to sound coherent. "Have you heard the Florida orange juice ads?"

"That's you?"

"Uh-huh."

"Wow! What else are you up to?"

"Hmm . . ." *Keep talking. Just keep talking.* "I was invited to join the union."

"That's good, right?"

"I think so. I can only accept union jobs now, but they pay a LOT more."

"Hey, now!" he said, giving me a high five. "And I've heard you sing. You have a really nice voice."

"Thanks. So do you. But, you know, it doesn't pay the bills."

"Doesn't matter. You'll figure out the money. Just sing." He turned to the bartender. "We'll have two coffees."

We sipped, and I told him about my dad. I told him about the

Drektors and the Resistance.

"That's Florida," he said. "I love the weather. It's great for tennis, but that's about it."

We sat and talked until the wine wore off. I wasn't nervous anymore. It felt like I'd known him forever. "Would you ever go back to Massachusetts?" I asked.

"To live?" I nodded. "Maybe," he said. "I don't know. I've thought about it." *Me, too!*

"Last call," said the bartender, leaning over the bar. "Can I get you two anything else?"

I looked at my watch. It was 2 a.m. "I didn't realize how late it is!" We'd been sitting and talking for four hours. "I gotta go. My mom's visiting. She must be having a heart attack." I turned my phone on. She'd left five messages.

"It *is* late. I'll walk you to your car."

We got there and stopped. I opened the door and looked up at him. He put his hand around my waist. My arms slid up to his shoulders. We kissed, and I closed my eyes. I felt connected in a way I'd never felt before. *This is real.*

"I have to go out of town," he said, stroking my hair. He leaned against the car and I leaned against him. "I planned the trip months ago. I have a tennis tournament, and then I'm going fishing with my fraternity brothers." *Daddy and I fished.* "We're sleeping on a boat, so I'll have limited Wi-Fi. After that, I promised my grandmother I'd visit." *If he's good to his grandmother, he'll be good to . . .* I smiled.

"That's nice." I didn't ask when he'd be back. I wasn't worried.

"I'll be back after the New Year. In the meantime, if you don't hear from me, know that I'm not ghosting you."

"When it's right, it's easy." I remembered the old man who tried to warn me about El Innombrable. No more games. *Talk about a 180!*

"All right," I said. "Happy New Year!"

His hand never left the small of my back. "Happy New Year, Alice." We kissed again. Driving away, I watched him standing there until I was out of sight. Sinatra's "Nice 'n' Easy" played on the jazz station. For the first time, it was just that.

26

Election Week

Thoughts of Peter came and went during the week before the election. It was a blessing he was unreachable, because I had to focus. First, the Drektors cancelled meet-the-candidates night. Their justification was our open house. Because some candidates met with unit owners privately—i.e., the party Lothario couldn't crash—they claimed there was no need for an official forum. All candidates were free to campaign on their own.

The Champion and I read the notice in the mailroom. "Can they do that?" I asked.

"No. They can't do a lot of things, but that never stopped them."

"They're afraid to face the music," I said.

"Don't get cocky, Alice," said the Champion. "They have closet supporters. And besides," she whispered, "their plan may not depend on campaigning."

Sunday night, four days before the election, the Bulldog called. "If I were you, I'd question the equipment maintenance fees budgeted for the Club House."

275

"Why's that?"

"They hired an outside company to maintain the new machines," he said. "And they're paying more than the going rate." *"They"? Aren't you a Drektor, too?*

"How do you know that?" I asked. "Aren't we meeting to discuss the budget tomorrow?"

"Oh. Right . . . I just saw a draft." *Yeah, sure.*

"Can you help me prove what the rate *should* be?" I asked. "Have you seen the bids?"

"Nooo, I just think you should ask about it."

"Well, thanks for the tip." *What are you up to?*

The next day, Joanna invited me over for lunch. "Those bastuhds aw gonna spike the maintenance fees," she said. "They're waiting to pass theyuh budget *aftuh* they get re-elected."

"What can I do?" I asked.

"Nothin', honey. At least you gawt the meeting. You'll go and ask yaw questions. I got the word out. If enough people show up, the Drektuhs won't dare mess with you. Come on, I'll go with you."

Joanna didn't need to recruit. Unit owners took notice as soon as the meeting was posted in the mailroom.

We arrived 10 minutes early. It was standing room only, and a man gave Joanna his seat. We'd never had a crowd like this. It was buoying.

After weeks of pestering, the Manager had agreed to discuss next year's budget with the Finance Committee on December 12th—three days before the election and two months behind schedule. The board was supposed to approve Condoland's budget before the year's end. Just putting it together usually took the

Committee a month, followed by the board's review, which usually took another month.

The Manager passed packets of papers around the conference table. "Since we're late on this"—*Who's fault is that?*—"I put together a draft budget for us to review."

"We create the budget together!" I said.

"She's right. This isn't how we do it," said another member.

"You said you didn't have time to work on the budget!" said a third.

"I said I didn't have time to *meet*," said the Manager. "It's been an extremely busy year. I'm trying to speed up the process, so we can finish before the election." *Cute.*

"Thank you fuh going above and beyond, Managuh," said Humpty Dumpty.

I shook my head. "Do you people rehearse your lines in advance?" *Did I say that out loud?*

Humpty Dumpty's eyes bore a hole in my head. I gathered my things before she screamed at me. If all we were was a rubber stamp, why bother? Then came the clapping. I looked up.

"She said it!"

"We're onto you people!"

"Cut the crap!"

This crowd had my back, and I was their mouthpiece. I put my laptop down and caught Sherlock's eye. He winked at me, and I cracked a smile. *The power of the people . . . is it enough?*

"Does everyone have a copy of the budget?" asked the Manager, ignoring his detractors. He looked at his watch and then at Humpty Dumpty. Ever so slightly, she shook her head. Emotions were running too high. If the Manager gave another bullshit excuse to leave the room, the Drektors would pay a price at the ballot box, and even Humpty knew it.

"Let's go over this proposal," said the Bulldog, "and see what questions we have." He gestured to me. I was always the person expected to speak up.

Is this why my mother wanted me to be a lawyer? I asked why legal expenses were tripled. "What assumptions support that estimate?" The audience leaned forward.

"Well, we've had a lot of . . . sensitive issues this year," said the Manager.

"Like what?" asked a Committee member.

"We can't discuss pending litigation," said the Manager.

"For the Finance Committee to recommend next year's budget," I said, "we need to understand your assumptions."

"She's right!"

Rage Man stood up. "We're not writin' you a blank check!" This was war.

"We're not asking for names, Manager," I said. "But the gentleman is right. If Condoland's legal fees are tripling, we need to know why."

Cheering from the spectators. The Manager sat lifeless, a marionette waiting for a Drektor to pull his strings. Humpty Dumpty stared at the handout, her reading glasses hanging from her neck. The Bulldog wiped his brow.

I was done tiptoeing. "Does the board keep the lawyers on the phone to . . . let's say justify secret board meetings in the Manager's office?" Humpty's head spun to me, her eyes wide. *Busted!* She started coughing. The Bulldog got up and excused himself. *Plausible deniability again?* Unit owners spoke over each other, absorbing my accusation. I tried to raise my voice over theirs. "If that's going on . . ." An aging hippy with long hair and a beard stood up. He flapped his arms, motioning people to be quiet until I could hear myself. "Thank you!" I mouthed. "If that's going on, then I suggest you stop it, because a) it's illegal, and b) we're not paying for it!"

"Does the Committee have any other questions?" asked the Manager from the land of Oblivion. *Excuse me? I saw them sneak out of your office into the garage!*

"Enjoy your last week!" someone shouted.

Bulldog returned to the room and slinked into his seat. I moved to my next question. "Tell us about the maintenance contract for the gym." It was a minor expense, but since the Bulldog alerted me to it, I was curious to see how it would play out.

"Not much to tell; we're using EZ Company," said the Manager.

"Can we see the bids," I asked, "so we understand our options?"

"We signed with EZ—Condoland III recommended them."

"You don't have competitive bids?" I asked. *Quelle surprise!*

"I don't know what to tell you, Alice. We were told it's a good company, and we went with the recommendation. Why find out the hard way?" The Manager was frantically trying to catch Humpty Dumpty's eye while she pretended to read the draft budget.

I stared at the Bulldog, imploring him to speak. Nothing. "What do you think?" I asked.

"Oh, I don't know," he said. "I'm not familiar with the issue." *You little—*

"Show huh the bid from EZ Company!" It was Joanna, standing on her chair. *Thank you, my friend!*

"I'd like to see it. How about you guys?" I asked the rest of the Committee. The door opened, and in walked the junior lawyer from the Bad Firm. She locked eyes with the Bulldog. *That's where he went.*

"Hello, everyone," she said. "I understand the Finance Committee is asking to see bids and contracts. You're also curious about legal expenses, is that correct?"

"You bet it is!" said Rage Man.

"It's our job to understand how and why our money is spent," I said.

"I need to consult with my clients—the full board—before anyone shares confidential information with this or any committee."

"We didn't ask for confidential information," I said.

"Well, that's your opinion, isn't it?" she sneered. *If we win, she's gone. I'll wipe that smirk off her face.* "Carry on with your meeting if you will, but the Manager and the directors cannot scrutinize litigation expenses with you." She turned, clicked her heels, and marched out the door.

"You heard huh!" said Humpty Dumpty. "And listen, what's the point of second-guessing every loyn item? The Managuh knows what things cost."

"I second," said the Bulldog. "Let's vote on the motion to adjourn the meeting—at least until the board consults with legal counsel."

What motion? You weasel! I looked around the table. Budget details were boring, and the attorney was intimidating. Committee members were unsure how to proceed.

"Maybe it's best to wait," said a member.

I'm losing them. "We don't have time to wait!" I said.

"I know," said another Committee member, "but I don't want legal problems."

Damnit! By a four-to-three vote, the budget meeting was adjourned. The Drektors won the budget battle by proxy. Thanks to the Bad Firm, they had "no choice" but to approve next year's budget sans oversight from the Finance Committee.

After that fiasco, I went to the gym to burn off steam. The room was empty. I did my three miles on the treadmill telling the Oracle what happened.

"They're feeling confident," she said. "The Long Island Lothario is here. He's been coming every afternoon for the last month, looking for votes."

"Where is he now?"

"Steam room," she said, "bragging about the renovation."

"How do people react?"

"You'll find out Thursday night."

"Why doesn't he come in the morning when it's crowded?"

"He leaves that to his wife. The businesspeople see through him." I shook my head. "You know she's been badmouthing you," said the Oracle.

"Whaddayou mean?"

"She goes to the exercise classes and then to the equipment room, bragging about her Prince Charming. When she mentions the election, your name comes up. I've heard her whine to new people that 'Alice is mean to me. I don't understand why. I've always been nice to her!'"

"You're kidding!"

"I wish I were," said the Oracle. "But there is someone who challenges her."

"Who?"

"Sherlock Holmez."

I couldn't help but smile. "What does he do?"

"He confronts her, asks about her husband. He does it with all the Drektors. He hands them incriminating articles and documents and asks them to explain. He gave the Long Island Lothario an article about the Mobster's conviction. At the top of his voice, Sherlock asked what qualifies a felon to be treasurer."

"Did he get an answer?"

"No, so Sherlock asked louder. Everyone stared. He drives the Drektors crazy."

"I'll bet!" I turned off the machine and stepped down. "Should I confront Mrs. Lothario?"

"No, you're doing what you need to do. Tensions are too high; just stay the course."

"Are we gonna win?" The Oracle put her hands on her hips and tilted her head. "I know," I said. "You can't tell me."

"Three more days," she said. "You're almost there."

On Tuesday, two days before the election, I walked around the loop with Cookie and the Champion. "Why are they so confident?" I asked. "Don't they see how many of us are onto them?"

"Because the ballot box is close to empty."

"How do you know?"

"Your friend Sherlock told me." I laughed. "Someone in the Office told him," she said. "The lower the turnout, the more ballots they can forge. They think it's in the bag."

"I can't wait to see their faces when we bring the ballots Thursday night!" I said.

"Neither can I," said the Champion.

My phone was ringing when I came in from the walk. I grabbed it before it went to voicemail.

"A few of us are goin' to the Restaurant," said Joanna. "Wanna come?"

"What time?" *I have to shower.*

"Six-thirty. You got an owuh. Come on! We'll have some laughs."

Tuesday was movie night, making it early bird night at the Restaurant. I met Joanna, Sherlock, and Paul Revere near the hostess station. We passed the Drektors' table on the way to ours. Drektors from all three Condoland towers were eating together.

"That's the public enemies table," said Joanna.

"Shh!" I said. "They'll hear you!"

"Good! I'll give those *gonivim*[23] a piece o' my mind."

Our table faced our oppressors. "Can we sit closer to the window?" I asked.

"Sorry, we're fully booked," said the Restaurant Manager. They laughed too loud, like they owned the place. Joanna was ready to blow a gasket.

"Two more days," I said. "Ignore them!"

Sherlock tapped my arm. "Alice, ees you new friend!" Rage Man and his very tall wife sauntered past the Drektors and sat by the window. He ignored his wife, growing increasingly agitated as he stared at the public enemies. *This should be interesting.*

"He's on the move," said Paul. Rage Man walked briskly toward the enemies table. He came up behind Lothario, who was busy stuffing his face.

He poked Lothario in the shoulder. "Thief!" he accused.

Lothario lurched from the table. He towered over his provocateur. "Prove it!" he said, and sat down.

"That's a guilty man's answer," said Rage Man. His associates

---

[23] Gonivim — Yiddish plural of gonif, a thief, dishonest person, or scoundrel

watching, Lothario had to save face. He got up, swung at Rage Man, and missed. The shorter man punched him—hard—in his paunch. Lothario doubled over, wheezing. Abruptly, he stood up, punching Rage Man in the face.

"You motherfucker!" screamed Rage Man, blood dripping from his nose as he staggered toward Lothario. "I'll make you rot in jail!"

"Do something!" I said to Sherlock.

"Ees no good to get between two fists. Ees Restaurant Manager job."

"He's cawlling someone," said Joanna. The entire restaurant watched—from a safe distance. *Schadenfreude.* This was the best entertainment ever. These two deserved each other.

"Heads up!" said Paul. Two police officers walked through the door and found two overweight, immature seniors swinging at each other. Rage Man stumbled backwards into a table. I heard glass shatter.

"Cops," Mrs. Lothario hissed at her husband. The "men" stopped fighting.

"Who threw the first punch?" asked a policeman.

"He did!" Three diners answered simultaneously, pointing at Lothario. *No love lost there.*

"He jabbed me first!" said Lothario. "And he provoked me."

"Come with us in the hallway," an officer told Lothario. "You two need to separate."

"Yes, Officer," said Lothario, his head bowed. It was the first time I saw him avoid attention.

Rage Man smelled fear. As the officers escorted Lothario out of the Restaurant, Rage Man yelled, "Everybody knows! You're going down, you son-of-a-bitch!" He caught up to them and spit on Lothario, who instinctively lunged, then pulled back. He was trapped.

"Gentlemen, if you'd like us to arrest you for disorderly conduct, keep it up," said one of the officers.

Rage Man's wife linked arms with her husband and pulled him back to their table. Mrs. Lothario followed her prince into the hallway to sweet-talk the police. Five minutes later, the Lotharios returned to the enemies table, sitting stone-faced as they finished their dinner.

Sherlock got up and spoke to the head waiter. He returned to the table like the cat who swallowed the canary.

"Tell us!" I said.

"The Restaurant Manager think Rage Man and Lothario conduct no acceptable. They banned from Restaurant for 90 days." *That's it?*

"Un-be-lieve-able," said Paul.

"You were right about Rage Man," said Joanna.

I pursed my lips. "Yeah, but so were you. I'm glad he's not my problem anymore."

Wednesday morning—the day before the election—my phone rang. I was working on a consulting project due the next day, but it was the Connector, so I answered it.

"Alice, I need advice."

"What is it?"

"I have beeen communicating with a uneet owner who leeves in Ea-ta-lee," she said. "I told her which candidates we support and why, and she agrees with me."

"OK. And?"

"She forgot to mail her ballot. She called me. She sent eet today through a courier, but she meessed the cutoff time. We won't get eet unteel after the election."

"Oh, that's a shame." We couldn't take any vote for granted. "But I don't think there's anything we can do."

"I have an idea," said the Connector. "The woman asked me to feel out the ballot for her."

"That's against the rules."

"I know, but I have her email geeving me permeession," she said.

"I dunno. I understand the temptation, but it's not kosher. Want me to ask——"

"The Champion? Yes, Alice. Please."

"Sure. Hold on. I'll conference you." I explained the situation to the Champion before adding her to the call.

"What's the verdict?" I asked. "Can the Connector vote on behalf of this woman?"

"No. I wish you could, but the Sunshine Law is clear: One unit owner cannot complete and sign a ballot for another."

"But she gave me permeession!" said the Connector. "What eef I attach her email?"

"Guys," said the Champion, "we agreed to do everything by the book, right?"

"We did," I said.

"Then we have to forfeit her vote. Understood?"

"Jes," said the Connector, deflated.

"Thanks, Champion," I said.

"Eet's just that we're playing by two deefferent sets of rules," said the Connector after the Champion hung up. "I hope we won't regret eet."

"One vote is not going to make or break the election," I said. "And even if it does, we can't become the people we want to replace." After our call, I wondered if I was being naïve.

That evening, I went out to grocery shop. Walking up to my car in the Condoland garage, I saw it had been keyed from the passenger door to the rear, over to the driver's side. *Assholes!* There was no camera near my parking spot, so I couldn't prove who did it, but I woulda bet money on Lothario. If the Drektors intended to intimidate me, they grossly miscalculated. I would do everything humanly—and legally—possible over the next 24 hours to remove them from the board.

27

Election Day

D ecember 15th. Election day! I slept fitfully and woke up early. One way or another, two years of work would end tonight. *They're gonna cheat. I know it!* Two cups of coffee later, I called the Champion. "If they get re-elected, I'm moving!"

"Good morning, Alice! You won't be the only one, but before you start packing, let's see what happens. It's probably not a good time to tell you, but—"

"What?" *Is she pulling out of the race? Did we lose the election moni-tor? Did—*

"I can't be there tonight."

"At the election? Why not?" I asked.

"Office holiday party. I can't skip it."

My chest tightened. "But you're the only one who can put the Drektors in their place!"

"*You* can do it. I've seen you do it."

"No, I can't. I don't yell. You get mad. I'm too polite. Nobody listens to polite. And you're a lawyer! I'm just a 'singuh.'" We both laughed.

"You were doin' pretty well just now!" said the Champion. "So, you think I'm a bitch."

"In a good way."

"Gee, thanks! About tonight. The election monitor is your go-to person. If you see anything you don't like, tell her. *She'll* be the bitch!"

"I hope so!"

"Are we ready?" she asked.

I looked at my watch and at my project. I needed time. *Maybe I can deliver it tomorrow?* "I'll check in with our people, but unless you hear from me, we're good to go."

"Thanks," she said. "I gotta get to the office. If you need me, text, but you got this, Alice."

"We'll see. Enjoy your party!"

My client gave me an extension. Reading through my election to-do list, I realized I was clenching my teeth. I added "relax" to the top of the list. Fifteen minutes into the "Ah Meditation with Wayne Dyer," my phone rang. *Damn it!* It was Sherlock. *Maybe it's important.* I answered while Dyer chanted, waiting for me.

"*Artista,* did you join a cult? What is that sound?"

"I was meditating." I stopped the recording.

"Better to meditate after the election," he said. "I need your help. Will you talk to my friend? He lives in our building."

"Today?"

"*Sí.*"

"*¿De que?*"

"He'll explain. It's about his business and the election."

"I don't understand."

"Just talk to him. Please. He needs your help with English."

"All right. I'll talk to him. *Oye,* you're telling people *not* to bring their ballots to the Office, right?"

"*Por supuesto, Artista.* I'm collecting ballots and proxies. I'll bring them tonight."

"Wonderful. Thanks!" He gave me his friend's number. "I'll call now."

The man was hard to understand on the phone. Because he was Sherlock's friend and thus likely not an ax murderer, I invited him over to tell me what he needed. Five minutes later, my bell rang. I opened the door to a man I recognized from the few times I'd been to temple. He recognized me, too, and looked as relieved as I felt. After the obligatory cheek kiss, I motioned to him to have a seat at my dining room table.

"*¿Café?*"

"*No, gracias.*" He tapped his foot, eager to get to it. "I am in the credit card processing business," he explained in Spanish. "Last year, I made a proposal to process credit card charges for the Restaurant." He showed me a copy of the proposal. It looked professional.

"Should I take notes?" I asked.

"Yes, please."

I opened my laptop. "To whom did you present?"

"It was the Manager, Her Highness, and the Mobster."

"Otherwise known as Dewey, Cheatem & Howe!"

"Who?"

"Nobody. Sorry. It doesn't translate. What happened at the meeting?"

"Highness said the Restaurant used another unit owner's company. She said she'd have to discuss it with Condolands II and III, but she was always open to opportunities to save money."

"She is?"

"I don't think so. The other unit owner was selling his condo. I didn't know that at the time. I just knew my proposal was very competitive. Why not consider it?"

"What were the savings?"

"I changed my mind about coffee—if it's no trouble."

"Of course not! I have to warn you, it's 'dirty water.'" That's what some Latins call American coffee.

"That's fine; I'm used to it. The savings were $400–$500 a month. The deal is peanuts for me. I did it to help our building."

"I understand. So, then what?"

"I got the contract, and I delivered the savings. Everything was going smoothly until the Office receptionist called. She asked if I'd received the ballots from family members living out of the country."

"How many ballots?" I asked, pouring the coffee. "Sugar?"

"*Sí, por favor.*" He took five packets. *That should calm you down.*

"Together, we own six apartments here." I shook my head. *You poor guy. You thought you got the business on the merits.*

"I see. What did you tell her?"

"That I hadn't received them yet, and I'd check with my family. That weekend, I went to the open house at that little lady's apartment—" He motioned how high with his hand.

"Florence Nightingale?"

"Yes. I listened to each candidate. They all said to bring the ballots on election night."

"Yep. Did the receptionist contact you again?"

"No. The Manager called. Same question. I told him they'd been mailed to me, but I didn't have them yet."

"Did he say *why* he wanted them?"

"No, and I didn't ask. He offered to overnight new ballots if they got lost in the mail—that happens sometimes in my country. I wish I'd paid more attention."

"You're paying attention now. What happened next?"

"Yesterday, Her Highness called. She said she 'needed' our ballots 'urgently.' I told her not to worry; I'd bring them to the election." He stood and paced in front of the window.

She threatened him. I know she did. "What did she say?" I asked, trying not to lead the witness. He turned, arms crossed. "She told me if I didn't hand her the ballots by 5 p.m. today, she would cancel my contract with the Restaurant."

I stopped typing and leaned back in my chair. "I'm sorry she did that, but I'm not surprised. How did you respond?"

He puffed air through his lips in disgust. "I told her I left my country because nobody can tell me what to do or how to do it. The same goes for her. If she wants to get another provider, I said she's more than welcome to do so, and I hung up."

"Good for you!" He flopped into his chair. "Listen, I don't know what's going to happen tonight, but if we win," I put my hands together and looked up to the ceiling, "you can present your services to a real board—an *honest* board. That, I promise."

He nodded. "Thank you, Alice. Sherlock told me I could trust you."

"Trust is earned." I smiled.

He cleared his throat. "My English isn't very good. If we win tonight, I want the new board to know what happened. Can you help me write a letter?"

"Of course. Do you mind if we do that *after* the election?"

"No, that's fine. You must be busy today." *That's an understatement.*

He kissed my cheek as he left my apartment. One more victim of Condoland's corruption. He didn't need the money. He offered to do us a favor, and that experience tainted his impression of America. He must have wondered if he made the right choice in coming here. *Damn them. We HAVE to win!*

I went downstairs to get my mail. Two men were carrying furniture from the service elevators into the lobby. I followed, watching them drop their loads into a nook where the most comfortable brown leather chairs had been. They removed the paper wrapping to reveal metal-trimmed, white *cloth* chairs. The Panamanian Princess was inspecting them. She saw my dismay.

"Ugly, *verdad?*" she said.

I nodded. "And how do we clean them?"

She approached. "Alice, the Decorating Committee no agree to this. The Drekorator says they are custom-made, but is no true. They come from a discount outlet!" *Oh, the horror!* She pointed. "*Mira*, the metal is chipped!" It was; the legs were a mess. She whispered, "Jew know what?" *Huh? Nah. She's M.O.T. [member of the tribe].*

"What?"

She came closer. "Her Highness paid Drekorator this morning. Ees a final sale." I looked at my watch. Four hours to the election.

The Party Room doors opened at 7:00 p.m. They were to stay open until all votes were counted and the results were announced. Sherlock and the Connector were meeting me at 6:45. I arrived at 6:30 to observe. Maintenance had set up a long card table with two folding chairs at the Party Room entrance, just off the lobby. The Office receptionist sat in one of the chairs, guarding the ballot box. She'd put blank ballots, proxy forms, and blue pens on the table for last-minute voters.

A steady stream of unit owners dropped their ballots in the box. Some waited outside the Party Room, others cast their ballots and went back upstairs. Her Highness arrived 10 minutes after I did. We happily ignored each other while surveying the table, watching the box. Sherlock and the Connector were right on time. I kissed them both, happy for reinforcements.

"Ready?" asked Sherlock, a twinkle in his eye.

"You bet I am! Hey, where's your cowboy hat?"

"Don't need it. Come, let's have some fun."

He was holding two thick stacks of ballots. Slowly, he removed the elastic bands around them, smiling devilishly at the receptionist as he dropped them into the box. *You're bad!* He handed her a folder. "These are the signed proxies," Sherlock said in Spanish. Her Highness stood on tippy toes, eyes on that box—the key to her financial future. *Trip!*

The Connector was next. She turned her 12-by-18-inch accordion folder upside down, and dozens of ballots and proxy forms fell onto the table.

"Italy?" I whispered.

"No, not eencluded," she said.

"You did the right thing."

"I hope so." *Me, too.*

The receptionist stared at the pile in front of her. "What's all this?"

"These are ballots and proxies from uneet owners who leeve overseas," said the Connector. "They asked me to deleever them on election day."

Her Highness plowed her way to the table. "You can't do that!"

"Why not?" asked the Connector.

"Because . . . because it's against the rules!" She looked at the receptionist. "Don't put those ballots in the box! You hear me?" The receptionist was on the verge of tears when the Party Room doors opened. A tall, athletic woman in her 50s walked out and sat in the chair next to her at the table. *Is she from the accounting firm?*

"What seems to be the problem?" she asked in a deep, measured voice.

Her Highness elbowed through the people around her. She reached the seated woman and stopped, shoulders back and chest out. "That woman dumped a pile of ballots on the table!" she said, pointing at the Connector. "She, she can't do that!" She spat as she spoke.

A drop of saliva landed on the seated woman's face. Her expression hardened as she wiped her cheek. *Gross.* "Who are you?" she asked.

"I'm the Condoland board president!" Her hands on her hips, she added, "I know your CEO!" *So, she is from the accounting firm.* Highness again pointed an accusatory finger at the Connector. "That woman's up to something. I want those ballots disqualified!"

The woman behind the desk stood up, her demeanor imposing. "I'm the election monitor," she said coolly. "The State of Florida authorized me to oversee this election, ma'am. I'll decide what to do with the ballots." She turned to the receptionist. "Help me count these ballots and proxies."

"There are 40," said the Connector.

"Noted," said the Election Monitor. She caught the receptionist and Her Highness exchanging looks. "I changed my mind," she said. "I'll count them, and I'll put them in the box." Seated again, she addressed the Connector. "Do you have a list of who sent you each ballot and proxy?"

"Yes, I do." She pulled it out of her purse.

"No, no, let me count them," said the Monitor. "I'll ask you for it if I don't count 40." She gave a warning look to the receptionist. *So, this is why cocaine packers work naked.*

At 7:01, the Connector, Sherlock, and I walked past the table and into the Party Room. We descended the grand staircase and saw Joanna waving. *She must have entered from the basement.* Using her purse, her blazer, and a sweater, she'd staked out seats for us with a clear view of the staircase. They were close to the table where the votes would be tabulated. We sat, waiting for the show to begin.

The Lotharios made their entrance a few minutes later. A dead animal draped Mrs. Lothario's spandexed shoulders. Her dress wrapped tightly around her, revealing her missing figure. She wore multicolored tights and six-inch platform shoes. Her husband was decked out in a tight, gold polyester shirt unbuttoned to reveal matching gold chains and a prodigious amount of chest hair.

"Should I tell 'em disco's dead?" asked Joanna.

"I dare you!"

"Let's wait," said Sherlock.

"You're off the hook," I told Joanna.

By 7:15, all the Drektors were there. The Panamanian Prince and Princess sat next to the Nightingales in the rear orchestra.

With no time to spare, the Lotharios separated to work the crowd. Their fake laughs echoed from different parts of the room. He shook hands and bootlicked. She joined the other Barbies. To-gether, they targeted women, complimenting their outfits, their hair, and jewelry while casually mentioning the blank ballots on the table upstairs. There was still time to change minds.

Having finished his rounds, the Long Island Lothario strutted to our corner of the room and sat facing us, taunting us. He spread his legs and smirked, his victory imminent. The Bulldog joined him, copying the pose like a boy imitating his hero. *Beavis and Butt-Head.* They joked and laughed while we seethed.

"I'd like to smack 'em," said Joanna.

"I'm worried," I said to Sherlock. "They think it's in the bag."

"The art of the con," he said in Spanish.

The Ceevil Engineer joined us, amused by the spectacle. "They came late," he said. "They think most people did not vote, and they weel vote *for* them. But look at Her Highness. Does she look confident?"

She looked like she'd seen a ghost. She paced near the counting table, biting her nails. At 7:30, Security closed the doors. All eyes followed the Election Monitor as she walked down the stairs holding the ballot box, then walked across the room to place it on the counting table. She picked up a small bell from the table and rang it. It sounded like the theater bell you hear when the curtain is about to rise. In Pavlovian response, unit owners took their seats.

"Where's the Champion?" Joanna whispered.

"Holiday party for work."

"Shit."

"I know." I closed my eyes and breathed. The Election Monitor was our last stand against unbridled corruption.

"Good evening, everyone," she said. "I've been appointed by the State of Florida to monitor your election tonight. I need two volunteers to count votes—no candidates, please. If you'd like to help, raise your hand."

Three or four hands went up. "You," she said, pointing at the Connector. "And you, in the back with the navy sweater."

"Who's he?" I asked.

"A retired lawyuh. Edguh knows him. Decent guy," said Joanna.

Both the senior and junior lawyers from the Bad Firm were there. Normally, they certified the election, but tonight, they were there to advocate for the Drektors and maintain their cash cow. They paced back and forth against the wall behind the counting table.

The two volunteers worked together while the Election Monitor observed. First, they recorded the ballots. The man in the navy sweater read each apartment number and name printed on the outer envelope while the Connector checked that name and number off on a master list. If a name didn't match the authorized voter of record, the ballot was put aside.

"What happens to the ballots they don't count?" I asked Joanna.

"Nothin'," she said. "Once the daws close, no new votes can be accepted."

Navy sweater called out the name of the Italian woman whose vote we didn't submit. The Connector and I made eye contact; she wanted to kill me.

"Joanna, that lady didn't vote!" I whispered.

"Howdaya know?"

"She asked the Connector to fill out her ballot and sign it, but we didn't because it's illegal. That's not her ballot. They forged it!"

"Say something!" she urged.

"What can I say? How can I prove it?" We listened.

"Steinberg, unit 1202," read navy sweater.

"That ees a dupleecate," said the Connector. They stopped to find the first Steinberg ballot, and both ballots were set aside.

"They did it again!" I said. A few minutes went by.

"Rodriguez, unit 329," read the second volunteer.

"Dupleecate," said the Connector.

I texted the Champion. "They're cheating. Help!"

She called me. "What happened?"

"Hold on." I walked into the basement hallway. "Remember that Italian woman—we didn't get her ballot, and we didn't include her?"

"Yes."

"She just voted! And apparently, Steinberg and Rodriguez voted twice. It's what you suspected. They stuffed the ballot box with out-of-towners. I don't know what to do. How can I prove it? Please, can you come?"

I heard music and laughter through the phone. She was talking to someone. "I have an emergency at home. I have to go." She came back to the line. "Ask the Monitor if she'll pause the counting. I'm on my way."

Joanna was waiting for me at the basement entrance. "What'd she say?"

"She's coming. I gotta talk to the Monitor." I ran to the counting table. "May I speak with you for a minute?"

"Yes?"

"Hi, my name is Alice. I'm a unit owner—chairperson of the Finance Committee." *What does that have to do with anything?* "I helped gather signatures to bring you here."

"I can see why." Her eyes were glued to the table. "I can't talk now. I have to watch the counting."

I persisted. "My friend—the attorney who sent our petition to Tallahassee—she's en route from a work event. Can we take a break until she gets here?" No response. I clasped my hands together, begging. "Please?"

"I'm sorry," she said, focused on the counting. "It's not possible. Once the ballots have all been sorted, we'll begin counting the votes." She glanced at my crestfallen face and added, "The duplicate ballots are slowing us down. Hopefully, your friend gets here before we finish."

I walked back to my seat. "So?" asked Joanna.

"They're not stopping." I texted the Champion: "Hurry! Not stopping!"

"Accident. Waiting for road to clear. You can do it, Alice!" she responded.

I have to try. "Hi," I said to the Election Monitor. "It's Alice again." She grunted. "The attorney I mentioned is delayed. "Just tell me, how many duplicates?" Sherlock and Joanna jumped up and stood against the wall nearest the counting table to hear the conversation.

"So far? Thirty." Her eyes were on the volunteers.

"What can we do!" It was a demand, not a question. She turned to face me.

"I don't know," said the Election Monitor. "I have no way to know which vote is legitimate."

I looked at the Manager. "Do you have signatures on file?"

He looked at Her Highness. She shook her head slightly, eyes wide under her baseball cap, face frozen. *Do you realize we can all see you?* "Unfortunately, we don't," he monotoned.

"If the unit owners are in the building," I asked, "can they come downstairs with ID to verify their signatures?"

The Election Monitor looked at her watch. *Does she have a date?* "Yes, we can do that. We'll take a break. You have 15 minutes."

"Let's call the unit owners!" I said to my friends. Joanna pulled out her phone.

"I call in *Español*," said Sherlock.

"Me, too," said Ceevil.

I ran back to the Election Monitor. "You have four volunteers.

We'll make the calls."

She gave us the four-page master list. We each took a page and dialed. In synchrony, Joanna and I switched phones with Sherlock and Ceevil when we reached Spanish speakers, and they did the same for English. Of the 32 duplicate ballots, only five unit owners were home. The Monitor gave them 10 minutes to come downstairs to identify themselves and their ballots. *It takes them 10 minutes to walk to the elevator!* One woman came down in curlers, but God bless them, they all made it.

The double doors flew open, and the Champion rushed down the stairs. She ran past us toward the Election Monitor.

"I understand we have a problem," said the Champion, introducing herself and trying to catch her breath.

"In my 28 years as an election monitor, I've never seen fraud like this. EVER."

"Take a load off," yelled Joanna. "We handled it! Well, Alice handled it, but we helped."

The Champion sat with us. She gave me a friendly push on the shoulder. "I told you you could do it!"

"I did what I thought you'd do," I said. "That's all—"

"She's cheating!" someone shouted.

"Who said that?" asked Joanna. We followed the voice. Her Highness stood on the left side of the counting table pointing at the Connector. *Again?*

"Excuse me?" said the Election Monitor, putting her body between the two women.

"She's cheating!" repeated Her Highness. Behind her, on either side, I saw a muumuu. Humpty Dumpty was using her friend as a shield.

"Ma'am," said the Election Monitor, hands on hips, looking

down at the accuser, "step back. I'm in charge now. This is not your election. You don't need to worry about anything." She stepped closer. "Do I make myself clear?" Her Highness retreated. She turned and sat front row center. The muumuu sat next to her.

"How dare she!" I said to Joanna. The Connector ignored her, intent on the counting. I couldn't. She'd gone too far. I got up, walked straight to Her Highness and pointed at the Connector.

"She. Has. Done. Nothing. Wrong! How DARE you accuse her!"

"Can't we all get along?" said Humpty Dumpty. *Now she wants to get along?*

"She's making false allegations!" I answered looking at Her Highness.

Her Highness stood and pointed her crooked finger close to my face. "You. Are. So. ARROGANT!"

"No. I'm HONEST. We've done EVERYTHING by the book. Have *you*?" I walked back to my friends. I'd never shown anger like that before.

"You told huh!" said Joanna.

"I know. I'm sorry, but I've had it."

Sherlock nodded approvingly, and Ceevil shook my hand. "She deserved eet," he said. *Yes, she did.*

Lothario still faced us, legs splayed, impervious to reality.

"I'll wipe that grin off yaw face!" said Joanna. He ignored her, pleased to have triggered at least one of us.

"Listen!" I said. We heard arguing in the back of the room, behind the staircase.

Joanna ran to the noise and ran back with reconnaissance. "It's the Bulldog. He's fighting with the owners whose votes were duplicated." There was a thump and then a thud. I raced to the sound.

A man lay on the floor, and the Bulldog stood over him, fists clenched. Dr. Nightingale rushed over to help the victim. *He's gonna have a shiner. And a very nice lawsuit!*

Dr. Nightingale helped the man up. He was holding the back of his head. "You're very lucky this room is carpeted," Dr. Nightingale told him.

"You'll hear from my lawyer!" the man said to the Bulldog.

"Everybody OUT!" said the Election Monitor. "OUT! Right now!" She rang her bell. "Get out and stay out! I'll let you know when the votes are counted."

I found my friends in the lobby.

"That was a first!" said the Champion.

"I'm worried," I said. *If anything else goes wrong, no one's there to set the record straight!*

"Don't be," said the Champion. "It's better this way."

"How's that?" I asked.

"The Drektors can't interfere from here, and I trust the Election Monitor. Come, let's sit down and wait." We sat under the funhouse mirror. *Apropos.* "We've done what we could, Alice. Try to relax."

I'd been losing to corruption since I moved to Florida, always wondering whom I could trust. But these last two years were different. My neighbors and I supported each other. Together, we fought back. *Whatever happens, I did my very best, Daddy.* I could scarcely breathe.

"I'll be right back." I put my ear to the crack in the double doors. The names of the candidates echoed as a man's voice read the selections from each ballot aloud.

"So?" Joanna asked as I rejoined my friends.

"I may be wrong, but I heard Fab Five names a lot more than

the other candidates."

"From yaw lips to Gawd's ears!"

"I don't want to get my hopes up," said the Champion. *I do!*

At 10:45 p.m., the Party Room doors reopened. We ran downstairs to hear what the Election Monitor was saying. "The counting is completed, and I'm going to announce the results. You're welcome back IF you can conduct yourselves like mature adults." *How embarrassing.*

Only a few dozen unit owners were left. My friends and I returned to our seats near the counting table. Thankfully, the leg splayers were huddling with the other Drektors in the kitchen. Humpty Dumpty was wrapping something around the Bulldog's knuckles.

"Thanks for your patience this evening," said the Election Monitor. "This has been an unprecedented election to say the least, but we have your results."

I felt my heart beat. "Whatever happens, you guys, it was worth it." Sherlock blinked his acknowledgement.

"I'm *farklempt*,"[24] said Joanna.

I couldn't read her. "You are?"

She slapped my arm. "Wasamadda with you? We gotta win!"

"Shh!" said the Champion, her index finger to her mouth. "Listen!"

"I will list the names in the order of votes received," continued the Election Monitor. "The first five are Condoland's new board members:

1. Paul Revere, 312 votes
2. The Champion, 295 votes

---

[24] Farklempt — Yiddish for choked up with emotion

3. The Panamanian Prince, 290
4. Florence Nightingale, 275
5. Harvard, 212
6. The Bulldog, 112
7. The Corpse, 84
8. Humpty Dumpty, 41
9. Her Highness, 29
10. The Long Island Lothario, 18

"Congratulations to the new board. You should now hold a brief meeting to elect your officers. I wish you the best of luck. From what I've seen here tonight, you're going to need it. Please excuse me, I have a flight to catch."

"We won!" I screamed, jumping up. "You guys, we won! We replaced the entire board!" We high-fived as Condoland's new board of directors took its place at the dais.

Joanna looked around. "Where aw those shmucks?" She was looking for the Drektors.

"They leave through the back door in kitchen to the basement," said Sherlock.

We looked through the pass-through window to the kitchen. They were gone. "They snuck out like cowuds," said Joanna.

"Like cockroaches," I said.

"*Exactamente*," said Sherlock. He rubbed his beard, smirking. "Eighteen votes." He was delighted by Lothario's demise.

We stayed in the Party Room while the new directors chose their officers. Paul Revere was elected Condoland's board president, and the Champion, our vice president. Harvard became treasurer—*Lord help us*—and Florence Nightingale, board secretary.

As soon as the roles were decided, the Champion got to work.

She approached the Bad Firm lawyers. They smiled sickly, like parasites seeking new hosts. "You're fired," she said. I strode to where the junior lawyer was gathering her things and looked her straight in the eye. This gloat, I deserved. She jutted her chin in the air, Mussoliniesque, and left the room without a word. *Bye, Felicia!*

The Champion found the Manager staring out the window. "I need the keys to the Office," she said.

"The keys?"

"Yes. You won't need them anymore. A security guard is on his way. He'll escort you to your office while you get your things. You may not remove your laptop or any files. Understood?" The Manager gaped, speechless. "Today is your last day at Condoland." The security guard was walking down the stairs. It was finally over.

By 11:15, only the Circle of Trust was left in the Party Room. "We have to celebrate!" I said. "You wanna come up for a toast?" It was late, but this victory was so sweet, it pushed my friends past their bedtimes.

The 10 of us entered my apartment like the Jamaican bobsled team winning Olympic gold. We'd beaten the odds, and we were ecstatic. Hoping for the best, I'd prepared for this moment. I took a bowl of strawberries and two bottles of champagne from my fridge. Sherlock helped me reach the glasses on the top cupboard shelf. Paul opened and poured, and we toasted.

"To the new board of directors!" I said.

"To teamwork!" said Florence.

"To Pawl!" said Joanna. "The King of the Jews!"

My phone beeped after everyone left. I had a voicemail from Peter. He was at LAX and wanted to know how it went. I put on my pj's and called him back.

"So?" he asked.

"We won! We kicked ALL five Drektors off the board. I still can't believe it!"

"That's amazing!"

"I know! How are you?"

"Sick of fish! And I miss you."

"Me, too. When do you get back?"

"Two weeks. I'm heading to Boston."

"Is your grandmother excited?"

"Are you kidding? She's been cooking my favorites all week. I'll be back after New Year's," he said.

"Oh, that's right. You told me that."

"What are *you* doing New Year's Eve?"

Do I say I have plans? No, what's the point? "I don't have plans yet." *Yet. Middle ground. Let's see what he does with that.*

"Why don't cha come home?" he asked. "Do you have to be in Florida?"

"No . . ."

"Come on, I want to spend New Year's Eve with you." *Ding! Ding! Ding! Ding! Ding!*

"I'd like that, too," I said.

"Great. I'll make it worth your while."

I hung up the phone and got into bed. My friends and I pulled off the impossible. I couldn't put it on my résumé, but this election was my greatest accomplishment. Living in Florida taught me to stand my ground, and for once, the good guys won! My dad would be proud—*was* proud. It took two years, but it was worth the wait. I thought about my conversation with Peter. I had a feeling he was worth the wait, too.

The Cocktail Party

Condoland was eerily calm after the election. From one day to the next, life there became stress-free. Things began to run efficiently, and the Drektors were nowhere to be seen.

Each day, the new board proved its worth. The directors hired a management company that set to work making long-neglected repairs and eliminating unnecessary expenses. The Good Firm now represented Condoland. Valet service was prompt, because side jobs could only take place on personal time.

Suddenly, I had a lot more time on my hands. The normalcy I had desperately wanted was anticlimactic. Since our champagne toast, I hadn't seen or spoken to anyone in the Circle of Trust, and I missed the comradery. I even missed our battles! Normal was . . . boring.

After the election, I went to see the Oracle. "It's time for you to care for others, and let others care for you," she said.

"Who are these 'others'?" I asked. *Peter Pan?*

She raised her eyebrows. "Alice . . ."

"I know, you can't tell me."

"Even if I could, what would be the fun in that?" *She has a point.*

When the Connector invited me to a victory celebration, I felt a flicker of the old thrill. Everyone would be there—Sherlock Holmez, Joanna Rivers, the Ceevil Engineer, and the Fab Five now on the board: Paul Revere, Florence Nightingale, Harvard, the Panamanian Prince, and the Champion. The new board got clearance with the Good Firm as long as they agreed—in writing—not to discuss pending board business.

We greeted each other like family at a reunion. Ceevil and the Connector were going to visit family in Buenos Aires. Paul was excited about his oldest grandson's upcoming bar mitzvah.

"Get this," said the Champion. "After the election, my toilet erupted. Erupted! I mean like Mount Vesuvius."

"Gross!" I said, putting down my plate.

"What happened?" asked the Prince.

"My husband was home. He turned off the water. You can't imagine. We waited 20 minutes with that . . . mess until maintenance came. They cut open the wall behind the toilet to check the connecting pipes." She had our full attention. "Know what it was?"

"A mouse?" asked Florence.

"Nope," said the Champion. "Anyone else?"

"Tell the damned story!" said Joanna.

"OK. They found a metal bar in the pipe connected to the toilet. According to the engineer, the only way it could get down there was if someone dropped it in from the roof. How it ended up behind our toilet, we'll never know."

"Those mothuhfuckuhs!" said Joanna.

"Yes, ma'am," said the Champion.

"Do you have to redo your bathroom?" I asked.

"Oh, yeah. But insurance will cover it. Let's change the subject. What's new with you, Alice? You seem particularly happy."

I was in such a good a mood, I forgot to mention my car getting keyed. "I've got a callback to be the voice of a big car brand—I don't want to jinx it, but it's a national campaign!" *Just what you imagined, Daddy.* "And I met somebody."

"Wow! Wow! Wow! Let's start with the guy," said the Champion. The women huddled around the couch, and I told them about Peter.

"I'm spending New Year's with him in Boston," I said.

"That's so exciting!" said Florence. "And your new career! You left your job, and look how your life changed!"

"Hey," said the Champion, "now that you're working from home and the election's over, I have a question for you. Cookie's mother had a litter, and her humans are looking for people to adopt the pups in about five weeks. Would you be—"

"Yes!" *If not now, when?*

"I didn't expect you to answer so quickly," said the Champion. "You know a dog's a big responsibility. I'd love for Cookie to have a sibling, but are you sure you're ready?"

"No. I'm going to do it anyway. It's time." Lucky for me, my heart overrode my brain. *The Oracle's right. It's better not to know until it happens.* And that's how I got Dennis—Dennis the Menace.

The men were having a conversation of their own. Their voices grew louder. We stopped talking and listened.

"How can they get away with eet?" asked Ceevil.

"I like see them in jail," said Sherlock.

"You wouldn't believe the hahf of what we found," said Paul.

"You talking about the Drektors?" I asked.

"Jes," said Sherlock. "Why they no punished?"

"I hear you," said the Champion. She took her wine glass and walked to where the men sat drinking. "But we've been over this. To try them in a court of law, we need proof—documents and witnesses." She took a sip. "And you know we have neither. As long as the Drektors live here, employees won't talk."

"What about the court of public opinion?" I asked.

Joanna nudged my arm. "*That's* an idea!" We joined the men.

"Guys, again, we've talked about this," said the Champion. "If you publicly accuse them of anything, they'll sue you! I'd like nothing more, but we have to let it go. Lemme put it to you this way: If you want justice, go to a whorehouse. If you want to get fucked, go to court. That's why I stopped litigating."

Did she just tell me no? "So, we couldn't use their real names, is that right?"

"Correct," said the Champion.

"And we can't, say . . . mention the name of our building, right?"

"Correct again."

"Or the town?"

"I wouldn't."

"Other than that, could we say whatever we want?"

"You're a riot, Alice. We'll just have to wait for karma to get 'em," she said.

"Yeah . . . karma," I said. *We'll see about that.*

Yiddish Glossary

Altah kahkers — Literally, old shitters. Figuratively, it means old people.

Biz a hindut und tzfuntzik — A toast wishing the person to live for 120 years

Bubbaleh — Term of endearment meaning sweetie, darling

Chaza — Pigs

Chutzpah — Intestinal fortitude, guts

Drek — Fecal matter

Farkakteh — Crappy, becrapped

Farklempt — Choked up with emotion

Fressers — Eaters, gluttons

Gonif — Thief, dishonest person, or scoundrel

Gonivim — Plural of gonif

Kibitzing — Informal chatting

Kvetching — Complaining

Mazel — Luck, fortune. Mazel tov means good luck.

Meshuga — Crazy

Nosh — Snack (n.) or snacking (v.)

Schmear — Bribe (v). Can also mean to spread something, e.g., schmear cream cheese.

Schnorer — Beggar—one who wheedles others into supplying his or her wants

Shiva — A period of seven days' mourning for the dead, beginning immediately after the funeral

Shmata — Rag

Shtick — A gimmick, comic routine, style of performance, etc., associated with a particular person

Shtick drek — Piece of shit, of no value

Tuchus — Gluteus maximus

Yenta — A woman who is a gossip or busybody

About the Author

Before writing women's fiction, Liz got an MBA in marketing and finance from Columbia University, followed by a career in financial services marketing and language research. In 2009, she threw caution to winds, quitting her job to become a jazz singer and voice actor. The pandemic afforded Liz a chance to revisit her bucket list, and she began to write for fun. *Alice in Condoland* is her debut novel. If you want to know when Liz's next book will be published, please visit her website, LizBieler.com, where you can sign up to be notified.

After more than 20 years in South Florida, Liz recently returned to Eastern Massachusetts, where she lives with her Westie, Cookie.